Lovingly RESTORED

KELSEY WOODS

Book Cover by Aleksandar N. – @blokowsky

Edited by Victoria Hadley – https://www.theromanticeditorialservices.com/

1st edition 2023

ISBN: 978-1-7390786-1-4
ISBN (e-book): 978-1-7390786-0-7

Content Warnings

To check content warnings for this book, scan the QR code below or visit: https://www.kelseywoods.ca/content-warnings

Contents

Chapter One

Isaac

There's no *good* time to interrupt your dad while he conducts a boring-as-hell project meeting, but when I sigh too heavily and every head at the meeting table swivels toward me, I figure now's my chance.

"What if we go in a different direction with the cabinetry?" I say, rubbing my sweaty palms on my jeans.

Except for my co-worker and best friend, Chris, and two other friends who aren't in my dad's pocket, everyone looks at me like I suggested we build a house out of papier-mâché. I swallow hard as the gaze of the man at the head of the table burns a hole in the side of my head.

"A *different* direction, Isaac?"

Matt Lauri, my father and the owner of Forward Construction, looks unimpressed, his mouth a flat line. It's an expression I'm familiar with.

I gesture to the pile of blueprints. "I'm gonna grab these."

I lift my butt off the squeaky rolling chair and slide the plans closer. The neat lines map out forty-eight identical kitchens. They look a lot like the forty-eight kitchens we did last year, too. If I have to build another vinyl floor, grey-paint, prefab town home, I'm going to scream.

"Since we haven't taken the trees on the property down yet," I continue, "we could reclaim some of the wood and incorporate it into the cabinetry. Not on all the units. Just some, as an alternative higher-end finish."

I grip the arms of my chair. Even though I feel shaky as hell, my idea is solid. It will only add value and give me a chance to build something that isn't cookie cutter like all the other homes we do. Hell, like most homes on the market. It's the type of work I'm itching to do. I offer a tight-lipped smile to the group of men, waiting for a nod of agreement from any of them. Instead, they shift in their chairs, avoiding my gaze, as they wait for the boss's response.

My father toys with his gaudy gold watch that glitters beneath the fluorescent lights. "That would take time we don't have."

I squeeze the plastic arms harder. "If I could borrow Chris, I could do it faster."

Chris gives me a *leave me out of this* look.

"Time is money, Isaac."

His signature phrase.

He shakes his head and laughs, "You'd think that my own son would know that by now. We can't all have the knack for business, I guess."

I wince at the dig, biting the inside of my cheek.

"Isaac, I can have prefab cabinets on site by Monday if I put the right pressure on the right people. This is the first job of the new year, and I want it done *fast*. Get that money in our pockets, am I right?" He rubs his thumb and fingers together until most of the middle-aged men and his suck-up assistant nod and chuckle at the thought of growing their bank accounts. Satisfied that the group is with him, he reaches over the table and drags the blueprints away from me. That's how everything feels lately. Beyond my reach.

"Yeah, I get it."

The words taste bitter in my mouth as I cross my arms over my chest, tuning him out. I can't pretend to be interested in a project that's the same as all the others.

I stare at the clock so long it blurs, the hour hand wobbling around eight p.m. When we're dismissed from the first project meeting of the calendar year, I rush to the exit. Mere seconds from my escape, my dad calls out, "Isaac, stay."

I sigh, stepping out of the way of the door to watch everyone else leave, listening to their conversations about weekend plans.

"Ooooh," Chris, my best friend and coworker, teases as he swaggers by.

I stick out my leg, smirking when he stumbles and glares at me over his shoulder.

Dad stands at the head of the table, alone. I'm surprised his assistant didn't stay. She treats taking meeting minutes like an Olympic sport.

"Yes?" I ask, leaning against the table on my knuckles.

"I think you already know what I'm going to say, so I won't drag it out."

Project manager. I've been stuck as a supervisor at Forward for years, waiting until some of the senior guys retire. Is this finally it? I fix my posture, reaching my full height. Several inches taller than my dad, I got my grandpa's stature. Maybe my recent suggestions haven't fallen on deaf ears. If we could lean into the restoration side of things, I think it could be beneficial for my father's company. I want this, and I think I deserve it. He pulls a thick document out of a leather folder and slides it toward me. The paper stops halfway down the polished table, and my small bubble of hope pops. I can read the capitalized bold font from where I stand.

NOTICE OF TERMINATION

Old coffee sours in my stomach, and the blood rushing in my ears drowns out whatever speech my father is giving.

I tear my eyes away from the offending document. "You're firing me?"

He simply gestures to the papers at the centre of the table.

"But that's–"

"It's what?" he snaps.

It's not fair. I'd been ready to say that it wasn't fair. And thank god he cut me off because that's something a child would say. It's his company. He holds the power to do with it as he chooses.

"On what grounds?" If he thinks I'll walk out with no questions asked, then he's stupider than I thought.

"You're in violation of our non-compete clause," he says, like I'm a rival and not his own damn son.

"In what fucking way?"

"All your side jobs."

The side jobs are the restorations I do on my own time. I work a minimum of forty hours for Forward each week, but I always make time to do the stuff that scratches the unrelenting restoration itch. I'm qualified in both carpentry and fine woodworking and love the work I do on the side. An afternoon with a banged-up antique dresser? That's what I'm talking about. Most Saturdays you can find me in Forward's shop. I replace everything I use, billing my clients accordingly. Inquiries for small projects are steady, coming mostly from word of mouth. Some of them are from people who used my grandfather for similar work.

I push my hair out of my eyes. "That doesn't affect my position here."

"I'm giving the project manager position to Ken. He's a team player."

My dad gathers his belongings, indicating our talk is over.

A team player? Also known as someone who keeps their head down and their mouth shut. It's a gut punch to know the position I've been waiting for is no longer available. I snatch the termination documents, preparing to rip the neatly stapled papers clean in half. But the stack is thicker than I thought, at least ten pages, and all I manage to do is lamely rumple one edge. My cheeks burn hot with anger and embarrassment.

When I flip him off with both hands his face turns crimson. He's still formulating a response when I storm out of the room, heart pounding from the confrontation. The behaviour is stupid and undignified, but he's not my boss anymore and, to be honest, he's barely been a father. Fuck him, and fuck Forward Construction. Ten years of my life? Down the drain. Chris is leaning against the wall outside the meeting room, pushing off and rushing to catch up with me when I pass him.

"Did you get it?" He asks.

I storm through the halls to the staff room, tossing a stainless steel travel mug with the company logo on it into the trash with a hollow thud.

"I got the exact opposite of a promotion. He fired me." I fish my keys out of my pocket.

They jingle in my shaking hand.

Chris stares at me, mouth agape.

LOVINGLY RESTORED

I drop my work keys with a clatter on the break room table and retrieve my brown Carhartt coat from the hook, heading for the exit of Forward Construction for the last time. When I push the metal door open, I halt at the sight of another West Coast storm that blew in during the meeting. A hallmark of winter on Vancouver Island. Chris joins me in the doorway, our shoulders filling the frame, his just below mine. My truck sits next to Chris's Jeep, two of the last cars in the lot. The sheeting rain is obvious in the glowing circles of tall security lights.

"Your work is beautiful, man. Ten times better than anything Forward will ever do."

I throw up my hands. "I don't expect every construction project to be some high-end, antique restoration. But could we do it once?"

For years now I've hoped my father would create a division of Forward that would allow me to sink my teeth into the restoration world. It's crystal clear that will never be part of his business plan. Even though I understand, it doesn't make it any easier to acknowledge that I wasted a decade at a business that doesn't value me or my skills.

"You don't need him," Chris says.

"I need his equipment."

The facility here has everything I need to do my side jobs. I won't lie, it's state-of-the-art. If I try to start out on my own...I've got nothing. The thought makes my chest tight.

"You've got to start somewhere. Don't worry, you can sleep on my couch if push comes to shove."

I try to relax my jaw, but my top teeth are hell-bent on grinding against my bottom ones.

"I'm not ready."

I pull my collar tight around my neck, steeling myself for the onslaught, and make a beeline for the truck. Water beads off my jaw-length hair, delivering the cold rainwater right against my nape.

"I've heard that before." Chris follows. "Listen, man, I don't want to talk bad about him because he's your family-"

"Never stopped you before."

He waves me off. "Your dad is an ass, Isaac. It's like he holds a special place in his heart for being douchey to you."

I catch my truck door as the wind tries to wrench it from my grasp.

"You don't think I know that?"

We both climb in our vehicles and start them up, rolling down the windows to continue the conversation without the shower.

Chris holds up his hands in peace, raising his voice so I can hear him over the rain pounding against our roofs. "I'm sorry. I think this could be good for you."

"It's good that I got fired? Thanks." I grip the steering wheel.

"Not today. Hell, the next few months could really hurt. But you two aren't meant to work together."

"You can say that again," I call, rolling up my window and driving away.

LOVINGLY RESTORED

Falling into a job with Forward after trade school was a no brainer, but the idea of working for myself has been swirling in the back of my mind for years. My mood matches the weather as I drive through the downpour, soaking in self-pity. The forest is thick on each side of the two-lane road. Tall conifers stretching up into the sky, thriving in the wet conditions, swaying ominously in each powerful gust of wind. On the outskirts of the small city of West Isle, it's easy to imagine I'm the only person on the road as I barrel down a straight stretch and try to leave some of my shit behind me. A brief flash catches my eye, but vanishes just as fast. I ease off the gas and run a hand down my face. It was probably a deer. Their glowing eyes are usually the last things you see before they go barrelling across the road right in front of your car. But then something comes into view, an outline of a small vehicle. I suck in a sharp breath, stomping my heavy boot on the brake.

"Shit!"

The anti-lock brakes kick in, and I skid across the slippery section of road. When I come to a stop, the only sounds in the cab are my shaky breaths and the pelting rain. Through the windshield, mere inches from my bumper, is the tail end of a tiny red hatchback, barely pulled off the road, blocking most of my lane. The death grip I had on the steering wheel leaves imprints of the leather stitching on my palms.

"Way too close."

As if nature knows I'm about to leave the safety of the truck, the rain intensifies into an all out deluge, overwhelming the whooshing wipers. I switch on my hazards and set out to see if the car is empty. Based on the way it's sitting there dark and quiet like it's part of the scenery, it's probably abandoned. As soon as my steel-toed boots reach the ground, the driver's side door flies open and a person stumbles out. The shadowy outline faces me, hesitates for all of three seconds, then marches in my direction with determination. Rain falls through the beams of my bright truck lights, blurring my vision. A petite, pretty, and *very* pissed woman is headed straight for me. Her eyes are narrowed, strides long, and before I can say anything, she launches a full force verbal attack.

"What in the ever-loving *hell* do you think you're doing?"

Taken aback by the strength of her voice, I stare down at her.

"Driving. In a straight line."

She's acting like I'm out here performing stunt moves instead of simply going home after work.

"You almost hit me, you ass! You need to *slow down*." She emphasises her last two words with sharp pokes to my sternum.

"Keep your hands to yourself," I warn, taking a step back.

She follows, ignoring my words. "And another thing..." The tip of her finger digs into my chest again, right between two ribs.

Oh, so this is how it's gonna be?

"No. No more *things*." I catch the wrist of the arm she keeps assaulting me with, holding it firm against my chest. Her skin is freezing cold like she's been out here for a while.

Her mouth pops open, like maybe she's used to telling people what's what. Like nobody ever bothered talking back to her before.

"Your lights aren't working. That, or you forgot to turn them on. Either way, that's pretty stupid."

"They work fine...usually. It broke down."

"Usually doesn't really cut it–"

I stop myself from lecturing her. She can't change it now.

"*Speaking* of lights, the high beams on your moronic monster truck are blinding me."

"Monster truck?" I throw my head back in amusement, crisp tasting rainwater filling my mouth. Is this girl for real? Her eyes are a warm brown, and even though she's squinting, her pupils are tiny points. Though she holds her head high, I don't miss the way her chin wobbles. Fuck, I don't want her to cry. I release her wrist, scrubbing a hand down my face like a squeegee.

I point my thumb over my shoulder, "That's an F-250 Powerstroke with a super cab and leather interior."

Her chin rises another inch.

"King Ranch," I add.

She scoffs. "Is that supposed to be impressive?"

No, but the monthly payment is. I grit my teeth at the thought of my upcoming last paycheque.

"Well, I'm done standing out in a storm. You gonna call for a tow?"

"Sometimes I can get it to start again."

Folding my arms over my chest, I tip my chin in the direction of the car.

"Give it a go, then."

She looks hopeful as she turns away from me, climbing into her car. Aside from being a bit shaken, she seems fine. I'm so fucking ready to get out of here.

"Yes!" she cries when it turns over.

I'm not a car guy, but my eyebrows knit together at the noise.

"Does it always sound like that?"

As if in response to my question, the engine launches into an unhealthy, high-pitched whine.

The acrid smell of burning plastic blows my way.

I cough at the stench. "Fan-fucking-tastic."

The squeal sharpens and sounds like it's about one octave from an explosion.

"Get the fuck out of that thing!"

I have no idea what the little death trap is capable of. She clamps her hands over her head like earmuffs as though *that* will solve the problem. I'm getting a sense of why she's out here in the first place.

"For the love of…" I haul her out of the seat, ignoring her protests. Tucking her behind me, I lean inside to cut the engine. I palm her keys and shut the door behind me.

"You can't drive this tonight. It's going to need repairs."

"What are you? Some sort of mechanic?"

She makes a move to grab her keys, but I raise my arm. Even if she jumped, she couldn't reach.

12

"No," I tell her, "but I have ears, and it's not safe."

"I'll call a tow truck. You don't have to wait around."

"Don't you worry. I won't."

I place the keys in her upturned palm, satisfied. I checked on her. She's fine. My duty is done, and now I can start my weekend of wallowing and damage control.

The warm, dry cab is heavenly, but I shudder at the thought of what my truck would have done to that car and the woman inside it. Water has forced its way through the lining of my coat, soaking the thick henley beneath. When I pull the waffle knit fabric away from my torso, it suctions back to my abs. I glance at the time. 9:02 p.m. How long will a tow truck take at this hour? I didn't think that through. She stands next to her car, shoulders hunched, cell phone by her ear.

If you're going to do something, do it right. The words of my grandparents find their way into my mind, and I know I'm not going anywhere yet. I sigh, my coat bunched around my elbows. When I shrug it back on, the sodden fabric of the collar touches my bare neck and I cringe.

She watches me approach while speaking into her phone.

"Get in the truck," I interrupt, not having the patience to say it any nicer than that.

A drop of rain falls off the tip of her nose when she looks up, processing my words. Her eyes narrow, sceptical of me and the authenticity of my offer.

"I d-don't th-think so."

She's freezing, and I almost left her here because I had a shitty workday.

I hold my palms up. "What are they even saying?"

She tugs the zipper of her coat towards her chin, but it has nowhere left to go.

"Um, it'll be a couple of hours."

Oh, hell no.

"Hang up."

I'm incredulous that she would stay out there for a minimum of two hours on an unlit road, in such harsh weather alone. She's tough.

"I'll wait in my car. I can take care of it myself. Go." She waves me off like I'm a nuisance instead of her last resort.

Leave her where another car could come by? One that might not see her until it's too late?

"I'm not going to do that. You can't run the engine for the heat, and you'll freeze. I'll give you a lift home."

She chews her full bottom lip before squeezing her eyes shut in resignation.

"Let's go, lady." I turn, knowing she'll follow because I'm her best option.

"Lady?"

"What? Are you not a lady? C'mon!" I clap my wet hands together twice.

Clapping at a woman? Mummo, my grandma, would be livid.

I wait at the passenger side, opening the door to cancel out my rudeness.

"How gentlemanly for a man who restrained me a few minutes ago."

"Yeah, because you've been a total angel out here tonight. Do you want a hand? It's a big step up." I gesture to the runner.

She rolls her eyes with practiced precision. "I think I can handle climbing into a vehicle."

"Suit yourself."

I walk away, desperate to get in and warm up. Mild coastal climate or otherwise, you can only be soaked for so long before it feels like the Arctic. By the time I hear her cry of surprise and whip around, she's already hit the ground, and it's too late for me to do a damn thing about it. I sigh, bowing my head. Why couldn't she have just accepted my help? She's a pile on the ground, sitting in a muddy puddle that seems conveniently placed for her landing pleasure. Tipping her head up to the dark sky, she slams her palms into the shallow water beneath her in a show of pure frustration and screams. I raise my eyebrows at the rawness of her release, unsure of what to do next. No judgement from me over her tantrum. She looks pathetic in wet, muddy clothes, and she'll be nursing a sore ass in the morning after that fall. Sinking down onto my haunches, my wet jeans stretch uncomfortably against my frigid skin.

"Can I help you into the truck now? While you're still in one piece?" I keep my voice low, trying to soothe her.

"I'm not sure I am." She winces, examining her hands. Jagged pieces of gravel cover the heels of her palms.

Her teeth chatter, and her shoulders shake. I extend my arm, and water pours over my hand, down my knuckles to the tips of my fingers. The amber hazards on my truck blink, each flash illuminates her face and reveals a distinct expression.

Embarrassment.

Pain.

Fear.

For the first time, I consider what it means for her to accept a ride from me. A man. A stranger. Here I am, worrying about her well-being if I leave her in the middle of nowhere, but it didn't cross my mind that she might believe *me* to be a bigger threat than exposure to the elements.

Male privilege much, Lauri?

"I know it doesn't mean much, but you can trust me. I'm on my way home from work. I'm Isaac." I sport the sincerest expression I can muster while wearing underwear that feel like they're straight out of the washing machine. My statement hangs between us.

"Ashlyn." She reaches up with a mucky hand. "And I suppose I have no choice."

I rise out of my squat, pulling her up with a bit too much force and nearly flattening her against my chest.

"Sorry," I mumble.

"That's okay."

She releases my hand and squares her shoulders towards the truck, ready to try again. Next to her, it *does* look like a monster truck. Hovering a few steps behind her, I decide to wait in case she's the world's clumsiest woman. She plants a black and previously white sneaker firmly on the runner, making an adorable grunting sound as she throws herself into the cab. She perches up there like she didn't scrape herself out of the mud a moment before.

"I did it." Her expression is smug as she settles into the cab.

"Congratulations," I say dryly, shutting the door behind her and thanking myself for spending on the leather seats.

Glorious dry warmth pours into the cab.

"Oh my god, I forgot how nice it is to have a heater."

Wiggling herself to the edge of the seat, she's pressed as close to the vents as possible.

"What, your car doesn't have heat?"

She glares over at me, "No."

My fingertips burn and tingle as they thaw, and I remove my coat the whole way this time, tossing it into the backseat.

"Can I take your coat?"

I sound ridiculous. Like I'm offering to hang her wool pea coat in the front hall closet before we enjoy a nightcap. Instead, we look like drowned rats in their natural habitat: a sewer.

"Sure." Her hands are still shaking as she eases the zipper of her pink windbreaker down. I don't dare offer to help, but it's painful to see how much she struggles with the simple task. The woman is halfway to hypothermia.

17

"Are you sure you're okay? I can drive you to urgent care or something."

"God, no. I just need to get out of these clothes and into a warm bed."

I groan, "I'm down for that."

Shit. Realizing how that sounded, I scrub my hand down my face. "Like, my own clothes. At my place. In my bed."

She looks at me like I'm an utter idiot, shaking her head as she pulls her phone from her pocket, tossing her coat to join mine. "I figured. Don't worry. I doubt that you're coming on to me looking like this." She gestures to her body with one hand.

I can't help but take a quick glance. Her long-sleeved, white shirt clings to her figure; whatever bra she's wearing does fuck all to hide how cold she is. The snug denim is so covered in filth that it's hard to determine the intended wash. She seems a few years younger than me, maybe mid-twenties, and she's pretty as hell. Even when she's mad.

"Perfect. It's dead now." She frowns at her black phone screen then tips her head back against the seat. "There goes my idea to text your face to a dozen friends for safety."

"That'll make my master plan a lot easier," I say as I push my wet sleeves up.

Her eyes flit down my arms, my torso. The dome lights cast shadows, accentuating purplish circles beneath her eyes and her slightly blue lips.

"That was a joke…"

A fucking dumb one, Lauri.

18

"Feel free to use mine to check in with someone."

If she calls a husband or boyfriend, even her dad, I'm asking to speak with him. What kind of shitty guy lets his girl drive around in a death trap like that?

We start the drive, comfortable in the silence, soaking up the heat pouring out of the vents. Her mood seems to warm with her body, but she mostly studies the rain pouring down the passenger window. She scans me more than once, but anytime I glance her way, she averts her gaze. When she yawns and my own jaw stretches in response, I cover my mouth to stifle it.

"Stop that."

"Can't help it. Long day."

"Same." I let out a long sigh. "You usually drive around so late at night for work?"

She turns to me. "Who said anything about work? Breaking down on the side of the road is more of a recreational pursuit. If I keep an eye on the weather, I can time it during heavy rainstorms for maximum enjoyment."

I laugh heartily when I realize she's screwing with me. For a few seconds, my mind empties itself of worry. We're approaching town, and even though this day is at the top of my shit list, I find myself wishing the drive was longer. Now that she's opening up and has dropped the tough girl act, she's not bad company.

"Seriously, though, what do you do?"

She fidgets with her hair. "I'm...a horticulturist."

"That's the science of plants and flowers and stuff, right?"

"Mm hmm," she nods.

"Wow, that sounds really interesting.

"Thanks. It is." Her voice is quiet, a small smile playing across her mouth.

"Are you going to tell me where I'm taking you?"

"I'll put the address in your phone."

She picks it up and holds it out to me, I press my thumb over the sensor reflexively.

She enters the address, and the truck's navigation system gives us directions that I don't need. I'm born and raised in West Isle and it's not that big.

Ashlyn's presence is enough of a distraction to keep my mind off the anger that's simmering below the surface. It won't be so easy to ignore once I'm alone in my condo. The rain is a light trickle, and, over the steady hum of the heating, I can hear her occasional sighs. I'm not even sure she realizes she's doing it. Asking her what's wrong seems pointless. We're minutes from her house. And I'm not in the headspace to listen to anyone's problems. We're just two people who probably never thought our days would end like this. I got her home safe, and she got me out of my head.

Her address is a well-maintained, low-rise apartment with a "no vacancy" sign on the lawn. A few windows are still lit, lobby armchairs and a row of metal mailboxes visible through the front doors. She unbuckles her seatbelt before I come to a complete stop, another sign of this woman's utter disregard for vehicular safety. When she opens the door, the overhead light switches on, reminding me of nightclub lights coming on at closing time. I hope I don't look quite that rough. She sure doesn't. Her hair dried into the colour of milk chocolate and her warm brown eyes are rimmed with natural lashes and smudged mascara. Now that she's recovered, I can see that her skin has olive undertones, and her outfit still shows her curves.

She rotates toward the centre console to retrieve her jacket, but I have the same idea, and my hand lands on top of hers. She's no longer icy. Her hand is smooth, small, and warm beneath mine. Without thinking, I brush my thumb over that soft skin. Her face flushes with colour, and she starts to smile, but then bites her lip like she's holding back. She's so flustered, it's as though I touched her somewhere far more intimate. The thought makes me shift in my seat as blood rushes to my groin. She wiggles her hand free, pressing it to her rosy cheek like she's checking her temperature. I open my mouth to say something, but the door clicks open while the words are still forming in my head. There isn't a hope in hell of me getting a properly formed sentence past my lips in the next two seconds. She steps down onto the runner, hops out onto the sidewalk, and then throws her weight against the heavy door. I wince at the strength with which she slams it.

"Okay," I say, sucking in a deep breath.

When I plug my phone into the charger, I notice the "create contact" page is open. Ashlyn's name and number glow at me.

"Huh." I pull on the back of my neck and look up in time to see her make her way safely into the lobby.

I'm losing my touch. The blushing makes sense. I drape my forearms over the steering wheel, watching her until she's out of view. After everything that happened today, flirting was the last thing on my mind. She obviously wants me to call her, but for what? To say thank you? To go out? Unfortunately, for me, I'm not really in a place for a relationship. I'd love to lose myself in a delicious distraction, but I'm busy digging myself out of a mess.

CHAPTER TWO

Ashlyn

"I'm a horticulturist," I mimic myself as I lock up. "More like an idiot."

I press my cheek against the door, watching the gold links of the chain lock swing back and forth like a pendulum. I'm not a horticulturist. Not even close. An amateur gardener, *at best*. What I am is a licensed practical nurse. Just like my mom. And I should be satisfied with that...but I'm not. I desperately *wish* I had the land, time, and skill to have my own flower farm. Something about my roadside rescuer seemed to encourage the lie, and there's no taking it back now.

Undressing is a struggle. My raw palms brush against my damp jeans as I remove them. I peel the denim off as gingerly as possible and still hiss at the pain. The steamy shower is bliss, even though my hands sting at first, and as I slide down onto my sore ass, I remind myself that I'm lucky. A bruised tailbone is nothing compared to what could have happened. I may do homecare now, but I've been in hospitals and seen the results of crashes. When my fingers are pruney, I scrub my hair and face, but the soap doesn't wash away the images of Isaac driving me home. A strong hand on the steering wheel, damp shirt stretching over broad shoulders, eyes focused on the dark road. Tucked into my bed, exhausted but safe, I squeeze my eyes shut and try to guess what his reaction might be when he notices my number. Will he toss his head back and let out that throaty, male bark? God, that sound heated me better than the butt warmer in his obnoxiously fancy truck. Marching up to him with the fury of a damp house cat was a dumb risk. But the way my body reacted when he took my wrist into his grasp and when he tucked me behind him as my car engine threatened to blow up? That felt more like a reward.

When dim light filters around the edges of my blackout blinds, I roll my neck and shoulders and groan. My muscles feel like they've been dipped in cement, stiff and heavy from my humiliating fall. Everything from my evening comes flooding back. The unsuccessful string of meetings with small farm owners as I searched for a space to grow flowers this spring, the engine making increasingly weird sounds, the spotty reception and worsening weather as the sun set.

"Damn."

My car is still sitting out there, and the very last thing I need is for my Saturday to be spent figuring out what's wrong with it this time. Three minutes passes before I check my phone with one barely open sleep-encrusted eye. I tell myself I'm looking up the weather...but I'm checking to see if Isaac messaged. The fact that he's the best thing that happened to me yesterday is very telling. There's a single email, so I scan the message, then read it more carefully.

"Oh my god. I got it!" I bolt upright, wincing at the pain in my tailbone.

I wiggle in my bed, a careful dance of celebration that doesn't jostle any of my vertebrae. After I type a quick response, accepting the job that will pay me a better salary than I've ever earned before, I make my bed and slip into my pink fuzzy bathrobe. A live-in nurse/maid/cook position is unconventional...and probably not legal, but the octogenarian's son is willing to pay the big bucks. And the house? Oh, the *house*. I toured it the day of my interview, and the hundred-year-old home made me swoon. It's everything my apartment is not. Rich wood, a brick fireplace, a backyard that's close to an acre. I creeped the address on Zillow after. It's had the same owner since the sixties, and the price they paid for it made my jaw drop. You would *never* find anything that price in West Isle anymore, not even a studio condo like my cousin, Anna's. I suppose if I kept to my original plan and went back to school to become a registered nurse, I might be able to afford a nice little house for myself one day. But my heart's not in it anymore, or rather, my heart is too involved. Everyone told me nursing would be the perfect job for me. Like mother, like daughter. But my clinical placement supervisors countered that by suggesting I was too sensitive, too easily attached to my patients. They weren't wrong. I've been wearing my heart on my sleeve for too long. Grief grips me for longer and longer with each patient I lose. Last year I took care of a gentleman for nine months, and when he passed on I had to take a leave of absence. We became good friends, and then he was gone. Guarding myself against heartbreak has not been my forte.

But you know what I've never cried about when they've died? Plants. Sure, it sucks, but it's not that big of a deal. It means you get to figure out where you went wrong and try again next time. Growing flowers from miniature seeds and creating living works of art is a straight up joy injection. Over the years I've taught myself about the flowers that thrive in this region of British Columbia, patiently waiting for the tender sprouts to emerge from the soil of the planters I've squeezed onto my postage-stamp-sized patio. I even took design classes at the florist and learned how to arrange my tiny crop of zinnias and gerberas to sell at the downtown farmer's market. Seeing the bouquets I grew and arranged go off with their new owners was everything. But I only had enough for one weekend.

Settling onto my loveseat with my usual plate of scrambled eggs, I click on my television. It's the Home and Garden channel around here or nothing.

"I'll take one of those, please," I mumble around my bite of cheesy eggs, pointing my fork at the screen.

I've tuned in at the tail-end of my favourite show, *Backyard Shakeup*. A drone shot of a transformed yard full of curved garden beds, mature trees ringed with mulch, bright blooms exploding out of raised garden beds.

My lips close over the tines. "Mmm! Freaking gorgeous."

The old house I'll be moving into next week could look like that. Currently, it's chaos with a side of neglect. When the credits roll, I mute the TV and hit redial on my phone to call the tow truck. No sense putting it off any longer.

After a minute of crackly jazz music, an unenthused woman answers, "West Isle Towing."

"Hi, my name is Ashlyn Carter. I called last night about my vehicle."

"You the one who changed her mind?"

"Er, sorry about that," I say.

"Mmm hmm. Civic, right?"

"That's right. I'll explain to you where it is–"

"The mechanic just got back to the shop. It should be at your address."

I open my mouth to interject, there's obviously some confusion, but she rattles off my licence plate and address accurately.

"Yes, that's correct, but I didn't–"

She hangs up on me. Rude.

The last of my eggs almost slip off the plate and onto the worn carpet as I spring up and speed walk to the living room window. My muscles protest at the burst of movement. Sure enough, my car sits at the curb, looking as crappy as ever. Dull paint, cloudy headlight lenses, but it's mine. I'm breathing a sigh of relief when I put two and two together. There's only one other person who knows about last night. The same person I have no way of contacting because only he has my number. The number he didn't use despite going to the trouble of having my car towed to my front door. The longer I stare at my car, drumming my nails on the chipped windowsill paint, the more it irks me. How am I supposed to pay him back? Does he think I can't *afford* to have it towed? Because I can. I'm only pinching pennies because I want to. And why not send a quick message? 'Thought it would be a good idea to tow the car after all, it cost this much, e-transfer me.' I picture the shiny black truck with the supple leather interior and glare at my snake plant, plucking a dried yellow leaf and crunching it in my palm. I can manage my own affairs, thank you very much.

"Anna, would you look at me? Please?"

She dodges my attempts for eye contact, angling her body away from me, arms crossed in a huff.

"Did I hear something?" She cups her hand to her ear.

"Yes. It was me, the serial oil change skipper. I'm right here. Forgive me!" I interlace my fingers under my chin.

"Forgive you!" She whips around, leaning across the wobbly coffee shop table.

Ha, made you look.

"Am I supposed to *forgive you* when you die in some type of roadside inferno?"

I already recounted last night's events, a slightly edited version, and she's livid that I didn't call her. For all the neatly organized parts of my life, car maintenance is not one of them. As much as I'd love to blame last night on the weather or that man, it's my fault. Plain and simple.

"I'll drop it on one condition." She holds a manicured finger up. "No, two. Two conditions!" She adds a finger.

"Okay. Go."

"One. You need to schedule a full inspection for your hunk of junk."

"It's running fine this morning..." I roll my eyes and let her go on.

"Two," a slow smile spreads across her face, "tell me more about the hottie!" She combs a hand through her highlights, resting her head in her palm.

Just like that, the fight is over.

"Nowhere in my story did I describe him as hot. You added in that detail to make it more salacious."

Anna shrugs. "Sounds hot to me."

"How can someone *sound* hot in a story?" I shove the last bite of still warm blueberry muffin into my mouth to stifle impending oversharing. She's reading me like a book.

29

She considers the question. "I dunno, but they can. The biggest giveaway is that vibrant shade of pink you're turning right now."

Great.

I surreptitiously place a couple of fingers on my throat. My pulse is fast for someone sitting on their bruised butt.

"He thought I was a hapless loser." I take a slow, purposeful breath, forcing my circulatory system into submission. "It was pitch black out there and pouring rain. All I could tell about him was that he was tall and hadn't shaved in a while. A beard can hide a lot of imperfections. Remember when Uncle Richard shaved his off, and we had to pretend we liked it?"

Anna slams her hand on the table before covering her mouth, trying to laugh inwardly and failing. A pre-schooler with blue eyes and a whipped cream moustache at the next table giggles like she's in on the joke.

"Those blue eyes were gorgeous," I say, savouring the last sweet sip of my London Fog.

Anna chokes on her latte. "I'm sorry, what?"

She leans so far over the table that I half expect her to crawl over it and take me by the collar of my sweatshirt.

"Hmm?" I feign confusion.

Shit.

I hoped to get away with a vague description and close the book on the subject.

She scans my face. "You're holding out on me, Miss Carter."

I take an interest in the foam at the bottom of my mug, but Anna won't let me off the hook on this one.

"Hot doesn't cover it. You win."

"I knew it!" She raises a fist in victory.

"At first I was really fired up, but then we had this intense sort of eye contact and, I mean, he *did* save my ass out there."

"Sounds dreamy."

I set my mug down too hard when I remember the cringe-worthy parts. "My God, Anna. I was so awkward. I blushed worse than I am now. I didn't even say a proper thank you!"

If I crawl under the table, I wonder how long the baristas will let me stay curled up under there.

"Ashlyn, sweetie..." She takes my hand.

"It's stupid. He was grumpy, anyway."

"That's always the way." She scrunches up her nose in distaste.

"It's not like we're gonna see each other again..."

We could if he calls.

The thought creeps into my mind like a wisp of campfire smoke that I try to blow away before it stings my eyes. We fall into a comfortable moment of silence for all the hookups that never happened. May they rest in peace. It must have been the adrenaline of the near accident that provoked my body's reaction to a man I knew for all of one hour. I haven't lit up like that over anyone in ages.

"Hey, one more thing?"

I refocus my attention.

"How did you get your car back so fast if you didn't tow it last night?"

I watch the gears turning in her crafty mind.

Screw you, Isaac Whoever-You-Are. Saying goodbye to people is hard, but you won't be one of them.

CHAPTER THREE

Isaac

My breath mixes with the steam of my creamy coffee in the crisp morning air, but I settle deeper into the plastic Adirondack chair on my tenth-floor balcony anyway. The coastal winter breeze on my bare arms is refreshing. It's waking me up after an almost sleepless night. West Isle stretches out below me, ending at the shore of the Pacific. A Maersk container ship floats in place, white caps playing around its rusty hull, and the dense dark clouds threaten more rain. The historic downtown core, most of the stone buildings over a century old, is surrounded by sprawling residential areas and higher density modern condos, like mine. I glower at the pretty city I grew up in all the same. I tossed and turned, replaying the conversation in the boardroom, thinking up all the satisfying ways I could have told my dad to get fucked. The air smells fresh after the cleansing rain. I want that for myself. A pressure washer to my brain to flush out all the emotions clogging everything up. My phone buzzes on the glass patio table next to me, and I'd be lying if I said Ashlyn isn't the first person that comes to mind. Until I remember she doesn't have my number. I wonder if she's already noticed that I had her car towed to her place last night. A mechanic buddy of mine owed me a favour from when I helped him fence his yard last summer.

"Hey, Chris," I say, trying and failing to inject some levity into my voice.

"Morning. Making sure you're okay after last night."

"That's very sweet," I deflect before sighing and choosing honesty. "Not great. But there's nothing I can do about it."

"No. But the ball's in your court now."

Yeah. But what am I supposed to do with said ball?

"It caused quite the stir," he says.

I glance at my watch. "It's been twelve hours. How can something 'cause quite the stir' that fast?"

"You know how gossip spreads at work."

"Aside from my dad and I, you're the only other person who knows. Is the gossiper on the phone with us?"

"You wound me. I can keep secrets, thank you very much. It was probably your dad's assistant. *She* knew about it ahead of time because of the paperwork. She probably mentioned it to someone in the office and then it got back to Berg who told Dean and, like I said, a stir."

Berg and Dean are two of our good friends who also work at Forward. I'd have told them today. Probably. It's fucking embarrassing.

"Good. I hope it pisses him off when everyone starts talking."

I slide open the glass patio door and step inside.

"People aren't impressed. Not that they'd say anything about it to him."

I drop my coffee mug in the stainless steel sink. "No. And they shouldn't. I don't want anybody else losing their jobs."

After a workout in my building's gym and a long shower I sit at my kitchen counter and wonder how long my dad planned to give me the axe? If he figured he'd never be able to force the love of doing things the good, old-fashioned way out of me, then he's right. I inherited a lot more than height from my grandfather. I spread a copy of my condo's lease out on the cold quartz bar, skimming through to find the clause about breaking the agreement early. Whistling low at the amount, I open my banking app. Paying the price end my lease early is better than watching my savings account dwindle every month. I don't want to dip into that money for overpriced ocean-view rent. This money is earmarked for the day I finally take a chance on starting my own company. I've put it off for so long. I send an email to the property management company to break the lease. Goodbye, condo. I'm not attached to the place anyway. It's

35

sparsely decorated, cold. There's one place I can get free room and board in this city, and while most thirty-year-olds would rather sleep in the forest than live with their grandmothers, I'm not one of them. Mummo and Pappa basically raised me after my mom left. I can use Pappa's old workshop to get myself started, and it'll only be for a few months anyways.

Ashlyn's name sits at the top of my contact list. I roll my shoulders, finger hovering over her number. My career might have combusted yesterday, but the girl made me laugh, and I could use some more of that. I type something out:

Isaac: Hey, hope you liked that surprise this morning.

Delete.

Isaac: Morning, wanna get breakfast?

Delete.

Isaac: How do you feel about unemployed men?

Jesus Christ.

What do I even bring to the table at this point? No job, about to have no house of my own, and a bad fucking attitude. A real trifecta. She'll have to settle for the car delivery. I was the one who insisted she hang up and come with me, so it was the least I could do. I had the lights changed and the screaming fan belts fixed, too. As I shove the lease paperwork back into the file folder, her wide brown eyes and glowing cheeks pop into my mind. I press the heels of my hands over my face and rub until I see stars. I need that pressure washer again. As lovely as she looked, as flattered as I am that she gave me her number, I need to focus on the goals I've avoided for too long.

It's been four, maybe five, weeks since I visited Mummo over the Christmas holiday. Too long. If I had to offer an excuse, I'd say mine is pretty good. Figuring out how to start your own business is fucking hard. When I pull up at the house, the neighbourhood looks different. West Isle's downtown and the surrounding areas have transformed during the last decade. Now that change is spreading into the older residential areas. Every time you drive down a street, there's something new. An excavator bumps over churned up soil in the front yard across the street. Solar panels protrude from a green roof on a newly renovated triplex. Rezoning application signage stands outside a century-old brick home. A tasteful mix of old and new in a neighbourhood is beautiful, but I'd sooner die than let my grandparents' 1930s Craftsman home become someone's house flip money grab. Someone like my dad. I rub at my chest as I exit my truck. Death might realistically befall me before I'll have the million dollars, minimum, that it will take to buy it. The price keeps rising.

With a duffel bag on each shoulder, I regard the single-story house on its corner lot, blowing air out of my cheeks as I take in the state of semi-disrepair. This area is wide awake with renovations, but Mummo's address looks tired. The butter yellow siding is faded and some of the planks need replacing. A brick chimney stack reaches up valiantly toward the mature trees on the property. The porch that had once been a focal point of the house sags slightly in the centre as if the wood has grown tired. *Thinking* about the work it needs is overwhelming. Actually getting it done seems impossible. I transfer my weight onto the short staircase, cognizant of my two-hundred-pound frame and the recent unrelenting rain. Aside from creaks of protest on each soggy step, it holds. The porch swing on my right hangs crooked, rust gathering on the silver chains. Building that swing was one of the first projects Pappa let me manage.

I let myself in with the key that's been on my keyring ever since I was old enough to not lose them. The snug living room is pure nostalgia. I hid amongst those overstuffed couch cushions as a boy, dragging clean sheets from the linen closet to create forts. Thick wool area rugs cover wide-plank hardwood, and a rough brick hearth frames the fireplace. The air smells of teak oil and laundry and...bleach? That's not right. The harshest things Mummo uses to clean are vinegar and dish soap.

I call out, "Mummo? I'm here for a visit!"

LOVINGLY RESTORED

An extended one.

I drop the heavier of the two bags by the door and slip off my boots, striding silently past the never used formal dining room in my sock feet. Through the swinging door of the closed concept kitchen, I hear faint humming. Bleach and singing in the kitchen? Mummo's on a roll.

"Where's the prettiest lady in West Isle?" I holler, pushing against the swinging door.

I freeze, eyebrows shooting up. A figure, and I mean a *figure*, is bent over the gas range. Black leggings hug shapely hips that sway with every aggressive scrub of the cooktop. That is *not* Grandma's ass. A familiar floral apron is tied snugly around her waist, a neat bow centred right above a round backside. I clear my throat, but earbuds poke out of the maid's ears, her music and steel wool scouring pad drowning me out. My dad hired a maid? Guilt washes over me. I should be doing more. It's not enough to take out the trash every couple of weeks and put up the Christmas lights and drive her to the odd appointment. Shaking out her arms and wiggling her fingers in pink, elbow-high rubber gloves, she straightens, stretching her arms overhead. A long, brown braid hangs down her back, grazing her trim waist. I gulp and pull at my collar.

Don't gawk at the hired help, Lauri.

"Excuse me!"

She shrieks and spins around, flinging a soaking scouring pad directly at me with impressive aim. It spirals towards centre mass, but I reflexively catch it, wincing when cold liquid splatters across my chest. Her gloved hands cover her heart, bumping into the range as she backs up as far as she can. I raise my hands in surrender, terrified of further onslaughts of corrosive chemicals as bleach-scented water drips down my right forearm. We stand on opposite sides of the kitchen, divided by a handcrafted dining table, and both our jaws drop.

No *fucking* way.

"What are *you* doing here?" Ashlyn's tone conveys that I'm the absolute last person she wants to see.

"Me?"

She fumbles in her apron pocket, withdrawing her phone.

"I trusted you! You *said* I could trust you."

I step around the table toward her, "Who are you calling?"

I have a sinking suspicion the number only has three digits and starts with nine.

She holds a hand up, warning me not to come closer.

"No, no, no. Please, wait. I can explain. This is my grandmother's house. I'm Isaac *Lauri*. Aada Lauri's grandson."

Why am *I* explaining myself? For years this was my home.

She tucks her phone and earbuds away and doubles over, hands on her knees, taking slow breaths.

"You scared the absolute crap out of me. I thought... I don't know what I thought."

"It didn't seem like anything good. Do you always consider the worst-case scenario?"

"During suspected home invasions? Yes."

I didn't mean to startle her. If I'm so worried about her feelings, I guess I could have messaged her like she'd evidently wanted me to. Instead, I'd called a tow truck.

Smooth.

"Sorry I snuck up on you. I wasn't aware that my dad hired a maid."

She narrows her eyes in confusion, "A *maid*?"

"Er, housekeeper?" I try again.

What's politically correct these days?

"I'm a *nurse*. An LPN. Matt—your father, I suppose—he hired me to take care of your grandmother."

"Oh."

I swear she told me she did something else for a living. I can't quite recall. That night was so weird. She tips her jaw up, and it reminds me more of the version of her that marched toward me and jabbed her finger into my chest.

"Your grandmother is in her room. If you don't mind, I have things to do."

Did she just...dismiss me?

She walks to the fridge and runs her hand down some sort of large calendar I've never seen before, pulling a pen out of the apron and making notes. Just when I think she's done talking to me, she turns her head and tilts it inquisitively.

"Why do you have a bag?" She nods towards the canvas duffel still hanging from my shoulder.

"I'm, uh, staying here for a while."

She laughs. The clear, feminine laugh I've been thinking of for weeks. This time I'm not laughing with her.

"Well, that's the plan. I've got it all worked out with Mummo."

That's a lie.

"Mummo?"

"My grandfather was born in Finland." I point at the ceramics above the kitchen cupboards painted with the white and blue crosses of the Finnish flag. "My grandmother is first generation Canadian, born to Finnish parents, and met my grandfather here."

"Of course. I thought I heard a light accent. That's a cute name." A soft smile plays on her lips but fades quickly. "He didn't tell me anything about that arrangement," she says, crossing her arms over her chest with finality.

I plaster a puzzled expression on my face. "Really? That's so *weird*." The lies keep rolling off my tongue. "What does it matter? You're here, what, a couple hours a day?"

Lines appear between her eyebrows. "This is a live-in position."

Live. In. Position.

I'm still clutching the stupid steel scrubber in my hand. I toss it across the room into the sink and wipe my wet hand against my dark jeans.

"Living here?" I clarify, as if she didn't just say that.

"That's right." Her fists take up residence on the waist of that snugly tied apron.

I don't have other options. My condo is gone, and if I try to have my dad alter her position, that will only cause more problems between he and I. I'll tell him about all this soon. Above all else, I need my grandfather's workshop. That's why this move makes so much sense. I need time to get my business up and running without my dad's judgement. The circle of people I'll be letting in on my plans is going to be real small. More of a dot than a ring.

I push my hair out of my eyes. "Guess we're gonna be room-mates."

"No." She shakes her head emphatically, braid swinging. "That won't work."

Is she honestly telling me I can't stay in my own relative's home? Not bloody likely. I drop my bag and grab onto the back of a solid wood dining chair, scraping it obnoxiously across the tile. Plopping myself down, I swing my feet up on the table with a thud like I'm marking my territory. If Mummo saw this, I'd get a wooden spoon whipped across my hard ass. Hopefully, Ashlyn doesn't believe in corporal punishment. Her eyes widen at my woolly socks and the left big toe that's peek-a-booing out of a hole.

Her nostrils flare. "Any idea how long you'll be staying?"

"Nope." I interlace my fingers behind my head like I'm settling in for a pleasant afternoon or thirty.

Her eyes travel from my threadbare socks along the length of my legs, pausing somewhere around belt buckle height, if I'm not mistaken. I raise an eyebrow at her, knowing the slim-cut denim doesn't leave a lot to the imagination. She tugs at the neck of her apron, and I bite my bottom lip to contain a grin. Yeah, I knew I noticed her looking me over in my truck.

"Fine. I guess you can stay here for a while," she concedes.

If she thinks she has any say here, she's wrong.

I bow my head to her in mock gratitude. "How gracious of you. It's lucky we already know each other."

"That's what I'm worried about," she mutters.

"Ah, it's not gonna be *that* bad, Ash."

She pins me with a look, and I'm not sure if it's because she knows that's a bald-faced lie or if she doesn't appreciate the nickname. She knows this situation has nightmarish potential. And *I* know she hasn't forgotten for one solitary second that I never called. Ashlyn plucks the steel wool from the sink and resumes her regime with renewed vigour. I look her over in that apron and catalogue the defiant look in her chestnut eyes.

I didn't call. But I really, really should have.

CHAPTER FOUR

Isaac

I linger in the doorway of Mummo's room, leaning against the dark wood frame and watching her in her armchair. The room smells of the woody florals of her Estee Lauder perfume. Of hugs and comfort and all things grandma. Pappa and I purchased that scent for her every Christmas. At the department store's fragrance counter, he'd give me an encouraging shove, making me ask the salesperson. He always let me keep the change. We wrapped the same blue box, and every year she'd act surprised. I've kept the tradition since he passed. How many more of those glass bottles will I get to buy? Since her Alzheimer's diagnosis last year, it's been hard to push those kinds of thoughts from my mind.

I follow Mummo's line of sight out the window, wondering if she's imagining the back garden as it used to be, because the state of it now isn't anything to gaze at. Noticing me, her warm smile extends all the way to her clouded blue eyes. A robin's egg kerchief covers much of her thick grey hair, and her gold wedding ring shines on her hand as she fusses with the scarf.

"Are you coming in or are you just going to stand there, Little One?"

She's called me that since I *was* a little one, but it stuck after I'd surpassed her height and then Pappa's.

I cross the room and kneel so we're eye to eye. "Hi, Mummo."

After I kiss her soft cheek, I sit on the foot of her firm twin bed.

"So, I was thinking I could stay here for a bit."

She raises one fair eyebrow. "Bored of the fancy condo?"

I brought her over to see it when I first moved in. She thought the elevator was too fast and refused to go on the glass-railed patio.

"What do you even do way up there in the sky? Look out the window?"

I smirk, not pointing out that's the activity she'd been partaking in a minute before. "Something like that. So, is that okay? Can I stay?"

I imagine a walk of shame out the front door, Ashlyn laughing at me being caught in my lies.

"How do you plan on earning your keep?"

I swallow. My keep? I *planned* to bust my ass trying to start a business from scratch.

Her eyes sparkle, "I have an idea. I'll write you a list."

"A list?" I scratch my jaw.

"Things are falling apart around here. Your grandfather is slacking."

Pappa died three years ago. Most of the time, she remembers that.

"Okay, Mummo. I'll take your list. Are Pappa's tools still in the workshop?"

"Where else would they be? The key is under a can of red paint in the garage."

She opens a drawer in the desk near her chair and rifles through it, presumably for a pen and paper.

"Your new personal nurse can help you with your list. Now who's fancy?" I squeeze her shoulder jokingly. "I wasn't aware Dad was hiring somebody."

Nurse Ashlyn. That's going to take some getting used to. It's at odds with how I'd pictured her in the weeks since our meeting. Broken down car, dead cell phone. Assuming that she was irresponsible and reckless was easy. Yet neither of those traits seem to fit this woman who cares for the elderly and scrubs their homes to boot.

"Catherine is friendly, strict though."

Strict? She better be treating my Mummo like gold.

"I think it's Ashlyn."

"Right, right. I knew that." She covers my hand where it still rests on her cardigan-clad shoulder. "Don't worry about being bored, Little One, I'll have a list of things that need doing before you can say go."

Between my new list and the woman a few walls away, boredom is the last thing I'll have to worry about.

The key is right where Mummo said it was, tucked under a dust-coated paint can with a rusty ring beneath it. She remembers where a tiny piece of metal hides but not the name of her live-in nurse. The mind is a funny thing. I rub the gold key against my pant leg and unlock the workshop door, leaning my weight against it until the sticking jam pops open. I breathe in a cloud of dusty air, violently coughing as I wave my hands in front of my face and force open the windows that will budge. The lights buzz as they warm up, doing almost nothing to cut through the February gloom. I squint up at the rafters; most of the cobweb-covered utility bulbs hang black and lifeless. Sighing, I brush my palm across the large table in the centre of the workshop, sending ancient cedar shavings to the floor. I lean against a wall between two filthy windows and slide on the heels of my boots until my ass hits the floor. When Pappa was my age, he'd already moved across an ocean, established his own business, purchased land, *and* had a wife and son. What do I have? A big truck payment and my old room at Grandma's house. Let's not forget a disgruntled roommate who looks at me with utter contempt.

My credit card is maxed out, the sun set hours ago, and the workshop looks a hell of a lot better. It's still old-school, which I love, but parts of it look like they belong in this millennium. Resisting the modern conveniences of the construction world had practically been a hobby for my grandfather. His devotion to doing things the old way is what got me into carpentry. It's probably what pushed my dad so far in the other direction. But it's a new era, and I'm going to embrace every comfort modernity can provide. Blending those older techniques and my experience of the current construction world should be the perfect pairing. I underestimated how hard it would be to work in a space that is so distinctly Pappa's. For every warm memory I have of watching him work under this roof, there's the acute hurt that comes with losing the man that was a hell of a lot more like a dad than my biological one. Pappa lived a long life, a good life. But I still wasn't ready for the news when he passed away in his sleep three years ago. How could I be? Naturally, that leads me to think of Mummo's fragility and the fate of the home I love so much, for so many reasons.

On my last trip out, I stocked the new beer fridge. There's a good dent in the row of pale ales, and another beer cap clinks to the floor, my reward for a job well done. The clean wood floors gleam, reflecting the brighter lights that hang above. I take a selfie with my fresh beer and the new table saw that sits on a modern workbench behind me, sending it off to my group chat with Chris, Berg, and Dean.

Isaac: New temporary home of Lauri Contracting and Restorations. Come to the Dark Side.

Chris: You must mean the Dark Age. Looks rustic.

Berg: What are the benefits like?

Isaac: The benefit is you don't have to work for an asshat any longer.

Dean: I thought you'd never ask. When do I quit?

LOVINGLY RESTORED

It's going to be okay. I can do this. Surveying my work once more, I kill the lights and secure the new sturdy lock. I'm sweaty, my back aches, and my childhood bedroom is calling to me. Living at Mummo's house won't be so bad after all.

Chapter Five

Ashlyn

"You need to get over here right now." I grip my phone in one hand and hug myself for warmth with the other.

"Should I bring Mrs. Peabody and her perm rods along with me?"

Anna recently became the owner of the most popular full-service salon in West Isle. Okay, it's the only salon, but it's modern and bright and always busy.

"No, obviously not. Come after work."

"Okay, she's my last client. Tell me what's going on."

"I can't."

I need her here, in person. I kick at a blackberry vine in a severely overgrown garden bed. The state of this backyard is a crying shame. That blackberry needs to be ripped out before it takes over. I can hear running water and laughter in the salon, and when a beeping noise comes through the phone, I know it's time for those perm rods to come out.

"That's my timer. Gotta go. See you soon."

I tuck my phone away and sigh in resignation as I make my way back to the house. Isaac Lauri looked just as good dry in the daylight as he did soaked on a stormy night. Touchable dirty blond hair, strong jaw, and a physique that says he knows all about hard work. While we aren't *total* strangers, Isaac is still a mystery to me. It's unsettling. Dropping his bag earlier spelled out a simple message, and propping his gigantic feet on the clean tabletop delivered it.

Back in my slippers, I check my calendar. Mrs. Lauri's medications and vitamins are tucked into a clear bin on top of the fridge, easy for me to see and manage. I've been working in her home for three weeks already and am settled into a routine that suits the sweet eighty-year-old. Now, all of a sudden, we have a third wheel. While I'm sure Mrs. Lauri doesn't see her own grandson as such, I sure do. I busy myself by making half a tuna sandwich and a nutritional drink for her lunch. Pills go into a tiny dish after I meticulously note the dosages and time. Less than a month ago, her meds were a mess. After a few phone calls with her family doctor and the pharmacy, I have everything perfect, and I'm not going to let anyone mess that up. Balancing the lunch tray, I push open her bedroom door with my hip. Her wingback chair is turned to face the square window framed with blue gingham curtains. She greets me with a smile. The powerful rumble of an engine travels through the house. For a second, I'm transported back to the night we met. The safety of being tucked into the rich leather seat, hot air sinking into my skin, Isaac's rich laughter as we chatted. The sound of the truck fades. It's good he's leaving, so I can focus on my afternoon. I hope he's headed to work and that he clocks long hours and has a gruelling commute. The less time we spend together, the better.

"Lunch time, Mrs. Lauri." I place the tray next to her chair and spread a white cloth napkin on her lap.

"Already?"

I hold the dish of pills toward her in one hand and a cup of water with a bendy straw in the other. "Can you believe it?"

"My stomach can." She smiles as she nibbles on the corner of her sandwich, some of her frosty pink lipstick transferring to the bread.

I have more in common with her than any other patient I've cared for. She was quite the gardener in her day. We've looked at several photo albums of her garden over the years. She and her late husband, Jakob, moved into the home in the 1960s, not long after they married. They were the second owners of the nearly one-hundred-year-old house. The backyard, the size of which is basically unheard of by modern property standards, used to be a marvel. I'm green with envy over how she'd filled it with her favourite plants but also a practical herb and vegetable garden. I never would have recognized the fresh-faced boy who appears in several of the images. Chomping a dirt-covered carrot the best he could with only one incisor or hiding amongst the delicate flowers in a way I imagined Grandma would *not* have appreciated. But now that I've seen the images and Isaac in the daytime, he looks a lot like his handsome grandpa. While she eats, I sit cross-legged on her bed to fold some laundry. I shake out a fluffy white bath towel, matching the corners together.

"I met your grandson today." She doesn't need to know it wasn't our first encounter. "I hear he'll be staying for a while…"

She finishes her swallow of sandwich and nods. "Yes, wasn't that a surprise?"

"Mmm hmm." I press my lips together and shove the folded towel into the laundry basket. "You could call it that."

I've got it all worked out with Mummo. That lying *rat*.

"Isaac lived here as a boy after his mother left."

I pause at the teak tall boy dresser, placing a pile of her unmentionables inside.

"Left?" As soon as the word is out of my mouth, I chastise myself. Talking about gardening and grandkids is one thing, but I don't need the nitty-gritty details.

"They fought like cats and dogs, especially after having Isaac."

This conversation is way too personal. I'm supposed to be separating myself and my own feelings from my patients, not delving into the secrets of their past. The thought of that happy boy in the photos being left by his mother is a punch to the gut. Eager to end the conversation, lest I bear more sympathy for the overgrown liar, I snatch up the lunch tray and laundry basket.

"I'll bring your tea in a little while," I say before leaving the room.

Anna's head bobs into view through the amber stained glass above the front door.

Thank god.

"Come in, come in." I push the rolled towel back into place at the gap under the door where cold air rushes in.

The gorgeous old house is a bitch to keep warm.

She hangs up her puffer coat and throws her arms around me. "Haven't seen you in a couple weeks."

"Right?" Her cheek is cold against mine. "I've been stuck here."

She lets me go. "This is tough living, Ashlyn. Need me to break you out? I bet we could take the old hag on, the two of us." She shuffles like she's in kickboxing class, fists guarding her face.

Anna finds a seat at the kitchen table, and I click the kettle on.

"You and the sweet old lady, that's a tough situation for sure."

"Well..." I wring my hands in my apron.

Anna's eyes round as she presses her hands over her heart. "Did she *die*?" Her last word is a mere whisper.

"What? Oh my god, no! What the hell, Anna?" I shake my head and pull three porcelain teacups down from an open wood cupboard. "Don't say stuff like that."

"What am I supposed to think? Be less cryptic."

Here goes nothing.

"So, remember the guy from last month? Isaac?" Why does saying his name seem to raise my body temperature a whole degree?

"Ashlyn. That's the most interesting thing that's happened to you in years. I obviously remember."

"I sort of gave him my number that night."

She gasps like I said I gave him road head on the drive home.

"Did he text? Did he call? Did you reply?" Her voice is squeaky.

Anna is spiralling, but I need her to be solid for me.

"No, will you shut up for a second?"

She presses her lips together, and there is, momentarily, a peacefulness in the kitchen where the only sounds are the water boiling in the kettle and the clock ticking above the back door. Then I hear the now familiar rumble of the big Ford truck vibrating its way down the driveway. The detached garage isn't far off from the kitchen, and the Old Country Roses teacups that I'd set out actually rattle.

"Ashlyn," she drags out my name, "what is that noise?"

I hear her, but I can't tear my eyes away from the window above the apron front sink. Seconds later, sauntering into view, is the impressive backside of one Isaac Lauri carrying an assortment of bags and boxes out of the garage. Every posterior muscle flexes under the weight of his cargo, and my mouth is dry by the time he disappears inside the other out building.

"Who on Earth," she joins me at the sink, "is that?

At that moment he exits the building, running his hands through that dirty, dirty blond mane. When his eyes flick up, they land right on mine. Of course they do. I make a choking sound and grab Anna's hand, ducking down and pulling her with me without a second thought.

"*That* is Isaac."

How the hell am I going to do this cohabitation thing when the man just, quite literally, brought me to my knees?

"So many questions. But brain is mush," says Anna next to me.

I explain quickly, not knowing how much time I have. What if he comes in the back door to the kitchen and asks me why we're playing hide and seek? "The man who hired me for this position is Isaac's dad. Isaac is Mrs. Lauri's grandson, and, as of today, he *moved in with her.*"

Anna creeps up into a semi-squat to peek out the window again.

"Stop that." I smack her butt over her black jeans. "That's *my* hot roommate."

She raises her eyebrows at me. "That's messed up, Ashlyn. What are the chances?"

I groan because she's right. West Isle is not a big town by any means, but this is too weird. Anna pours the tea for me while I remain in a puddle on the clean kitchen floor, admiring the gleaming tiles, even if they're icy cold.

"So, what are you going to do?" Anna asks.

"Nothing. I want this job. I *need* this job. It pays well, and you know how bad I want to have something bigger than my apartment."

I can't care less about the square footage of the actual house. Give me some soil to sink my hands into. I crave the pressure of cool earth around my fingers. I'm already hoping this job extends into the spring and summer and I can find the courage to ask Mrs. Lauri to do some yard work. All of this is temporary, but I can't help myself. I stare out at that yard every day, and it's such a waste.

An hour has passed, and I've already listened to Anna's hair salon gossip, given Mrs. Lauri her tea, and helped her get into bed for an afternoon rest. I cleaned the kitchen within an inch of its life and, of course, glanced out the window about three hundred times. I'm gripped with a wild curiosity about what is in that out building and what Isaac is doing inside.

"You don't think he's, like, hiding anything in there, do you?" I ask, sinking into a dining chair with my second cup of tea.

"Like what?"

"Contraband?"

"I can't with you. Those are bags from a hardware store, weirdo."

"Great. So, it could be saws and tape and those long plastic things that go on your wrists."

She tips her head to one side, "Zip ties?"

"Sure. Those."

Anna tucks her phone in her pocket and places her teacup in the sink.

"Are you leaving? Don't. I'm not above begging."

"You live here, and apparently, so does he. You're going to have to get used to each other. Be cool."

I fan my face. "I'm not cool. I hang out with old people. My favourite game is backgammon. I think prunes are delicious."

"You could quit," she says. "Or call the boss man and complain."

Something doesn't really seem right about checking up on Isaac like that.

"No. I can do this." I clap my hands to psych myself up. "He's only hot because he's mysterious or whatever. That'll get old real fast."

"I cannot agree with you on that last point. Sorry. I have eyes."

I'm not even doing a good job of convincing my cousin, let alone myself.

"When it comes down to it, we're all adults here. Three mature adults. Living together."

She grabs her purse off the counter. "I'll leave you adults to it and let myself out."

And then she leaves me with my elderly patient and my unreasonably hot and unwelcome roommate.

CHAPTER SIX

Ashlyn

After much deliberation, Mrs. Lauri chooses the navy nightgown over the indigo while I turn down her sheets. I want to give her the agency to choose her own clothing, but it's not always easy to be patient at the end of the day. We sing our way through brushing our teeth and secure her thick hair beneath a silk nightcap. I read aloud a chapter of her murder mystery novel, and she's snoring softly before I can finish. After tucking an extra quilt around her legs, I sneak from the room, though I've learned that even a small aircraft won't wake her. Talkative the whole day, it's obvious her mood was elevated by Isaac's arrival. What grandmother doesn't love an extended visit from a loved one? If there's one thing that helps patients that you can't get in a pharmacy, it's important people in their lives. That connection and support is priceless. As annoyed as I am about having an unexpected male roomie, this is a net positive for Mrs. Lauri, and that's what my job is all about.

Isaac made himself scarce all day, maybe due to my less than warm welcome. Whatever he's been doing in the mystery building kept him occupied, and that's fine by me. With any luck he and I will orbit around each other with minimal interaction. It's for the best. I keep a tight ship with his grandmother's care, and I don't really need anyone stirring that up. Shuffling into the kitchen to get a snack before turning in for the night, I stop in my tracks, the swinging kitchen door hitting me in the ass. A large male is rummaging in the cupboards. I feel like I'm witnessing a bear crashing a picnic? You know, if I was attracted to bears. Flattening myself against the door, I wonder if a person in a fluffy pink robe and a hair mask will pass as part of the decor. Men aren't *that* observant.

"What the hell did you do with my cereal?"

Okay, this one is.

He continues his scavenging, moving on to the next cupboard.

"The Lucky Charms? Froot Loops?" I list off some of the children's cereals I'd found during my kitchen clear out.

"Either. Both."

"I assumed those were for small children. How many nieces and nephews do you have?"

"None. I'm an only child. Why do you assume *I* don't have kids?"

He looks over his shoulder at me with those crisp blue eyes, and I wish like hell I wasn't wearing my bathrobe. I bristle at the thought of Isaac with a whole family and steal a look at his left hand. Bare.

He abandons his search, turning to face me. He's tall enough that when he leans back and folds his arms, his hips are level with the counter.

"Do you?"

He winks. "Not that I'm aware of."

I roll my eyes. *How endearing.*

"The cereal is mine." He runs his hand through his hair, a move that's sexier than it should be for a guy who just made a weird joke about illegitimate children.

"*Was* yours. I regret to inform you they were well past their expiration."

Regret to inform you? Was I notifying the cereals' next of kin?

His face falls, and he places his hands over what are probably rows of visible abs. "You're killing me. I'm starving."

On cue, his stomach growls.

"I tackled the cupboards and pantry this week. There were a lot of items going bad."

"Makes sense," he sighs. "Do you need to get in here?"

There's more than enough room for us both, but this is a healthy distance. The last time we were too close in his truck I'd done idiotic things like blush and offer my phone number without prompting. The knowledge that I was so unappealing to him that he couldn't even send a text makes me cringe. I've tried to forget it, but the memory is as fresh as an unopened box of cereal.

"I'm only here for a snack. I ate supper with your grandmother at five." I glance towards the clock behind him that reads ten o'clock.

"Five? That's not supper time."

"It is for your grandmother," I snap.

He'd know that if he'd been around the past month. If I had a dollar for every elderly person I'd cared for whose family barely visited, I'd have a whole damn acreage for my flowers.

I tighten the tie around my waist and fold my arms across my chest. Isaac is wearing the same clothes as earlier but is now filthy. If he tries putting his feet on the table again, I'll hit him with my slipper, European grandma style. I bet Mrs. Lauri has tips. His snug jeans are dusty on the knees and ass, his shirt wrinkled, and the musk of a hard-working man reaches me as he moves. He rubs at the scruff on his jaw before drawing his phone out of his pocket.

Would you look at that? He still has it. I bet he deleted my number.

"In that case, I'm gonna order pizza. What do you like?" He walks to the fridge and reads the number off a faded, pizza-shaped magnet.

We aren't going to have some late-night, roommate-bonding pizza party. If he called me up a few days after our meeting, yeah, I'd have grabbed food with him. But a month has gone by, and he isn't some mysterious guy who saved my ass, he's the grandson of my patient. There are some definite personal/professional violations going on here. I open a cupboard that *was* the picture of organization before Isaac attacked it. My spine tingles as I stand on my tiptoes for the box of granola bars I placed up there after my last grocery shop. My hand meets the bare shelf. Craning my neck, I can make out the bottom of the tipped over box, just out of my reach.

Shoot.

"You like olives? Pineapple?"

"Neither." I lie, continuing to reach while the arches of my feet cramp from my efforts.

I want a snack. Is that too much to ask?

"Okay, plain pepperoni?"

My fingers graze the edge of the box, so close, and then it slips back from my fingers. "I don't think it's a good idea, Isaac." His name comes out in a sharp burst, frustration over his arrival and my elusive granola bars compounding to make my voice edgy.

My calves give out, and I lower myself back onto flat feet, sighing in resignation.

"Pizza is always a good idea." His deep voice is right behind me, his shadow sweeping across the butcher block counter to merge with mine. He reaches into the cupboard and snags the box, bringing it down to my level.

"Coconut or peanut?" he asks, offering me the open package.

His arms are around me, his biceps grazing my upper arms.

I grit my teeth, "Why are there only two left?"

"Sorry. I was hungry earlier...I didn't know they were yours."

I snatch the last two bars, fully aware that pizza would taste a whole lot better.

"Don't make this awkward. We can still enjoy each other's company, right?"

"The only company I need is your grandmother."

It sounds silly, even to me. Obviously a twenty-six-year-old woman needs more than that.

"Let's keep it professional," I say.

Rich laughter catches me off guard, loud in the confines of the closed concept kitchen. Isaac tips his head back, long throat exposed, Adam's apple bobbing. I hate the way that sound affects me.

"It's just pizza, Ashlyn, I wasn't asking you to go steady."

Any trace of resilience leaves me, and I wince. We nearly made it through day one without the topic coming up, but here we are. The elephant is in the room. I sort of wished an African mammal *was* between us. For a guy who isn't interested, he's standing real close. So close that I can smell hops on his breath and know he's chewing cinnamon gum to cover it up. He licks his full lips, and I catch a flash of the pale pink gum tucked between his white teeth. I scowl way up at him, unwilling to break eye contact first lest it be a sign of submission. He may be related to the owner of this house, but I belong here too.

He lowers his voice to a whisper. Hot, spiced breath fans against my forehead. "You almost got me hot with the fuzzy housecoat, though."

He touches the neckline of my robe, rubbing the material with his thumb, brushing my collarbone with one callused finger. My skin flushes at the contact, embarrassing evidence of our one-sided attraction. Arousal and anger wars in my chest. I can't help but think he's screwing with me. Is this another power play like earlier? I smack his hand away, the sharp sound distinct in the quiet room. He recoils, stuffing his hands into his dirty jean's pockets, having the decency to look embarrassed.

"Goodnight." I infuse enough venom into my tone to be a warning.

I storm out with my measly granola bars clutched in my sweaty palm, probably melting the chocolate chips.

CHAPTER SEVEN

Isaac

I open and close my mouth, an uncanny resemblance to the plastic guppies in that magnetic fishing game, but nothing good comes out. Ashlyn leaves, the kitchen door swinging shut and the sound of her slippers fading. Once she's out of earshot, all the right words pop into my head. Ground-breaking things like: *Sorry* and *I'm a jerk* and *I've had at least three beers on an empty stomach.* Not that the last one is an excuse for my behaviour. Instead of going after her, because she's fucking scary when she's mad, I order a large barbecue chicken pizza and finish the entire thing alone in the kitchen. No big deal, I'm used to eating by myself. Bachelor life. Mummo needs a nurse, that much is obvious, and the last thing I need is to drive her away or give her a reason to call my dad to complain. I'm a moron, and I have to do better at keeping my hands to myself. I manage to shower even though there is some sort of creeping plant hanging in there. At one point a vine wrapped itself around my wrist while I shampooed, and I nearly bailed. I swear it was out to get me.

When I'm out of the bathroom and ready to sleep, I stand outside my childhood haven. The place I sought whenever my dad and I butted heads is right behind the three-panel, solid-core door. More recently, After Pappa passed, I stayed here for weeks so Mummo wouldn't be alone. That was years ago, and it's bizarre to be back. My damp feet conduct a chill through the threadbare runner, and the too small towel around my hips is weak protection from the draughts. I turn the cool brass handle, but it sticks. It's then that I notice the soft light seeping out from under the door into the hall.

"Oh, you're kidding me," I say under my breath. I lean in, placing my lips close to the door. "Ashlyn."

No reply.

"*Ashlyn*," I growl. "It's obvious you're in there. I can see the light."

I want to keep my voice down for Mummo, but my restraint is waning.

"Who is it?" Her voice is light and sweet.

Who the fuck else would it be?

Give me strength.

"That's *my* room, Ashlyn."

"Sorry. I didn't know it was yours," she echoes my earlier apology about the granola bars.

I bang my fist, just once, against the door. It bounces on its hinges, and her response is a barely audible yelp followed by an aggravating lilt of laughter. My old mattress has lumps in all the right places. I've memorized where the floors squeak and how to silently open the stubborn sash window, a skill honed by more than a few nights of sneaking out.

It's mine.

The only room left is the primary bedroom. Cold, stale air whooshes toward me when I enter. My skin is covered in goose-flesh, but I'm hot with annoyance. I chuck my bags towards the bed, overshoot, and they sail over the queen-sized mattress, thudding onto the floor, missing the tall brass lamp in the corner by a hair.

"Damn it!"

I have a whole other chain of expletives I'll save for a time when my grandmother isn't sleeping nearby. I glare at the shared wall, picturing *her* on the other side, comfy and cozy.

Is my name on the door? No. But Isaac Lauri is sure as shit written on the second-grade bowling trophy on the shelf above the desk. There's also a handful of Playboy issues hidden beneath the mattress, so I send a prayer to the pornography gods that she's not a nosy roommate.

Sleeping in my grandmother and grandfather's room, a space they shared for decades, seems all wrong. Even Mummo relocated to the guest room not long after he passed. Logically, it's a room with a bed and all the other makings of a place to rest, but the remnants of their love are here. Mismatched picture frames sit upon each surface, holding memories and catching dust. An oval frame displays a photo of a strawberry blonde in a striped bikini with a chubby toddler in her lap. I run my thumb through the dust, revealing the face of my mother, who I only know from pictures. The photo evokes no memories. I should probably have mommy issues over something like that, but any gap that her leaving caused was thoroughly and lovingly filled by my grandparents. I only wished her departure hadn't created such bitterness in my remaining parent. Maybe that was always there. Perhaps that's what made her leave. She didn't have any family. I suppose it made sense to leave me in a town that had loving grandparents.

I slip into pyjama pants and fall back on the bed, a solo trust building exercise between myself and the antique furniture. The handmade quilt is covered in dust and my nose tickles when I pull it over me. I'll wash it all tomorrow. Since when does offering to share a pizza with someone who said they were hungry imply something more than eating? My laughter when she mentioned keeping things professional was forced. I'd extended a proverbial olive branch, and she turned it into a lecture on personal boundaries. The soft quilt backing curls into my fists, but it's the silky texture of her skin that's trapped in my mind. The way her hips rocked as she reached for her measly granola bars. Too hungry to only take one, but too stubborn to enjoy a proper meal with me. Her curvy butt managed to fill out the fabric of that robe in a way that shouldn't be possible. I tried to avert my gaze and keep my distance, but I'm human, and the damn box wasn't going to leap into her hands. She pulled me in like a tide to shore, and the warmth of her back seeping into my chest made it hard to go back out to the chill of the sea. The quilt tents over my hips. I groan, annoyed with myself for getting aroused by a woman who had all but told me to fuck off. I roll over, trapping the hardness against the mattress. I'm not touching a boner that she's responsible for. And that apology I'd been planning? That's not gonna happen.

CHAPTER EIGHT

Ashlyn

The mist from the spray bottle catches the light, and a rainbow arcs through the air before the moisture settles on my growing palm tree. Water droplets roll along the dark, waxy leaves. Fresh shoots erupt from the top. This plant likes his new home. I was enjoying it here too, until an oversized house-guest came in and took things a step too far last night. I scoff, bouncing onto my bed, trying to quash down the annoyance I feel every time I replay the encounter. I'm being paid to be here, and he's, well, I'm not sure what he's doing. It's hard enough to figure out my patients and their care, let alone navigating their extended family. I leave my door ajar to hear when Mrs. Lauri wakes from her nap and settle back against the headboard with my book. I scan the page to find the right spot. The main male character just cornered the heroine backstage, and things are about to get *juicy* in the shadows of stage left.

"How's Punk Rock *Cock*?"

I gasp, snapping the book closed. This man is a walking adrenaline rush. He needs to wear a bell. Between sneaking up on me and that four-letter word from his mouth, my heart is racing.

Isaac leans against the doorway to my bedroom in a way I'm sure my punk rock hero did in Chapter Five. I slide the book beneath my thighs in an attempt to hide the semi-nude man on the cover.

He laughs, pointing in the vicinity of the book. "Nothing I haven't seen before."

The navy blue henley he's wearing does nothing to camouflage his muscular arms and broad chest. I scan the length of his legs, ensuring I blink at his belt buckle. I'm *not* going there.

"What are you doing in my room, Lauri?"

I'm not sure why I used his last name like we're bros. Isaac and I are *not* on the same team.

"*My* room, you mean." He gestures to a couple sports trophies on a shelf. "But you knew that."

I swallow. Of course I did. The room has male written all over it. I can guess what's under the mattress, too. Obviously, I had no clue that the original occupant of said room would need it. When he showed up yesterday and announced he was staying, I thought about offering to trade... but then he pissed me off. First, he ate my snacks, then he touched me. But it wasn't that finger on my collarbone that bothered me. It's the way my body lit up from the contact of that solitary digit.

I shake my head to clear the memory. "Looks like it belongs to a *little* boy. I'm not switching."

"The little boy grew up." A smirk tugs at the corner of his mouth, and I swear his chest swells.

He looks around the room, noting the alterations. The seven-foot-tall palm tree, my clothes in the open closet, the full bedding change. Sleeping in the sheets of an unknown person was a no for me.

"Can I help you?" I lace enough sarcasm into my voice, so he knows I'm not offering to assist him with anything.

"Yes." He unfurls a pair of jeans. An obvious, orange bleach stain extends down one leg. "Wondering if you knew how to get rid of this?"

"That," I circle my pointer finger, "is permanent."

He looks crestfallen, full bottom lip protruding. I note that a grown man pouting should revolt me, but the shape of his lips only makes me wonder how they'd fit against my own.

"Damn. I thought you'd know a laundry trick."

I stifle a laugh. "A laundry trick?"

As though women received a handbook of such information at the onset of menstruation. Or worse, is he coming in here expecting I'll *do* his chores? Forget it.

"Nope, that's bleach, unfortunately, the damage is done."

"How unfortunate that someone *threw bleach at me.*" He balls up the fabric and chucks it toward me, but I dodge.

"I thought you were an intruder. It was an automatic reaction."

"Remind me to not sneak up on you if you're cooking in case you have a knife."

"Smart. I keep them real sharp."

"Are you aware of how hard it is to find jeans with a thirty-five-inch inseam?"

"Um." I gesture to my legs that don't come anywhere near the end of the bed. "The distressed look is fashionable." I have to lighten the mood. For the plants. I'd hate for them to wilt from the awkwardness.

"Spring is coming. I'll turn them into cut-offs."

His delivery is deadpan, and while I endeavour not to burst into laughter, the mental image of a pair of blond hairy legs in booty shorts breaks me. Laughter bubbles out of me.

"I don't think you have the ass for it." I crane my neck, pretending to steal a look.

"I think you know I do." His warm grin hints at dimples beneath his scruff.

I cover my mouth, trying to get myself in check. Flirtatious banter, or whatever this is, can't happen. It goes against what I told him last night. He made his choice, and I won't be an afterthought because our living situation puts me right under his nose.

"What are these all about?" He walks over to the fern in the corner.

Putting the largest plants in my room was my way of not imposing. That was before I learned how much of a plant lover Mrs. Lauri is. Since then, they've spilled over into the rest of the house.

"They're called plants. Green, use photosynthesis, enjoy water?"

He frowns at me. Those Arctic eyes are so damn inquisitive. "Hold on."

Something is going on in that obnoxiously handsome head of his, I just don't know what.

My heart skips a beat as I remember my lie about my career. If I'm not willing to share a pizza with him, I'm sure as hell not sharing my dreams either, so I press my lips together and pick some lint off the comforter.

"What's this one called?" He tousles the fronds of a fern.

"It's a Maidenhair fern, and don't touch it."

He laughs, "What? Is it going to wither and die under my touch?"

"You never know."

If the plant feels anything like I did last night, it's not unlikely that the whole thing might combust.

"I like it." He looks right at me while he flicks the tip of a leaf, trying to get a rise out of me.

I am the picture of serenity as I ignore it.

"You should have seen Mummo's plants," he says.

"I did. I mean, she showed me pictures. Everything was so beautiful."

While I'm conjuring images of robust rhododendrons, Isaac makes himself even more at home, plunking down on the foot of the bed. I hug my knees to my chest, drawing my feet further from the heat radiating off his hips. This house is always so cold, yet Isaac emits heat like he's recently vacated a sauna.

"Are plants a hobby of yours?"

"Something like that." I fiddle with the elastic at the end of my braid, bristling at his use of the same word my mother does when speaking about my love of all things flora.

He tips his head.

"What do you do?" I turn the questions back on him.

I've been wondering since we met. What job does a guy have where he can afford that beast of a truck but doesn't have anywhere to be in the middle of the day on a Thursday?

"By trade, I'm a carpenter."

Oh, God. Why does he have to have a hot job?

"Cool. What do you usually, um, carpent?"

Carpent? Oh, my flipping God, Ashlyn.

He bites his bottom lip, eyes sparkling with amusement. At least one of us is entertained by my inability to remember common words.

"I studied Fine Woodworking and general carpentry, but I mostly enjoy restorations. Bringing old houses and furniture back to their original state. I can do a lot of different things."

Every home and garden show I've ever watched runs through my mind like a highlight reel. My stomach somersaults as I glance at his hands. Can those big mitts actually hone chunks of wood into something ornate? I'd imagine most materials are pretty malleable under his influence. Women, for example.

Clearing my throat, I drag my eyes off the two fingers I'm perving over. "You must love it here then. Your grandmother's house is lovely."

He rubs the back of his neck. "Thanks. I do. It...needs a lot of work. Mummo's making me a list." He sounds tired at the prospect.

"Believe me when I tell you she's working on it." Mrs. Lauri showed me the list earlier. It's double-sided.

He gives me a 'oh, shit' look. It's cute and vulnerable, and I wish he wouldn't.

"Do you run your own business?" I ask.

He stiffens, like I corrected his posture.

"No." The bed groans with relief as he stands.

Apparently, that topic isn't up for discussion. At the door he pauses, one of those large hands wraps around the unpainted wood frame. He inspects the woodgrain and drums his fingertips in a simple rhythm.

"Come out and see the workshop one day. I can show you some things I *carpent*."

Couldn't let that one slide, could he?

"If I have time." I sit back against the headboard and pretend to read, feigning disinterest.

"Make some." The floors creak as he walks away.

I try to enjoy the rest of my downtime, but my eyes skim the same sentence over and over, and the rock star keeps trading the guitar for a tool belt. Instead of a stage, he's standing in a tiny bedroom, full of plants, and one very screwed nurse.

CHAPTER NINE

Isaac

I'm sitting on my bed, laptop open on my legs, when an email from the bank hits my inbox. My stomach flips as I read the message from the loan officer, eyes darting from line to line of the tiny text. My business line of credit was approved. I stare at the zeroes and swallow hard, raking a hand through my hair. That's a lot of money. A lot of responsibility. Banks, lawyers, insurance. Employees, payroll, site safety. But this is what I wanted. What I've been putting off for way too long. I've been drowning in a sea of adulting, and it's paying off. Berg and Dean are in; they transferred me the money that claims their place as co-owners, and they've signed all the paperwork. I'm working on Chris. He's younger than us, and it's scary to leave a sure thing. I get it, but I refuse to leave his ass behind. Some of my oldest contacts, friends of my grandfather, have spread the word about my new venture, and I'm receiving more inquiries than I can handle. Only a week living with Mummo, and I'm figuring things out.

"Isaac Lauri!" The voice of my feisty roommate comes flying down the hall.

"Jesus, now what?" I say under my breath.

Over the last week, Ashlyn has taken to hollering my full name whenever I do something that isn't to her liking. Unfortunately for me, that's a lot.

"Yes?" I call, pulling on a white t-shirt and leaving my bedroom in search of the impossible to please woman.

She pops her head out of the utility room off the kitchen. It houses the hot water heater, the ancient washing machine and dryer, and other odds and ends. "Get in here."

I can only see about half of her face, but it's enough to tell the general vibe is 'pissed'. Why are small angry women so scary...and hot? I step in to join her.

"You left your laundry in the washer again, and I need to throw a load in."

While I feel a strong urge to make a load related joke, I figure that type of humour isn't her speed.

"So? Switch it over," I say, leaning against the laundry sink.

Her eyebrows arch. "I'm not doing that. I get paid to do *two* people's laundry around here: my own and your grandmother's. Stick to the schedule. It's on the fridge."

Not the fucking schedule again. That calendar I saw her consulting the day I arrived? It's so much more than I could have ever imagined. It's not a schedule; it's a fucking flight plan. And it's laminated.

"Ashlyn, you're very good at your job, and Mummo loves you, but can't anything be done organically? Not every single thing requires a fucking colour-coded schedule."

Not only do I have my to-do list from Mummo, but it only took Ashlyn a matter of days to get my name on the refrigerator schedule.

"That's where you and I differ, I suppose," she says.

Eager to end my scolding of the day and switch my laundry, I step around her, but she moves the same way, accidentally blocking me.

She rolls her eyes, "Get out my way, you big oaf."

Oaf? What the fuck.

"Turn to the side," I tell her.

"What the hell will that do?"

"I don't know, make you smaller."

Her voice is shrill. "What is *that* supposed to mean!"

I laugh. It's too easy. I'm not going to tell her that I wouldn't change a damn thing about her body. We're fumbling around each other, the inward opening door hemming us in. Her soft hips brush my legs, and the floral and vanilla smell of her shampoo fills my nose. Ashlyn holds her arms awkwardly, trying to afford herself some personal space.

"Let me out of here, Isaac."

"I'm *trying*," I grit out.

With exasperation she tosses her arms up, accidentally swiping the box of detergent off the shelf behind her. Fine white powder spills across the linoleum and over our feet.

She covers her mouth with both hands, brown eyes wide. "Oops."

What a fucking mess, and I don't even mean the stuff on the floor.

"I'll get the broom," she says. "It's behind you. Excuse me."

"I know where the broom is."

Her telling me where things are in my own damn house irritates me. The powder sticks to my socks but is slippery at the same time. Where exactly does she want me to go? There's no room to back up, and I'm tracking soap all over the place.

"Let me do the laundry, and then I'll go."

She speaks under her breath, "None of this would have happened if you'd stuck to the schedule."

Holy hell.

This woman isn't on my nerves, she's *in* them. Why did I ever think we'd be able to manage this living situation? We're too different. I have about twelve things I need to do, and dancing around while being berated isn't one of them.

I'm *done*.

I grip her waist, lifting her with ease. "Up we go." I plant her on top of the big dryer with a hollow bang.

"What do you think you're doing?"

Personally, I think she sounds a little breathy. My lungs are doing some type of squeezy thing too, but that's due to the powerful smell of the spilled laundry soap. Right?

"Laundry." I wink at her. "Chores *are* fun."

I begin transferring the wet clumps of clothing.

"This is highly inappropriate, Isaac Lauri."

There she goes again. I'll protect my middle name with my life lest she start using all three of my names.

"I'm just trying to stick to the schedule, Ash," I say, sweet as honey.

She huffs and crosses her arms, and even though she's scowling, she looks damn cute perched up there. I fish out the last piece of laundry from the bottom of the drum, a particularly small pair of boxer briefs, unfurling them in front of her before tossing them in.

"For goodness sake," she says, a pink tinge blooming over her nose and cheeks.

It's so easy to get a rise out of her, and I've been doing it every chance I can. If she's going to nag me and make my life some sort of chore-laden hell, then I'll bother her the best way I know. Relentless flirtation. What's the worst that can happen? I throw the boxers in the dryer, closing the door. Ashlyn lifts her legs at the last second to avoid them getting slammed.

"Happy now?"

She nods stiffly, apparently out of smart things to say.

With her on top of the big appliance, we're eye level. She's erased the scowl off her face. Or maybe I did that. It occurs to me that if our eyes are aligned, other parts are too, and that has blood rushing to my dick way faster than it should.

"Oh," I say, slapping my forehead with my palm, "I almost forgot."

I smirk as I lean toward her, reaching for the dial.

She glares. "Don't you dare."

I'm about to set the machine to rumbling right under her ass, and she knows it. Aware that the big appliance packs a punch. It isn't some eco-friendly, whisper-quiet, new-fangled model. The burly beast vibrates its way right across the floor when it wants to. I look her dead in the eye and rotate the dial. The machine comes to life, filling the room with noise. The wet clothing thuds within the drum, the zippers and snaps clank on the metal. Even standing this close, you need to raise your voice to be heard.

"Get me off here, Isaac." She tries to poke me in the chest, her signature move, but I block her.

She can't slide down, not with the way I'm standing between her legs.

I cup my ear, "What's that?" I'm almost yelling. "You want to get off? You want me to get you off, Ash?"

A grin spreads over my face at my play on words while she shifts around, the shuddering machine beginning to affect her. Her eyes flutter close, and I'm keenly aware of my hardening dick pressing against the buttons of my fly.

Fuck.

Does she have room in her precious schedule for *self-care*? Because she fucking needs it. Ashlyn is the most tightly wound twenty-something woman I've ever met. What would it be like to see her unravel? I consider that for a moment, growing jealous of a major appliance. It's way too easy to picture her round ass squirming on my lap as she rolls closer to release. My fingers twitch at my side, eager to slide up her thighs and complement the oscillations beneath her. Her chest rises and falls more rapidly than normal, and my own breathing mimics hers. If I don't get out of here, I'll do something we, or at least she, might regret. The last thing I need is to give her a reason to contact my dad.

"Okay, ride's over."

I grab her around her waist again, the buzzing transferring through her body to mine. I mean to put her down right away. To deposit her back where she started and leave, laundry complete. But the delicious weight and warmth of her is hard to relinquish. Sliding her down the length of my body feels better than it should, and I'm acutely aware that she can probably tell how hard my dick is. Does she notice all the tension that's been building between us this past week? She looks up at me, wet lips slightly parted, examining my mouth. The sweet sigh that passes over her lips brings me back to reality, and I let her go. She falls a couple inches to the ground, gasping in surprise at the sudden movement. She already expressed to me that she didn't want to get involved like *that*. If she changes her mind, great, but I'm not going to bully her into it like this. Stepping through the mess on the floor, I squeeze my way around the door. Escaping from the tiny room and the woman I'm quickly learning has more control around here than I care for. Whose house is this, anyway?

CHAPTER TEN

It's one-part boredom, one-part curiosity, and one-part palpable sexual tension that propels me toward his workshop. A couple weeks have passed since he first asked. Most women wouldn't have lasted a day.

Ashlyn Carter: Paragon of Discipline.

Did other women get personal invites to Isaac Lauri's workshop?

Weeds brush against my jeans as I trek through the overgrown yard. The workshop has a barn vibe going on, minus the red paint. One end of the building has double doors that open toward the garage. The weathered wood and single-pane sash windows look like something you'd see hanging in an overpriced vintage store. A carving above the door says: EST. 1965. So the workshop isn't part of the original property, but was probably built by Isaac's grandfather. The whine of heavy machinery cuts through the evening. Despite the cool air, I have to wipe my palms on my white fuzzy cardigan.

When I pull open the heavy door and step inside, the change in temperature is overpowering. Warm air rushes towards me as I take it all in. Hand-hewn plank flooring, thick rafters suspending strings of glowing industrial-style bulbs, the shelves cluttered with old-fashioned tools. The last light of day seeps in through the windows. I'd pictured a sparse and sterile work environment full of steel toolboxes and shiny wrenches with a cold cement floor. That's what they always display on the home improvement shows. Everything new, top of the line. Instead, the space is cozy, and I immediately love it.

Isaac is bent over a modern table saw, tight jeans stretching across his behind. He raises his arms over his head, and my eyes are drawn to the inch of skin that appears. His jeans hang low on his hips, black boxer briefs sit flush against his lower back beneath the prominent muscles on either side of his spine. I'm a complete creep for noticing those are the same briefs he brandished at me in the laundry room. The workshop is a hell of a lot larger than the utility room, but I'm not sure it's big enough to house the tension mounting between us lately. I can see the house through the window. That's where I'm supposed to be. It was dumb of me to come. If I turn around and leave while the saw still buzzes, he won't even notice. I turn on my heel, but because I have crappy luck, it stops. In the silence my ears ring. Even my own breathing seems loud.

"Making a break for it?" His deep, warm voice starkly contrasts the metallic whine of the saw.

"Nope, just got here."

He looks me up and down, which is fair considering the once over I gave his backside. Why else did I change into these tight jeans and look in the mirror five times before I came out here unless to turn his head? Whenever he smirks at me like that I can barely look away.

"You're gonna get dirty," he says.

"P-pardon?"

"That white sweater is gonna get dirty in here."

My brain is doing its damndest to turn this into some weird woodworking fantasy.

"I won't touch anything," I say, stuffing my hands in the impractical cardigan pockets.

"Gonna be hard to not touch anything while you're helping me."

He hooks his thumbs into his belt loops, tugging the waist of his jeans ever so slightly lower.

"Help?" I squeak. "I couldn't. I don't have a clue about any of this." I flap my hands erratically around the room.

He takes a couple steps closer. "No experience required. C'mon, let me show you a few things."

"You said show. Not do."

"It's more fun to do it."

His words twist themselves like ribbons. I imagine a couple things that I wouldn't mind him showing me at all. I'm not naïve enough to think Isaac's near constant double entendres are accidental. It's obvious he does it to rile me up. It works like a charm. His blue eyes plead down at me, and I soften alarmingly fast under his persuasion.

I lay my sweater over the back of an antique tufted armchair. Shedding the layer is a relief under the heat of the machinery, lighting, and Isaac's gaze. Steel-toed work boots give him a boost in height that he doesn't need. I'm almost giddy looking up at him. When Isaac raises his chin in the table's direction he was working at before, I follow him.

"This is a table saw."

I press my lips together.

"Er, sorry if you already knew that."

I laugh at his discomfort. "No, explain it like I'm five. This is all new to me."

"Okay, deal. You're going to make some cuts on these boards for me," he continues.

"Cuts! I don't think–"

"Ashlyn, trust me. Please?"

If I could trust him the night we met, surely I could trust him now, so I nod again.

"Safety first." His face is serious as he grasps my shoulders and turns me to face him. I close my eyes instinctively as clear, plastic safety glasses descend over my face. He's gentle as he nestles the arms of the glasses behind my ears. A tingle runs through my body until it disappears into the planks beneath my feet. With my eyes closed, I sway. I open them to balance myself. The glasses must be comically large on my face. He opens his palm, orange foam ear plugs inside.

"Now these."

"Is this really necessary?" I roll my eyes.

In a second I'll be wearing a hard hat and high vis vest. This is probably the whole reason he invited me out here. See how stupid we can make Ashlyn look. Fun game.

"I always use protection."

"Good one." I snatch the earplugs and shove them in my ears.

If I wear these all the time I won't have to listen to his steady stream of sexual innuendo.

"Are you ready?"

I shrug. "As I'll ever be."

"Face the table."

I swallow and turn, hating the way I obey the order. The table comes up almost to my chest. He reaches for a crank, turns it a few times, and the table drops several inches. Isaac moves behind me, and I can't stop the shiver that runs up my back at his proximity. Years have gone by since I let a man get so close to me. Now, in a matter of weeks, it seemed like I'm constantly close to one.

He slides a piece of wood over to the blade. "This is a one by six," he says close to my ear.

The foam earplugs filter out the ambient sounds of the shop. His voice is muffled, but I can still hear the deep tones. It's like he's speaking *inside* my head.

He offers a triangular pencil to me. When I take it, our fingers brush, and a quick shiver runs up the top of my spine.

"Cold?"

I shake my head, examining the pencil that feels foreign in my hand.

"Alright, Ash. You look like you're ready to carpent."

My right elbow shoots backward into his gut. Of course his entire core is rock hard. He grunts, and the sound makes my stomach and thighs clench. Warm hands press against my shoulders, squaring my body to the workbench.

"No horseplay in my workshop," he says against my right ear.

"Okay." My voice sounds raspy.

"Make a mark... right...here." He shows me the spot with his thumb, fingers splayed across the wood.

Whose hands are that big? It's unnecessary. I brush the pencil along the board, his thumb as my guide.

"Harder. We need to see the mark while we cut."

I go over it a few more times until the charcoal is visible. The pencil transfers to his skin, and I like the way it feels to make a mark on him.

"Wait," he says.

Out of the corner of my eye, I watch his hand slide over my shoulder. I open my mouth to ask him what he's doing when he grasps my braid in his fist and lifts it behind me so it's well out of the way of the saw. He's being safe. It's his job. But it's also incredibly sweet. He could have told me to move it myself, but he didn't.

"I'm gonna start it up now. It's not too loud until the wood hits the blade. Ready?"

As I nod the motion tugs my braid where it's caught between my back and his broad chest. He flips a switch, and the machine takes on life. Even though I expect it, I startle and lean back. Isaac is *right* behind me. There's nowhere else to go. Screaming steel blade or six plus feet of solid carpenter? It's hardly a choice. Gratitude courses through me that the sound covers up my deep breaths and hammering heart. I swear I'm not *trying* to turn this into some dirty late-night version of *Backyard Shakeup*. That line between my personal and professional life is fading. I need to redraw it using a jumbo Sharpie and not some weird wood pencil. He stands his ground, letting me lean back on him, seemingly unbothered by the closeness. He taps two spots on the plank.

"Hands right here."

I do as he says, and he covers my hands with his own, applying firm pressure and guiding the movement. Our hands working together to push the plank toward the inevitable. I watch with wide eyes as we inch closer and closer to the whirring metal teeth. They bite into the wood, the steady sound morphing into a high-pitched whine. Particles of dust float in the air around us, tickling my nose. It's the smell of wet forest and winter air.

"What type of wood is this?" I ask, not daring to turn my head and take my eyes off our work. I'm mesmerized by the way the blade slices through the wood.

"What's that?" His breath brushes the hairs on the side of my neck.

"WHAT TYPE OF–" the machine shuts off mid-sentence.

I pluck out one ear plug and start over at a more appropriate volume.

"What type of wood is it?" I brush my hands together and turn to face my new carpentry instructor.

"It's cedar."

Of course it is. The rich colour, the woodsy scent. "I should probably have known that."

His eyebrows dip. "What's the plant that runs along the side of the house in the shade?"

"Um." I let my eyes close for a moment and picture the space. "English yew."

"See. You know your stuff. I know mine."

The professional persona force field I built around myself these last couple weeks is faltering. This little lesson, his care for my safety, him ensuring I understand that it's okay to not understand everything. It's like an electric fence has been shut down. I'm still not certain it's safe to cross it though.

"I love the smell."

"It's manly, right?"

I huff a laugh and pull out the other earplug. "It's...Christmas-y. It reminds me of my fireplace at home during the holidays. Of my family."

He's staring at my lips while I talk. God, it would be too easy to let my eyes slip closed again. To pretend we aren't a one-minute walk away from his grandmother's house and let him kiss me. He would, right? If he doesn't, I'd be the idiot standing here with her eyes closed and lips parted in fucking eye protection. I swerve around him to retrieve my cardigan, slipping it on and wrapping it around me even though I'm more than warm. I need another layer between us. Protection from Isaac, instead of protection from the elements.

"Aren't you gonna help me cut a few more?"

"Uh, no." I hold my hands up. "I've got to, um, check on my plants."

He rolls his lips like he's trying to not laugh.

"They're finicky."

His eyes crinkle. "Is that so?"

I nod. "Mmm hmm."

I'm goddamn breathless, and all I've done is stand in one spot. My mind is running in circles, though. Images of me laid out on the workbench and Isaac stripping off his shirt flash in my mind. The gleam in his eyes holds similar secrets. I want him to stop looking at me like that...I think. I don't understand what's happening between us at all. My brain-to-mouth filter must be loose because the question I've been asking myself for weeks rolls off my lips and into the tension fraught air.

"Why didn't you call me?"

I press my lips together a second too late and bite my tongue hard in retribution. I sound vulnerable and needy, like he owes me an explanation. His silence is torturous, lengthening between us. I'd give anything to have the noise of the table-saw back.

"The timing wasn't right." He becomes intrigued by a layer of sawdust on his clothing, brushing it off with annoyance.

What does that even mean? That he was with someone? Did he just go through a breakup and that's why he moved in here?

"Are you seeing somebody?" I should have asked *before* I offered my number.

He shakes his head, arms crossed over his chest protectively.

"*Were* you seeing someone when we met last month?"

His jaw ticks. "No. I wasn't in the right place to start something serious."

I almost laugh. This is the same guy who joked about not being sure if he had any kids. Who walks around the house like his full-time job is flirting.

"Who said anything about serious?"

He rakes a hand through his hair. The expression on his face tells me that's not what he expected to hear. Honestly, it's not what I expected to say. It popped out, my mouth filter is still loose.

"Is that what you're into? Casual?" His tone lacks enthusiasm. I sense judgement. It makes me want to pry up a floorboard, crawl beneath it, and hope he nails it back down after me.

I backtrack. "I don't usually, I mean...I thought we could get to know each other better?"

"Ashlyn, you can't even do laundry casually. You almost broke out in hives when I ate an expired yogurt. You're telling me that if I called you last month, a guy you met on the side of the road, that you'd have been content to, what, have a casual hook-up?"

I've never actually had a one-night stand before. That doesn't mean I *can't*.

"Maybe." I try to appear confident, standing as tall as possible. A futile effort in the presence of this man.

He's scrutinizing me with his clear blue eyes again. "I don't buy it," he says, matter of fact.

My mouth pops open. Who made Isaac Lauri the expert on what type of relationships I am or am not capable of having? He doesn't know my sexual history. For all he knows, I'm the fucking *Queen* of casual. He busies himself around the workshop, ignoring me. I don't know shit about carpentry, but even I can tell these are make-work tasks that he's only using to distract himself from our conversation. A man that can't handle talking about his feelings for five minutes. Shocking. It shouldn't, but it hurts like I'm the latest victim of the table saw.

"Tell me how much I owe you for that tow."

That gets his attention. His back is to me, but I hear him draw a deep breath through his nose as he bows his head. He lets the air out so slow I see his shoulders shake.

"That's *completely* unnecessary," he says.

"It's necessary to me. I don't want to owe you anything."

He turns to face me, and everything in his body language is tense. Taut neck muscles, firm set jaw. I think of the abs that stopped my elbow in its tracks.

"Ashlyn," his voice is strained, "it was a favour. A friendly gesture after an inconvenient night."

"You know what would have been a friendly gesture?" My voice rises, shrill like my engine that night. Why am I letting my emotions run so high?

"I bet you'll tell me." He pinches the bridge of his nose.

"Calling! Calling would have been nice instead of some weird act of chivalry whereby you assumed I'm incapable of taking care of myself or my crappy vehicle. And I'm sorry it was *inconvenient* for you!"

He points a finger at me. "It wasn't like that at all!"

He loses his composure, slamming his fist against the thin board we cut together. Splintering beneath his fist, the pieces clatter against the floor. The triangular pencil falls from the table. I watch it sit there, immobile and stuck. Kind of like Isaac and I. Frustration radiates off us. I have to get out of the workshop before we take our anger out in a way we can't take back. Because we aren't looking at each other like we hate each other. Quite the opposite. I fantasize about tossing a wrench at his stupidly handsome face, but also figure a ferocious fling on the floorboards would go a long way to blowing off some steam. My sweater feels like a straitjacket, so I push at the door with an adrenaline-fuelled shove, but it doesn't budge.

"Pull."

"I *know*!" I shoot daggers at him, pulling this time and charging out.

Gulping the night air calms me. Outside, away from the smell of Isaac and fresh-cut cedar, my mind begins to clear. No more visiting the workshop. No more chats with a man sitting at the foot of my bed. *Absolutely* no more shared laundry. There's chemistry between us, that's for sure, but the equation is off. I enter the house, going straight for my purse and pulling out several fifty-dollar bills. If Isaac won't tell me how much the tow cost, fine, I'll still pay him. I won't owe him anything, and I'll make sure I never do again. I let myself into his room, tossing the money toward the bed, watching the red rectangles flutter down to the duvet. The way they land askew irritates me, so I march over to stack them up and place them on the end table instead. I won't leave the money thrown about like a damn strip club. When the pile is neat, I remember his words. *You can't even do laundry casually.* Tears sting my eyes. He's right. That's who I am.

Another stack of paper catches my eye. Before I consider that it might be something confidential, I've already scanned the heading. You can't *unsee* something. It's a bank statement, clearly labelled: Lauri Contracting and Restoration. This must be new. I asked him if he ran his own business last week, and he'd said no. Things start falling into place, my brain filing my thoughts like tiny folders. Isaac recently moved in with his grandmother, hardly going anywhere except for the workshop. I'd bet this stack of money and more that he's had a big change lately. I try to drum up the anger from before, but it won't appear. Instead, there's a sense of camaraderie and a bit of pity for a guy who's been down on his luck. A guy I've been barking at to keep up with his chores. I slip out of the room and head for the bathroom to shower. Washing the remnants of this masculine Christmas smell off my skin will help me cool off. God knows I need something to take my core temperature down a few degrees. How long am I going to lay in bed tonight replaying every word of this stupid fight? Is that how it's going to be for the next who knows how long? Flirt, fight, retreat, repeat?

CHAPTER ELEVEN

Isaac

I try to keep the corners of my mouth from creeping upwards, but my mouth splits open into a grin so wide my
cheeks ache. Staying annoyed with my type-A roommate is
too hard when she does cute stuff like this. The tidy stack of
cash that first appeared on my end table after our spat in the
workshop has just turned up neatly rolled into the crotch of
my cleaned and impeccably folded boxer briefs with a note that
reads:

*I did your laundry, now **you** owe **me**.*

I tried my damndest to return her money. Slipping it into
the cover of her smutty romance novel didn't work. The next
morning the bills reappeared under my windshield wiper. I
snuck back into the kitchen like a fucking ninja while she was
washing Mummo's hair and tucked it into her apron pocket.

It's the most fun I've ever had with one hundred and fifty dollars. Neither of us has said a thing about it out loud, but we've dared each other to with furtive glances.

I had no idea it would be such an enormous deal that I towed her car. I'll take the fact that I had her headlights and belts replaced to the fucking grave. That she didn't notice either repair is a testament to the fact it needed doing. I'm not proud of my part in our spat, though. I acted like some hot-headed Neanderthal who lost his favourite club. Her line of questioning brought out the deep-seeded frustration I've been bottling up. Interacting with Ashlyn drives me up every wall of the house and along the sloping roof, too. Some mornings I receive the silent treatment, other days we play cards with Mummo after supper and make small talk. I've seen her check out my biceps one moment then glare at me the next. If you ask me, she doesn't have a clue what she wants. Casual hookups haven't been my thing for years, and Ashlyn doesn't seem like the type, but I'm not sure how much longer we can dance around the palpable sexual frustration.

In the kitchen I snag an apple from the fruit bowl, biting into it then running a finger down Mummo's handwritten list, contemplating which item I should tackle. Halfway down I find something promising. After checking the workshop to see what I have on hand, I head to the closest hardware shop. It's small, locally owned, but the only thing I need is paint and some chains. The roads are calm on a Sunday morning; the fresh green buds on the tips of the trees are poised to blossom, and there's more blue than grey in the sky for a change. Soon, pink and white flowers will burst open in droves, signalling the early spring of the West Coast. The front window of the store sparkles and displays hand lettered signage and a pyramid of paint cans. A bell jingles over the door as I enter, the sound of small business and Sundays with Pappa.

Mr. Umber, the long-time owner, shakes my hand over the counter. His smile deepens the grooves along his cheeks.

"Isaac! Good to see you around here. What can I help you with?"

"Looking to get a couple gallons of paint today. Fixing up a porch swing for Mummo."

"How's she doing?"

"Not too bad, thanks. Well enough to have me doing chores."

Mr. Umber laughs with his thumbs hooked in his suspenders. He's only a few years younger than my grandma. Still working and keeping busy. Pappa had done the same thing. Never truly retiring. It kept him sharp.

"Still working with your father at Forward?"

I hesitate before deciding honesty is the best policy with someone I've known since I was too small to see over the shop counter.

"I've moved on. He let me go."

His bushy eyebrows sink. "I don't like the sound of that at all, Isaac. Sorry to hear it."

"I'm trying something new..." Before I can second guess it, I reach into my back pocket for my wallet and draw out one of the business cards that came in the mail.

I hold it out. "I'm starting my own business with a few friends."

Mr. Umber lifts the card up, sliding his glasses down from his forehead. He nods his approval. "Looks sharp. Can I hold onto this?"

"It's all yours."

That wasn't so hard. Truthfulness was a relief.

The swing has a new lease on life, but the reveal is bittersweet without my grandfather. Sanding and painting took a few days, fresh chains replace the rusty ones, and a new cushion covers the seat. It's a beautiful March day, but as I lean against the wobbling porch railings, all I see is another project waiting for me. I'm waiting for Ashlyn to bring Mummo out. Something about reapplying lipstick. I comb my hands through my hair, still a bit damp from my shower. We found an old photo in an album of Mummo and I sitting on the swing when I was a pre-teen with legs and ears too big for my body, and we thought we'd recreate it today. I even found a shirt in a similar shade of blue to the one I wore in the original. I don't know how many more photos I'll take with her. It's getting hard to swallow when the door swings open and Mummo steps gingerly over the threshold. Ashlyn is by her side, both of their house slippers shuffling on the rough porch planks. I cover my smirk with my fist. Without a doubt, she is the oldest twenty-six-year-old I've ever met, and it's adorable. Her hair is pulled up high on her head in a long ponytail which makes me think of her smooth hair on my fingers in the shop. Her leggings cling in all the right places. We've barely spoken to each other the past week. Not about anything important anyhow. Instead of being adults and acknowledging our disagreement, neither of us is willing to make a truce and admit our parts in that disaster. We're like a couple on the rocks, keeping it together for the kids, except our dependent is in her eighties.

"Okay, Mummo." I rub my hands together. "This wasn't at the top of your list, but I redid the swing."

She's silent for a beat, taking it all in, I assume.

"What do you think?" I raise my voice a bit in case she has a hard time hearing.

Ashlyn steps forward to support her elbow. "Isn't this nice, Mrs. Lauri? The weather is getting much warmer, we can have tea out here soon."

I hold the swing steady so Mummo can sit down safely then I ease into the seat next to her. In that old photo my head was level with hers. Now she feels small tucked against me as I hug her to my side.

Ashlyn uses to her phone to snap some photos of us. She glances up at me. "It looks amazing, Isaac. Really. You do beautiful work."

Her genuine compliment catches me off guard. I'm grinning at the sincerity before I even realize it. "Thanks. If you're going to do something, you do it right."

She nods, "See. I knew you appreciated my desire to do things the right way."

I'm deciphering what that really means and trying to ignore the way her saying the word *desire* makes me so hot when I register an odd sound. At first, I'm confused while I look for the source. Then my eyes settle on Mummo, who sounds like she has a cry caught in her throat. The keening, grief-stricken moan comes from deep within her. She hides her blue eyes with her wrinkled hands, and her slight shoulders are shaking against me. Mummo removes her hands from her eyes and looks around.

"Jakob, is that you?" she asks in a croaking voice.

My heart sinks. That's Pappa's name. I follow her gaze to the overgrown lawn, wondering if she sees a man that reminds her of her late husband.

"Nobody is there, Mummo, it's only us."

"I'm talking to my husband!" Mummo snaps, leaning away from me.

The strength of her voice floors me. How do you remind someone that their husband has been dead for years without being a complete ass? Ashlyn is outwardly unruffled, but I see the layer of sadness in her expression. I guess she sees this a lot in her line of work.

"What's happening to her?"

Ashlyn sighs, "She's hallucinating, likely."

"Did I do this? With the swing?" I haven't seen Mummo like this before.

"No, no. This can be common. Honestly, triggers that cause these reactions can pop up anywhere." She kneels before Mummo, establishing eye contact. "Mrs. Lauri, it's Ashlyn. I know you think you see Mr. Lauri. He's not there, I'm so sorry." She places her hands upon Mummo's shoulders.

I shove my hands in my pockets, glancing at a particularly wide space between two floorboards. "I thought she'd like it."

"Isaac."

When I lift my eyes to meet hers, she says, "She does. She will. This isn't your fault. You can't tell how people will react to certain memories."

I nod and rub at the lump in my throat. Swallowing with strep throat would be easier. Moving to help Mummo stand, I cup her elbow, but she wrenches away from my touch with surprising strength. The whole swing sways with her sudden movement.

"Don't touch me!"

I throw my hands up to show her I mean no harm.

"I can take it from here, Isaac. Give us some space?"

With absolute competence and strength, she lifts Mummo to standing and leads her indoors, murmuring comforting words and promises of hot tea in her ear. I'm left alone on the swing, rolling my neck and groaning at the stiffness settling into my shoulders. Mummo's words are on repeat in my head. How many times has this happened? Has she spoken like this to Dad?

Was an episode like this the catalyst for hiring Ashlyn? Mummo's behaviour fills me with questions and overwhelms me with respect for Ashlyn. The interaction drives home how needed she is. Having a relationship with Ashlyn could be a mistake. A breakup could compromise Mummo's care. She needs her job, I need the workshop, and I need some damn focus. I won't jeopardize that for any of us.

CHAPTER TWELVE

Ashlyn

If there's one thing I've learned from my mom's career, and now my own, it's that each day in health care has the potential to be different. Some are easy, some funny, some sad, some hard. Unfortunately for all the people living in this house, we've had about a dozen of the hardest days all shoved together. Mrs. Lauri's hallucinations of her late husband got worse before they got better. Sitting in doctors' offices, standing in pharmacy line ups; life the past few weeks has been a never-ending waiting room. However hard it was for me, I know it was harder for her and Isaac. Even with the respite nurse coming in for a few shifts while I escaped back to my apartment to sleep and take care of my mental health, I'm frazzled. Isaac has tried to support her, to support me in whatever way he can. The way he watches over her, visiting as much as his work allows, shows me my assumptions about him being a detached relative were so wrong.

Isaac and I have endured the pressure from all sides. His work, my work, caring for the house. Instead of crumbling under the weight, it seems the wrinkles in our confusing relationship have smoothed. He looks at me like I'm a miracle worker half the time, when I'm simply doing my job. What I'm paid for. An unspoken truce formed between us. That, and we're too tired to acknowledge the currents of magnetism that still swirl around. Darting glances at each other in the bathroom mirror when we brush our teeth side by side. Goosebumps that raise along my arms when he brushes past me in the kitchen during breakfast. Gravelly goodnights when I watch him disappear down the dark hall to his bedroom while I sit in the living room watching home renovation shows. Isaac stopped being an inconvenience long ago. Now he's an exercise in self-restraint.

I curl up on my bed with a warm tea, rubbing my eyes and groaning at the grittiness behind my lids. The tiny font of the flower seed germination guide in my lap blurs again. Fed up with my forlorn looks and sighs of sadness as I gazed at the backyard, Mummo finally told me to do what I pleased with the space, offering me a hearty 'good luck'. I'll need it now that spring is here. When I find a spare moment, I'm going to slice my way so hard through those weeds they won't know what hit them. Stretching and yawning, I turn up the music in my earbuds and dance my way off my bed, snagging my towel off the back of the door and trying to summon an iota of energy. The original jadeite green fixtures in the only bathroom in this house are dated as hell, and I love them. Off-white hex tiles cover the floor except for the fluffy grey rugs placed strategically to keep our feet warm and dry. I turn the knob and get a couple steps inside the bathroom before the wall of humidity hits me. The large silhouette behind the semi-opaque shower curtain stops me in my tracks. I cut the music that prevented me from hearing the running water. The overhead fan hums steadily, losing the battle against the swirling steam. Isaac's head peeks over the curtain rod. The house is not scaled for him, and I bet he needs to stoop to avoid the shower nozzle. My breath whooshes out of me, and it's a struggle to pull more into my lungs. The correct reaction is vacating the room, not standing here and considering the stature of the person in the shower. Not that I'm thinking about his *size*. Except now I am.

God, what a perv.

"Fucking plants everywhere," he says while shaking a leaf off his wet fingers over the top of the curtain rod.

I hug my towel to my chest like maybe it will keep my heart from hammering its way out.

"I appreciate your desire to preserve water by showering with a friend, but let's save that for summer water restrictions, babe."

Babe? What happened to Ash? I like the way it sounds way more than I should. He peers around the edge of the curtain, thoroughly amused and not embarrassed in the slightest. Why would he be with a body like that? Beads of moisture pepper my forehead, and it's not the result of the humidity in the air. My response, frankly, is ridiculous because all I really see is his wet face and an adamantine arm.

"Jesus," I whisper.

"Whatcha praying for?"

For something heavy to fall on me.

"I'll go." I take a miniature step backwards.

"You don't *have* to go if you don't want to."

The statement is awfully close to a challenge, and it snaps me out of my stupor.

"I think you have the water too hot; the steam seems to be going to your head," I scoff.

"Which one?"

"Isaac!"

He roars with laughter because, yet again, he's managed to get a rise out of me. I back out, slamming the door behind me, muffling his laughter. How will I ever forget that image? That man is a distraction and a half. Yesterday, I found myself with pruney fingers and a sink full of lukewarm dishwater thanks to his masculine wiles. Isaac and his friend, Chris, who's equally easy on the eyes, were hauling lumber from Isaac's truck to the workshop. Apparently, I can't multitask quite as well as I thought when someone is hefting huge planks around like they're kindling for a campfire. These daydreams are obviously fuelled by a serious lack of balance. A crush on an attractive man borne out of forced proximity and circulating pheromones. I need a night out.

LOVINGLY RESTORED

That evening, the sky is dusky, mourning doves finally quieting down in their nests. I settle onto the porch swing and let it sway me. Soothed by the silent gliding motion, I draw up my knees and savour the moment. This has become my favourite spot in the house. Anna's face appears on my phone screen, and my lips curl into a grin as I accept the video call.

"Hey, sweetie. What's up?"

"Not much. Enjoying the new porch swing."

"Aw, I saw the pictures you sent. It's really pretty. Must be nice to have a handyman at your beck and call."

I wish. The thought pops into my mind.

I lower my voice and the volume on my phone, not wanting to be overheard. "He's different than I thought."

"How so?"

Flirtatious. Headstrong. Gorgeous.

"I don't know. He's not as grumpy anymore." I let my head tip back, releasing a foot so I can push myself into motion again.

"Why would he be when he gets to live with you?"

"Believe me, I've not been the best roommate. I put him on my chore chart."

Anna snorts. "You didn't."

"I absolutely did." I long yawn stretches my mouth, "I'm tired."

"You've been working hard. It will be worth it when you get your place."

My savings account isn't looking as juicy as I'd like. Real estate prices only keep climbing.

"Anyways, I'm calling to ask if you want to go out tomorrow night."

Catching up on sleep should be my top priority, but I'm overdue for fun.

"I'd hate for you to break your curfew..." she says slowly.

My eyes narrow. "I know what you're doing."

She shrugs dramatically enough for me to see her shoulders come into the frame.

"I don't *have* a curfew. Isaac is going to be here."

Mentally, I run through my to-do list. I was going to take Mummo to get a haircut somewhere. A better idea pops into my mind.

"I'll go out."

She gasps.

"*But*, you have to do me a favour beforehand."

I can't believe I hadn't thought of it before. A smile plays across my lips as I listen to Mrs. Lauri chat behind me in the kitchen while Anna cuts her hair. Doing this at home allowed me to wet her hair safely in the comfort of her own bathroom and avoid the stresses of the busy salon. Anna hurried over after work this afternoon and forced me into the shower first so she could trim some layers around my face and blow my hair out before our night on the town. How long had my cousin been bugging me to go out with her? Probably too long. I'll have a drink or two, dance with cute guys unrelated to my patient, and let loose. Living in a beautiful old house with a senior citizen and simultaneously fighting and flirting with Isaac hasn't exactly been checking all the boxes in the recreation department. I'm tense. On edge. Okay, horny.

Anna stands behind Mrs. Lauri, a gleaming pair of rose gold scissors in one hand and a black, fine-toothed comb in the other. They've been chatting non-stop about anything and everything. My cousin chose the perfect profession because not only can she make anyone look amazing, but she has the gift of the gab that gets them to open up to the point that she's joked she should also charge a fee for counselling. It must be her special skill set that has Mrs. Lauri talking more than I've ever heard. It doesn't seem to upset her at all to tell stories about her late husband, who she's been calling Jakey or "my love". She even shared some funny anecdotes about Isaac, the "Little One", a nickname that makes Anna snicker every time she hears it. There's nothing remotely small about that man...and I'm guessing that applies everywhere. I shiver at the thought even though I'm standing over a pot of steaming cream of broccoli soup. Ladling some into a shallow bowl for Mrs. Lauri's supper, I watch as my talented cousin holds out an oval mirror and Mrs. Lauri gazes at her reflection, turning her head side to side, admiring her fresh look. A broad smile spans her face and lights her eyes.

"Thank you, young lady. What do I owe you?"

"It's on the house."

"Guard your purse," I tell Anna. "She's one of those grand-mas that'll slip at twenty into your bag if you're not looking."

Anna laughs. "Sweet, where do I sign up for one of those?"

As I'm stirring the soup in the bowl, blowing on the surface, I see Isaac and Chris cross in front of the window over the sink. I guess we'd all been too busy chatting and laughing to hear the truck. A moment later they enter and Chris surveys the room, wiping his hands against his thighs to clean them, but his pants are so covered in sawdust that it makes no difference. Isaac steps up behind his friend, filling out the doorway. My stomach does a stupid somersault at the sight of him, at the way I have to tilt my chin to look up. In a couple hours I'll be out at the bar, dancing with Anna, and this man will be the last thing on my mind. Chris's eyes settle on Anna since she's the only unfamiliar face in the room, and I jump at the chance to introduce them.

"Chris, meet Anna, my cousin."

"Hi," Anna says, offering him her hand.

Chris doesn't hesitate to take it. "Nice to meet you."

Isaac rounds the table to kiss Mummo on the cheek, causing Mrs. Lauri to giggle and bat at his chest.

"Mummo, you look beautiful!"

"What is it with men saving their affections for when they are at their filthiest? Pappa did the same thing."

"This is your doing, I take it?" Chris turns to Anna, leaning over the back of a dining chair.

"Yep. I can make anyone look fantastic. I could do you next."

I suppress an eye roll.

Chris clears his throat. "I'm more of a barber guy. But, are you saying I don't look fantastic now?"

"Dirty tradesman aren't my type." Anna shrugs, a grin tugging at her upper lip.

Isaac laughs. "We're in the wrong house, man. We need to go somewhere where we're appreciated."

Mildly wounded, Chris appeals to me, "Don't I look fantastic, Ashlyn?"

"Yes, so gorgeous, Prince Christopher." I place a hand by my mouth and fake whisper to Anna, "He's terribly insecure, needs his ego stroked constantly."

I place Mrs. Lauri's cooled soup on the table, so she can stay on schedule.

"Help yourself, by the way, Chris," I call over my shoulder.

Chris looks slightly apologetic as he fills a bowl to the brim.

Anna's shaking out the black cape and sweeping up the silvery strands of hair into a neat pile. When she looks up at me again, there's a gleam in her eye.

Oh, no.

"Isaac, what do you think of Ashlyn's hair?"

Isaac's soup has a big dent in it despite the steaming contents. He abandons his supper and leans against the counter, arms folded, head tipped to one side in appraisal. Self-conscious beneath his gaze, my cheeks warm, and I tuck my new layers behind my ears. Silence dominates the kitchen, except for the occasional clink of Mummo's spoon against her bowl. Isaac saunters toward me, reaching down to untuck the strands of hair from behind my ears. Grasping a section between his fingers, he slides them down, right to the freshly trimmed tips until they fall from his thumb and forefinger and tickle the side of my face. The last time he touched me in this kitchen I smacked his hand away. Now? Stopping him is the last thing on my mind.

"It's beautiful, too." His voice is a low vibration.

Maybe I won't go out tonight. I'll just...stay in. Lay myself naked on his bed and see what happens. No. I shake myself from my stupor, sneak around him, and pull a bowl down from the cupboard to serve my own meal. Mrs. Lauri has an empty seat next to her, so I take it, hoping she can protect me from his intensity.

"Soup's delicious, babe." He finishes his with a noisy slurp, foregoing his utensil.

Chris and Anna look at each other. "Babe?" they both mouth.

Isaac's tongue darts out to devour one last drop. I shove my spoon in my mouth, forgetting to blow on the thick soup. I hiss, letting some heat out of my mouth. It's a poignant reminder that if I'm not more guarded, I might be the one who gets burned.

Grabbing this dress from my apartment earlier seemed silly, but the little black thing oozes sex appeal, and I'm glad I did. The form fitting silhouette hugs my curves, ending a few inches above the knee. It's sexy enough when I'm standing still, but when I walk, a six-inch slit appears up my right thigh. I slip on a leather jacket, filling a jade-coloured clutch with the front door key, my cell, cash, ID, and my lipstick. I stare down the drugstore bag that contains an unopened package of condoms. Isaac's comment in the workshop still rankles. If he thinks I'm too serious and straight laced to enjoy no strings attached sex as a full-grown woman, he's *wrong*. I rip open the box, taking a condom from the strip and shoving it next to my lipstick. Now *that's* the purse of a woman ready to have a night of fun.

Heels clicking along the hardwood, I make my way to the living room where Anna, Isaac, and Chris sit chatting. Heads turn in my direction when I enter. The look on Isaac's face, iron tight jaw and narrowed gaze, is intense.

What the hell is he thinking?

Crossing the threshold into the room, the toe of my shoe catches. I stumble, recovering by sheer luck, but my clutch slips from my hand. The magnetic closure pops open as it lands on the carpet, the contents spilling haphazardly at Isaac's feet.

"Happens to me all the time," Anna says.

I appreciate her attempt to save me from embarrassment, but I'm already bright red. House slippers are more my speed these days. Isaac spreads his thighs, leaning forward from his reclined position to collect my things, his fingertips pausing millimetres above a shining foil packet.

Shit.

Tension radiates off him. His shoulders look tight, and while his head remains down, he glances up at me. "Just one?" He raises a thick eyebrow.

"That's all it takes," I say with all the bravado I can muster.

He bites his lip like he's holding back.

"If you two are finished staring at each other, the cab is here," Anna says.

"We weren't…" I start, but it's not worth it. "Let's go."

I'll be at the bar soon, and I can burn off the tension that's been building in our close quarters.

"You be careful tonight," Isaac calls out as we make our way down the stairs to the front yard. He stands in the doorway, watching our car until we're out of sight, and his warning makes me want to do the exact opposite.

Infinity is the only establishment that has a designated place for dancing in West Isle. It's just different enough from the pubs and bars that host local musicians and serve craft beer. The music tonight features remixes of modern rock songs, and the crowd is thick. Exposed brick lines the wall behind the bar, the rows of liquor bottles arranged on live-edge shelving.

"Why don't we do this more often?" I scream.

Anna shakes her head. "What!"

There's no point trying to talk. That's not why we're here anyways. The answer to my question is obvious anyway. We don't do this anymore because I'm boring. I know it, and Isaac knows it. A wave of resistance rolls over me at the thought. I don't want to be uptight and high-strung. Not tonight. Swirling the ice of my third mojito with my straw, I suck back the last sips of the citrusy rum.

I bounce off my barstool the best I can in a tight dress. "C'mon."

The songs are blending together, and I've lost track of how long we've been dancing. I pull my hair off the nape of my neck then fan myself to dry the sheen of sweat gathering on my hot skin. The drinks have kicked in and the confidence coursing through me is the confirmation that this night out is exactly what I needed. Anna nudges my arm and gestures behind me. A moving wall of muscle is dancing close to my back, black tee tight around his biceps and bold tattoos climbing from the v-neck onto his throat. I recognize him from the line up outside. My glance is all he needs to snake his arm around my waist, an open palm rests boldly against my lower stomach. My eyes go wide and Anna shrugs and smiles as if to say, 'You do you, girl!'

His arms are strong, and he keeps us moving in a steady rhythm with the music. As far as guys at clubs go, he's cute and a good dancer.

"I'm Jason!" His cologne is strong; the heat of the club amplifying the scent.

"Ashlyn!"

His hold tightens on me, and a bead of his sweat drips onto my bare shoulder.

Gross.

I push the rude thought away. I'm sweaty, too.

"You come here often?"

"Not lately."

His eyes are so dark it's hard to make out where his iris ends and the pupil begins. So different from looking into Isaac's blue, white-flecked eyes. Good. Different than Isaac is *good*. A wave of nausea overcomes me. Alcohol, heat, and Jason's cologne are a powerful trifecta. The beat fades before another deeper bass line takes over. I peel his hands off my churning stomach, but he mistakes my action for wanting to turn to face him. Spinning me around, he adjusts his grip. Dizziness encircles me, the flashing lights blurring. Jason is pressing his groin against my thigh, hardness obvious beneath his dark jeans. Okay. That's enough. I lift my head to tell him I'm done being dry humped, but we aren't on the same page. Parted lips descend upon me as he leans in for a kiss. Horrified at the thought, I turn my head at the last moment and the sloppy smooch lands on my ear instead. Anna grabs my elbow, signalling to Jason that it's time for us to go. This is why you take a sidekick to the club. He sneers at me before waving me off like he isn't interested. The pressure against my thigh a moment ago told a different story, but whatever. My stomach clenches again. I have to get off the dance floor.

Anna clutches my arm. "You okay?"

"Those drinks were strong. I'm too hot." My speech sounds slow.

"I think we should get some fresh air," she says, rubbing my back.

We snake through the writhing bodies, my pumps sticking to the black flooring in spots where syrupy drinks were spilled. Anna has a good grasp on my hand, and relief courses through me when I see the exit. Why the hell did I pack a condom? Being grinded on by Jason grossed me right out. There's no way in hell I'll ever go back to a stranger's place to have sex or invite one back to my apartment. Apparently, I'm not a one-night stand kind of girl. I spend my days working with people triple my age, reading, and gardening. It appears that my clubbing life is over. Isaac, the instinctive bastard, is right. And that pisses me right off. I shift my weight around, trying to relieve the throbbing in the balls of my feet and the hot spots on my baby toes while I wait for Anna to grab our coats. I spot Jason fully lip locked with a curvy blonde. He sure got over my rejection quickly. Anna pushes my leather coat towards me, and I fold it over my arm as we escape the stifling heat and noise of the club.

"Put that on."

"I'm still hot."

"You're sweaty. Put it on so you don't catch a chill."

I fumble around in my clutch for my phone.

"I got it." Anna pulls her phone out, adjusting it around her hoop earring.

"It's ringing busy," she says.

I'm not listening, too busy scrolling through the contacts in my phone. Isaac is saved as 'Roomie' alongside a photo of a monster truck. I set that up the day he moved in. In case of grandma-related emergencies. The mojitos make it seem pretty hilarious, and I giggle as I press dial.

Anna shoots me an annoyed look. "Jesus, you're a lightweight."

I've been the designated driver for her countless times, and you can bet she's way sloppier than I am.

"What are you doing? I told you the line was busy."

The phone rings in my ear. Once, twice, three times.

Shit, what if he's sleeping?

"Ashlyn?" His voice is deep and clear. Not groggy at all.

"Hey, Isaac. Anna, it's Isaac!" I wink at her.

"For fuck's sake." Anna's eyes roll to the back of her head.

"Ashlyn, are you there? You okay?"

"I'm fine! I danced with Jason! He was super sweaty and kissed me." I pop a hand over my mouth.

"That's nice." His tone of voice tells me he doesn't think it's nice at all.

"Maybe I'll bring him home tonight, whaddya think?"

Anna groans, palming her forehead.

There's a pause before he answers. "Not to my fucking house."

I squeeze my bare thighs together at the timbre in his voice.

"Okay, Ashlyn." Anna attempts to pry my fingers off the phone.

"Hey, I'm talking!"

"Give. It. Up."

Her grip is freakishly strong, and she wins the tug of war.

"Hey, it's Anna...sorry about that...she doesn't get out much."

I cross my arms over my chest, irritated that I can't hear what he says on the other end.

"That would be good... I wouldn't say she's *totally* drunk, but–" She turns away from me.

"I resent that!"

Anna turns to shush me. "We're at Infinity. I know, I just called, and it was busy. Okay, we'll be out front."

She shoves my phone towards me. "Put this in your bag. Unless you'd like to drunk dial someone else. Your mom?"

I wrap her up in a bear hug. "I'm sorry, Anna! I'm no fun."

She wriggles her arms out from under mine and hugs me back, resting her chin on top of my head and patting my hair. "You're good, babe. I had lots of fun tonight."

"So, what's the plan? Are we heading back in?"

"Definitely not. Isaac is coming to get you. I'm meeting friends from the salon."

"What? Nooo. Let me come, too!"

"Next time." She side hugs me, and we lean against each other, seeking relief from our throbbing feet. "We had fun while it lasted. Next time, dinner and a drink. No more mojitos for you."

"They're my *favourite*."

"Shocking."

The rumble of the black truck reaches me right before it pulls up to the curb. Turns out that parking your ass on cold concrete serves the dual purpose of numbing your butt cheeks and sobering you up. Leaving the cloying concoction of perfumes and aftershave instantly settled my stomach. The tires stop inches from my tender toes, and the tinted passenger window whirs down.

Even over the chatter of people outside the bar, I can hear his gruff voice. "Get in."

Maybe it's the way he ordered it, or the fact that his assumptions about me were aggravatingly accurate, but I don't think I will. I stand, the ache in the balls of my feet reminding me why I sat down in the first place.

"I'm not ready to go home yet." I tighten my leather jacket around me.

He leans further over the centre console toward the open window. "I'm not playing this game again, Ashlyn. We've already done it once, and it ended with your ass in the truck."

Anna hangs back, staying out of it.

A bald bouncer, dressed in head-to-toe black approaches us. "This is a no parking zone."

"I'm not parking. I'm picking someone up," Isaac says with gritted teeth.

This night was supposed to be about blowing off steam and forgetting about Isaac, but all this outing did was rile me up further. Here I am with him. Again. The man is inescapable, and that adds to my bitchiness.

I point to the truck then turn to Anna. "This is the monstrosity that nearly killed me."

"Yeah, yeah. And then the handsome driver escorted you home. Traumatic." She tries to herd me toward the truck.

"Seriously, you need to move along," the bouncer says.

"I'll move *along* when I've picked her up."

"Doesn't really seem like she wants to go with you, buddy."

I press my lips together when I see Isaac's jaw clench and the fake smile he plasters on his face. The bouncer steps over to me and places a heavy arm around my shoulders, pulling me tight to his side, making me stumble slightly in my heels. The driver's side door clicks, and I gulp. Isaac strides around the front of his truck, and my stomach swoops at the sight of him in a big grey hoodie that emphasises his broad shoulders and strong arms. A black ball cap is pulled low over his eyes. His steel-toed work boots don't really go with the outfit, but it tells me he grabbed the first shoes he could find in his rush to come get me the moment I called. The bouncer is smarter than he looks, because he lets go of me as Isaac reaches us.

"I've got her now, *buddy*." Isaac stares him down until the man glances pointedly at the no parking sign once more and returns to his post by the bar doors.

Isaac places his hands tight around my waist and yanks me toward him, so our bodies are flush. It's the closest we've ever been, and, of course, we have an audience. People are looking our way.

"Ashlyn, I came out to get you in the middle of the night. *You* called *me*." His eyes smoulder as he leans in close. "Get. In. The. Truck."

That bouncer might have crumbled under Isaac's show of authority, but *I* won't.

In search of a little control, I glance up at him, licking my bottom lip and pressing my abdomen against his hips.

"Or what?"

What can I say? I'm not good at taking orders.

Isaac's answer is an action. The bright streetlights over my head flip, and my breath whooshes out of me as a muscled shoulder bears my weight. I squeak, but don't scream. I don't want that bouncer coming back thinking I'm actually in danger. Although, maybe I am in trouble with the man beneath me.

"Bye, babe," Anna says, swatting me on my ass.

Isaac unceremoniously drops me into the sumptuous leather seat, blood rushing from my head.

"Night, kids, don't have too much fun," she sings, slamming the door and giving it a tap.

I wiggle around in the seat and drop my condom-filled clutch on the floor. My hair is in my face, and my dress rode up several inches from being manhandled in front of dozens of people. I find the button for the window and roll it up, desperate to be out of the view of the curious onlookers. Isaac gets in and looks me over. The slit of my dress teeters on the edge of obscenity. I tug on the hem, but since I'm sitting on the fabric, it doesn't make much difference. Blowing some hair out of my eyes, I glance at my disagreeable driver. He's pushing his sleeves up over his forearms. When he grabs the steering wheel, activating all sorts of corded muscles that ought to be illegal, I practically whimper. If it wasn't for the enraged expression on his face, he almost looks cuddly. What would it be like to hug him while he wears all that soft squishy fabric?

"Glad to see you got in," he says.

"Like I had a choice." My voice is too loud, ears still recovering from the club.

His skin glows from the colourful marquis, eyes tracking down to the slit in my dress then back up to my face. I gulp, heat rising in my cheeks. I won't avert my gaze. I'm not ashamed. My empowerment only grows under his perusal. He breaks eye contact first, and a sense of satisfaction slithers through me. His knuckles pale as he grips the steering wheel and stares straight ahead.

Chapter Thirteen

Isaac

"**A**shlyn?"

I wave a hand through the direction of her far off gaze. She's lost in thought and seems tired. I grab her seat belt and draw it snugly across her lap, clicking it into place, knuckles brushing across her hips. The contact breaks her back to reality.

"I could have done that myself."

"Yeah, yeah. You like to do everything for yourself. Drink this." I hold out a bottle of water and pull away from the curb, flipping off the bouncer even though his back is turned. The decision to take the scenic route is easy. I want her to drink that water and sober up the rest of the way. Selfishly, I want her to myself for a while.

I was waiting up for her. Chris and I enjoyed some beers and talked business. After the tenth time looking at my watch, he called me out, asking me what time Ashlyn's curfew was. There's something good about knowing everyone is safely home before I head to bed. Since I moved in I've been walking around checking doors and windows each night. I have Mummo and Ashlyn to think about. I'm not the "man of the house", or some shit, but I can't seem to quell that protective urge. Hell, it started the night I met her, and it was even stronger when she walked out the door in that head-turning dress with a condom in her purse. When she called at 12:30 in the morning, I answered on the first ring. Her slow, relaxed voice told me she was at least buzzed. Good, I wanted her to enjoy her night out and relax. Hadn't I told her she needed to stop trying to be so controlling? Then she mentioned *Jason* had been sweating all over her and kissed her, and my happiness turned into jealousy. *I* hadn't even kissed her yet. And that did something to my head, heart, and dick all at once. Despite telling myself that it wasn't any of my business who Ashlyn got with, my body disagreed. Chris stayed to keep an ear out for Mummo, and I hightailed it out of there like the house was on fire.

"How you feeling?" I ask when she places the mostly empty water bottle in the cup holder.

"Better. It was boiling in there. Thanks."

"Check the glove box."

When she opens it, she gasps and I'm suddenly smiling.

"Are you serious?"

She tears into the granola bar wrapper, moaning at the first bite. I may have grabbed her a snack on the way out, too.

I rub the back of my neck. "Listen, I'm sorry I went off on you back there. It doesn't matter what time it is. I'll come and get you if you need a ride, okay?"

Her mouth is still full of peanuts and granola.

"Okay, Ashlyn?"

"I understand," she mumbles.

Now that I see she's alright, there's something I want to ask her.

"Did you mean what you said?"

She finishes the last bite and takes another drink of water.

"About what?"

"On the phone, you said you wanted to bring someone home tonight."

I can't think about it in too much detail.

"Oh." She tucked some hair behind her ear. "I was dancing with that guy–"

"Jason."

She cringes. "Good memory. I was dancing with *Jason,* and thought about the stupid condom that I put in my bag when his erec–"

Nope.

I clamp my palm over her mouth to cut her off. "Let me stop you right there."

She giggles, ducking away from my hand which is now sticky from the remnants of her snack. "I would never bring someone

134

back to your grandmother's house. I don't know why I said that. I'm sorry."

I scrub my hand over my face. "You don't have to be sorry about wanting to have fun."

"I would have used my own apartment."

The *location* isn't the problem. I'm wracking my brain to figure out how to tell her that when she keeps talking.

"How do people *do* that? Just go home with strangers? How can you trust someone you know nothing about to..." she waves her hands around like she can't think of the right word. "Treat you right?"

Christ. I rub a hand over my face. She's going to be the death of me. Treat her right? I'll show her the definition of being treated right. At a red light, I glance over. Her heels are off, legs tucked beneath her, that dress riding up. The darkness of the cab makes the contrast between the black fabric and her skin more obvious. She nods in the intersection's direction; the light turned green while I was ogling her.

"So, you wouldn't have minded if I went home with someone?" Her face fades in and out of visibility with each streetlight I pass.

That's *not* what I meant.

Screw it.

"I would mind." I rub my jaw. "Not because I'm judging you, but because I'm jealous."

There it is. Something about sitting side by side in a dark moving vehicle makes people open up. Level playing field or some shit. Her mouth pops open, and I glance at her lips. The lipstick is worn off, leaving her mouth the natural shade of pink I'm used to seeing. I imagine kissing those pink lips and wonder if any other parts of Ashlyn are the same colour.

She crosses her arms over her chest and huffs. "I guess you were right."

On any other night I'd make her repeat it, just to bother her. "Right about what?"

"That I'm too...controlling to be able to be casual. That I'm boring."

"I *never* said you were boring."

"Well, I am."

I can't stand how dejected she sounds. Ashlyn may be a homebody at heart, but she keeps me on my toes and makes me laugh. She treats my grandmother like gold. A boring girl wouldn't have me walking around the house sporting a semi half the time. A boring girl wouldn't talk to plants and keep them in the goddamn shower. She's worried about being treated right and being able to trust someone? A dangerously half-cocked plan forms in the most primitive part of my brain. She reaches across the console, placing her hand on my thigh, the heat of her palm penetrating the soft fabric.

"I don't want to be boring, Isaac."

Oh, Jesus.

She grips my quad, the pressure travelling right to my crotch. My mind came up with the plan, but it's my dick that makes me say it.

"What if you had the best of both worlds?"

"Both worlds?"

"Being *treated* right. Good sex with someone you can trust. That you're safe with."

The idea of Ashlyn getting it on with some drunk fumbling idiot is too much to bear. A condom can only keep her safe in one sense. I cover her hand with mine. We're pulling into the driveway, and I'm more aroused than I've been in ages, the loose sweats doing nothing to hide it. If we had the time, I'd park us at the beach and show her how non-boring she is, but Chris is waiting. I need a minute to compose myself before we go inside. Minutes have passed since I spit out the half-assed idea, and I'm thinking she's gonna let it slide. Breakfast tomorrow will be awkward as hell.

"Did you have someone in mind?" Her voice is soft and breathy, and any progress I'd made on losing the raging boner is undone.

"I do." I shift in my seat, gently moving my thumb across the back of her hand like I'd done the night we met. The ticking sounds of the cooling engine are loud in the dark garage.

"This is my job." She gestures toward the house.

"Look at me, Ash. No matter what happens between us, it won't jeopardize your job. I promise. That comes first. Mummo is the most important person in the house."

She nods. "Good, that's good."

"I'm working here, too. I need the workshop. I'm only going to get busier."

"So this is...beneficial for everyone?" she asks.

I pull at the neckline of my sweater. "Lots of benefits."

Barely contained lust is painted on her face. The cab light dims and leaves us sitting in near total darkness.

"Can you tell me some of them?" Her voice is a mere whisper.

"No," I rasp, "but I can show you."

With the lightest pressure, I guide our hands from their position on my thigh, upwards. Toward the unignorable erection that tested my patience half the drive. My heart pounds, the thick hoodie and nerves working together to make me sweat. Her fingers brush the edge of my painfully hard dick. I can't see her facial expression anymore and I don't want to influence her, so I remove my hand. She doesn't hesitate. Her warm palm settles over me, and I think I might die. Then she squeezes, and my soul does leave my body for a split second. What a way to go.

"Jesus, Ashlyn."

"That does feel like a big benefit."

For the thousandth time, I curse myself for not calling her months ago. It takes everything in me to stay still in my seat and not thrust my hips up against her hand like a horny teen. I focus my energy on the woman next to me, reaching out to cup her face. Her jaw fits nicely between my thumb and forefinger as I tilt it up, angling her mouth to mine. She smells like mint and citrus as she sighs. The heat of her breath lures me the last inch, and I brush my mouth across hers, whisper soft. It's only half a kiss, but she moans, and I twitch against her hand, which only makes her moan more deeply. I want to get her inside the house so fucking bad. Slipping my hand to the nape of her neck, I pull her against my mouth, turning the pressure into a proper kiss. A tingling sensation works its way down my spine. This is gonna be good.

"Help!" A loud cry comes from outside the garage.

We jolt apart like children caught with their hands in the cookie jar, wrenching our necks towards the house. Muffled shouts come from inside. Mummo and Chris, maybe, but it's hard to tell. We fly out of the truck, my arousal long gone as we race to the back door. Ashlyn runs barefoot across the rough gravel and weeds ahead of me. At the back door, she bounces on the balls of her feet while I fumble with my keys. When I get it open, she pushes past me.

"Jesus, wait, Ashlyn!"

The last thing I need is her running into potential danger. Why didn't I hold her back and go in first? Where the fuck is Chris? I follow her through the dark kitchen as my eyes adjust. When we reach the hall, I see Mummo standing in her long nightgown, pointing to her reflection in a wood-framed mirror. Chris is there, a freaked-out expression on his face.

"Help, Jakey! Help! There's a woman here, she'll hurt me!"

She screams again. Despite the lack of danger, my heart picks up speed at the genuine fear rolling off her, at the alarm in her voice.

"Mummo, that's not a woman. That's you in the mirror. It's a reflection!" I say, trying to reason with her. My voice is shaking, the panic still fresh in my veins.

Ashlyn steps forward, cautiously touching Mummo's right arm.

"Hi, Mrs. Lauri, you sound scared. You saw a woman? That must have been so frightening."

Ashlyn's empathy is otherworldly, and I probably said the wrong thing. Again.

"Let me get rid of her," she says. "Isaac, pass me the blanket from her chair in her room."

I rush to grab the cream blanket and hand it over.

"Here, Mrs. Lauri. Let's get rid of her. You go away, awful woman!" Ashlyn drapes the blanket over the mirror. "There, there. I'm here to help you. Can I help you get back into bed?"

"Is she gone?" Mummo croaks, tears streaming down the lines in her face.

"Yes, Mrs. Lauri."

Any bit of strength Mummo had in her voice is gone. "I'm so cold."

"Let's get you back to bed."

Chris places a hand on my shoulder. He and I stand in the hall, listening to Ashlyn begin to read aloud to my grandmother. My stomach churns like a cement mixer as Mummo's mortality weighs heavy on my mind.

CHAPTER FOURTEEN

Ashlyn

"**T**his is my fault."

I pace back and forth, wishing my room was bigger, so I could burn off this nervous energy.

Isaac shakes his head. "Stop apologising." He reaches out to intertwine his hands in mine when I cross in front of him. a pass. I take hold of him and finally stop.

"If you hadn't had to come pick me up because I was being irresponsible, this might not have happened."

"You know that's not true. Both that it's irresponsible for you to have fun with a friend and that you could have prevented this by being here."

He rubs his thumbs over my trembling hands, the sensation grounding me. Inhaling deeply, a sense of calm returns.

"You told me that the hallucinations and anxiety are hard to manage and will not get better. Chris was about to call me. We were only ten minutes away."

I rub my eyes with my palms, smudging my makeup. After the night I've had, I probably resemble a rabid racoon.

"Can you sit now so I can check your feet?" Isaac's voice is strained.

"My feet?"

I glance down to see a faint trail of blood drying on the floor where I've been pacing.

"I-I didn't even notice. What kind of nurse am I?"

"The kind who had a bit of a fright and who can't have everything under control. Sit." He points at the bed.

I scoff at his comment but sink onto the bed anyway, the discomfort in the soles of my feet increasing by the second now that I'm aware of them. I should have taken my chances running in the heels.

"Here," he pats his lap, "put your feet on my legs."

The first aid kit I keep in the kitchen lays open next to him. When did he even grab that? Lifting my feet up, I gingerly place them across his lap, tugging at the hemline of my skirt.

"Don't peek up my dress, Lauri."

He rolls his eyes at me. "Believe it or not, administering first aid is not one of my kinks."

"Feet might be."

"They aren't," he says, smirking and shaking his head as he looks at the damage. "There's only one deep laceration. I'll disinfect it."

"Laceration? Okay, Nurse Isaac. Maybe I'm not needed around here."

"Please. I have Occupational First Aid Level 3. I've seen some pretty gruesome injuries on job sites."

I wince at the thought of all those sharp, heavy things in the workshop. Has he ever been seriously injured at work? I bite my lip against the sting, trying to focus on Isaac's warm and spicy smell instead of the acerbic scent of the disinfectant. He's being so gentle, cradling my foot with those big hands. Somehow, his care is more intimate than our kiss in the truck.

"That should do it." He rubs my shin in a comforting motion.

The adrenaline is gone, Isaac's steadfast reassurance replacing it. Hip to hip, both feet on the floor like a high school couple with strict boundaries for having "friends" in our room, we sit at the foot of my bed. The door is closed, though, so I guess we're being rebellious.

"I think we should call it a day. You've been up for a long time."

I nod, not bothering to point out that he got up even earlier than me. "Um, I need…"

How do I ask this without sounding like I'm trying to pick up where we left off? As sexy as that would be, we both need rest.

Curiosity dances in his eyes. "What?"

"I need you to unzip my dress. Anna did it up for me earlier." I tuck a strand of hair behind my ear.

His deep exhale borders on a moan. I rise from the bed, cautiously putting weight on my feet; the cushion of the bandages helps.

I keep my voice light. "It's only a zipper, Isaac. I'm not asking you to undress me."

"You might not be asking. But I'm still going to think about it."

Oh. I press my thighs together, wondering if I have the strength for this after everything we'd discussed in the truck. How serious is he about it? Or is this a simple surge of testosterone borne out of jealousy from Jason and the bar bouncer? Maybe by breakfast he'll pretend this never happened. The bed creaks under the weight of his body as he stands. Heat radiates from him, sinking into my bare upper back, as he fumbles with the dainty gold zipper.

He growls with frustration, "Could this be any smaller?"

"That's what she said." I wiggle my shoulders.

"We both know that's not true," he replies, placing a heavy hand on my shoulder. "Stay still."

My stomach flips at the memory of his heat and hardness under my palm. No, Isaac is anything but small. The teeth of the zipper open wide, and he drags his fingers sliding along my spine. I imagine his view. My hair resting upon my upper back, the black lace band of my strapless bra, the curve of my waist, and the line of my matching panties.

"Done," he says, voice almost strangled.

I turn, hands pressed against my chest to keep the dress up, the spaghetti straps dropping off my shoulders. I watch his throat work to swallow, the muscle in his jaw pulse, his blue eyes dragging over me. The thought of the trouble hooking up with Isaac might cause does nothing to douse the flames that lick their way up my thighs. My well of willpower has run dry. I raise up on the balls of my feet to get closer to his perfect lips, wincing and sucking air through my teeth at the pain that shoots through my arches.

"Careful," he says, banding strong arms around me, lifting me enough to take the pressure off my feet. "*Please* be careful."

I draw a shaky breath. "I don't want to be careful anymore."

I tried to be careful when it came to Isaac. But I'm tired of that now.

He lowers his mouth over mine, those strong arms still secured around my bare back, kissing me with a passion that quickly has me forgetting I even have feet. I'm simply floating. Kissing him back takes zero thought, my lips moving over his, parting readily when the tip of his tongue swipes across the seam of my mouth. I whimper when he pulls away, too full of lust to be embarrassed by the wanton sound. He presses me into his chest, and he's as cuddly as I thought. Isaac's chest is strong. The space between it and his arms is warm and safe. I know I'm going to agree to his suggestion. He *is* the best of both worlds. Since the first night I met him, Isaac Lauri has brought me a sense of safety. It's no wonder that our passion is off the charts.

"I have to go, Ashlyn."

He's at least as aroused as I am, his hard-on pressing against my abdomen. I understand, though. We're exhausted. There's blood on the floor, for god's sake. He sets me down softly and strides to the door, hesitating for a fraction of a second before he shuts it softly behind him. I limp over and turn the lock for no good reason. It's more to keep me in than to keep Isaac out.

The black dress flutters to the floor at my sore feet. I slide a hand down my bare stomach and beneath the waistband of my wet panties. The cause of my neediness is mere steps away. Isaac's been popping unbidden into my bedtime thoughts for weeks. Until now, he's been unwelcome. I've denied myself every release, screaming into my pillow with frustration when I couldn't seem to erase the pictures of Isaac in the shower, on my bed, in front of me in the damn laundry room. But now? I welcome him. He destroyed my defences, dismantled them reason by reason, and made me a proposal that is impossible to turn down. It's an Isaac Lauri highlight reel playing in my mind as I recline on my bed, putting my head at the end where my feet usually go. When I let my fingers slip between my soft lips, finding the pleasure I've disallowed myself for weeks, I sigh with relief. I smooth my hand up and down, cradling my clit between my index and middle fingers. My eyes bore into the shared wall. Is Isaac as desperate for release? Has he touched himself recently? He left the room minutes ago with a memorable erection in his sweats. My pussy clenches at the thought of him pulling the waistband down below his balls and handling himself. I tighten the space between my fingers, squeezing the source of my pleasure. Working myself faster, my breaths become ragged. I constrict around nothing, consider fucking myself with my fingers, but decide it would be a poor substitution for what I really need.

He's right there, he's so close.

I think of Isaac in the next room, long limbs sprawled on the bed with his dick in his hand, and grow wetter.

Come with me.

I will imaginary Isaac to finish. Visions of him grunting and coming in his fist is all it takes for my pussy to flutter and bliss to roll through my body like a wave. I moan loudly as the orgasm takes its toll, not caring if Isaac hears, and kind of hoping he *does.*

Isaac seeps into my dreams. A hot, restless sleep made up of friction-filled moments. When I wake, I'm knotted in the sheets. My feet touch the hardwood, and I flinch. Picking a foot up off the floor, I examine the shallow scrapes on each sole. Isaac did a good job bandaging them. I hobble out of the bedroom. Laughter and the smell of butter and onions drift down the hall, amplifying my hunger. Isaac and his grandmother are in the kitchen side by side, heads bent over a well-loved cookbook. She points at a handwritten note she made in the margins long ago.

"If you're going to do something, you do it right, little one."

I smile at the quote. The same one Isaac said the day he revealed the restored porch swing.

He kisses her silver hair, bending to reach, "I want to do it right, Mummo."

I don't want to invade on their private moment. Isaac glances over his shoulder, the intensity in his eyes pinning me to the spot. He's shirtless, wearing pyjama pants low on his hips, drawstrings untied and dangling. I can't help but stare. How does he maintain that body with his diet of children's breakfast cereal and several servings of my suppers each night? Dense hair, darker than the blondish strands on his head, dust his chest. I follow the trimmed trail of hair, down to his hips, where it looks like—I gulp—he's commando. Flashes of last night's solo session come flooding back to me, and I burn with embarrassment at my fantasy of Isaac handling himself. He reclines against the counter, fully comfortable being on display.

"Mornin', Ashlyn. Sweet dreams?"

My eyes snap away from his groin.

Shit.

He's wearing a wolf-like expression. Like he caught a lone sheep wandering far from the safety of its flock. How loud *was* I last night? Maybe I do care if he heard my moans through the thin walls of the old house.

"Why don't you sit and give those feet a rest." He gestures to the table.

"I'm fine."

"Liar," he whispers.

"Okay. I fold, it hurts like a bitch." I only mouth the last word.

I shuffle to the table, and he's got the chair pulled out for me before I even get there. He does the same for Mummo, so we're seated across from each other.

"Do you have supper plans on Monday?" he asks, returning to the pots and pans he has going on the stovetop.

"Supper?" I say dumbly.

"Yep. The meal you tend to eat at four, maybe five o'clock?"

"Early bird supper is where it's at. You've never complained."

He smirks. "Do you want to eat supper with me on Monday? I looked at your Bible...I mean calendar, and there's a respite nurse that day."

"Hilarious."

I glance at Mrs. Lauri, who's watching us with amusement. "That sounds like a lovely idea, Ashlyn."

I smile sweetly, but my teeth are pressed tightly together. What is this? Two against one?

"You have to add milk to her oatmeal to thin it out," I tell him.

"I know that."

"And if you don't stir it hard enough it sticks to the pot."

He folds his arms over his chest. "Can you stop?"

I drop my head into my hands, examining the tabletop. There I go again. Trying to keep everything under control. A full mug of milky tea slides across the table, stopping between my elbows. I almost cry as the sweet scent of Earl Grey fills my nose. Isaac smooths his hands over my shoulders and squeezes my trapezius muscles. I lean back, the heat of the cup sinking into my palms, letting him work out the knots. I'm practically drooling at the sensations.

"Thank you."

I don't even know what I'm thanking him for. The tea? The massage? The care?

The heat of his hands on my bare skin makes me realize my robe is still hanging on the back of my door. I limped my way in here wearing a snug tank top and sleep shorts. And much like Isaac, I'm commando too. My nipples tighten beneath my top.

"Well?" He sways me with his hands. "Supper?" He's still waiting for my answer.

Mummo is folding cloth napkins across the table, no longer paying us attention. I envision my calendar in my mind. Monday, she has a specialist appointment out of town.

I lower my voice, "What about Mummo? You saw what happened last night."

"She thinks it's a great idea. Right, Mummo?"

She lifts both her hands in a thumbs up.

Seriously?

"We can stay in. Is that a yes?"

Why does he have to sound so hopeful?

"We eat supper most nights together, Isaac."

Of course, he has a rebuttal. "You always cook. This time I'll make the meal."

"You're cooking?" My eyebrows shoot up.

"I can cook."

"You're probably burning the oatmeal right now."

"Oh, shit."

"Mouth, young man!" Mummo cries.

He takes two strides to the stove and cuts the flame. "Sorry," he says sheepishly.

Carefully, I stand and join him by the stove. He ladles the oatmeal into a bowl and adds the perfect amount of milk.

"*Someone* distracted me."

He leans closer to brush his lips on my earlobe. His hot breath tickles my skin, and I quiver.

"Did you forget to put something on this morning?"

My thighs pressed together involuntarily.

"Stop it. What would you cook for me?" I ask.

"Don't worry about it. Are you coming?"

I fricking hope so.

"I live here, so–"

"Perfect. It's a date."

A date? Did he and I have separate conversations in the truck last night? He specifically used the word casual.

I face him, crossing my arms over my breasts. "It's not a date."

"I'm the one who invited you, so I think I should know." He mirrors my position, and I do my best to ignore his bulging biceps.

"It can't be a date unless both parties agree."

Even in this, I'm trying to control everything. I had no issue bringing myself to orgasm with Isaac in mind, but I won't give the guy a date? Hardly seems fair. To either of us. What are we going to do? Just hook up in our bedrooms at night and ignore each other the rest of the time? That hardly seems possible.

"Don't think so hard about it, Ashlyn."

"How did you–?"

"You always play with your hair when you're nervous." He leans down so his breath tickles the shell of my ear. "Do I make you nervous?"

"*No*," I scoff, turning away from the counter.

I'm not nervous. The level of arousal I'm experiencing is downright inappropriate for this time of morning, especially with this half naked man's grandmother present. I place her oatmeal down in front of her along with a spoon and folded napkin. Isaac pours some scrambled eggs with diced onion and melted cheese onto a plate and holds it out to me.

"See? I can cook."

Not only was my tea made to perfection, but this breakfast is exactly the one I prepare for myself several mornings a week. I accept the plate and scarf down about half of it immediately. All that dancing and orgasming used up a lot of energy.

"I need a shower."

Isaac's eyes light up, and when he opens his mouth, I hold up a finger in warning. "Don't."

Moments later, I've got my robe and towel in hand, heading for the bathroom when a car slowing along the curb outside catches my eye. Isaac's dad. He's shown up like this before to visit his mother, but not with his son and I in our jammies.

Usually, Isaac is tucked in the workshop or gone from the house entirely. I hastily shove my arms in the robe and tie it tight around my waist.

I pop my head into the kitchen, "Put some damn clothes on," I hiss.

"I am wearing clothes." He gestures to his pyjama pants.

"More clothes. Your dad is here."

A flash of anger or annoyance, I'm not sure which, fills his eyes.

"What do you want me to do? Wrap myself in aprons?"

I roll my eyes at the image and sigh. "I just want everything to seem professional."

"Everything *is* professional, Ash. You're not doing anything wrong."

Then why does it feel that way? I'm so worried that the second Isaac's dad comes in here, he's going to know exactly what is going on between us. Guilt washes over me, but I breathe it away. Isaac is not my boss, and we're two consenting adults. Besides, it's only casual. It's not like I'm shacking up with him forever or something.

The staircase creaks.

"If you want to forget about...us, we can do that." He tugs on the back of his neck. "The last thing I want is to make your job harder."

My shoulders are creeping up around my ears. I'm going to need another massage. Isaac's suggestion of us forgetting about each other sounds ten times worse than Mr. Lauri's judgement.

"I don't want to see him. It's complicated between us. Can you distract him for a minute for me?" His blue eyes are pleading.

Fantastic. That's an unanticipated twist in the family dynamic. I love blending together dating *and* messy father-son relationships with my work.

"He knows you're living here...right?"

Oh my god. Have I unknowingly been keeping a secret from my boss?

I take another peek at his bare chest and the muscles wrapping around his ribs. That heat in his eyes says, 'the last thing I want is to forget about you.'

"He knows. And he hates it."

I'll unpack that later.

Mummo scoffs, "Too bad for him this is *my* house."

The front door swings open, so I step out of the kitchen, leaving Isaac and his grandmother there.

"Good morning, Mr. Lauri." I clutch at the front of my robe in feigned modesty.

He doesn't return my greeting. "I thought everyone would be up by now."

We *are* up. Does he think I'm talking to him while I'm sleepwalking?

"Finishing up breakfast now."

"Seems late."

"Nope, right on time." I work to keep my eyes centred in their sockets.

"I'll join my mother while she eats then."

There are only two ways out of the kitchen. Through the door right next to me, or out into the yard.

"Um, wait!" I scan the room, looking for inspiration.

"What?" Mr. Lauri fiddles with the briefcase he holds in one hand.

"I need you to look at the fireplace for me. I'm wondering if you can show me how it works?"

He screws up his face like I just asked him to hold a scorpion. "That fireplace hasn't been used in years. It's filthy."

"It's been cold in the evenings. Especially for your mother. And there's a draft that comes under the front door."

I gesture to the damp rolled up towel on the floor.

"Old houses are draughty."

I stick out my bottom lip, but based on the perma-scowl he wears while I pepper him with home maintenance questions, it has no influence. Not long after I started working for him, I called him about installing a ramp on the front porch, and he wasn't interested in the slightest. Now that I know his son is a freaking carpenter, it ticks me off that he hasn't hired Isaac to do such an imperative job. Empathy as well as DIY skills obviously skipped his generation.

"Too bad. I love sitting by the fire at night. Don't you?"

I hear a thud somewhere in the direction of the bedrooms and release the breath I'd been holding.

"I prefer electric. It's easier. What was that sound?"

"That's...the house settling. I adore old houses. Their sounds, their imperfections. So much character," I gush.

He scoffs. "This house needs so much work it's hardly worth keeping. The neighbours across the road have the right idea."

"The people who bulldozed their house?" I ask, trying to keep the horror out of my voice.

"That's the one."

There's no way Isaac and his dad are on the same page about what to do with this house when Mrs. Lauri passes. They don't seem like the type to have family meetings. I step aside, allowing him to pass now that the coast is clear.

"I was about to go get ready. Call if you need anything, Mr. Lauri."

"Time to get dressed for work now, don't you think?"

Jesus, no wonder Isaac doesn't want to see him.

"Oh, and Miss Carter, while I have you. My mother's hospital appointment on Monday, you're free to take her to that, right?"

I open my mouth to speak but can't think of what to say. Even Isaac knows I have that day off. She's had this appointment on her calendar since before I met her, and we'd discussed that he would accompany his mother to this one. It's at the hospital two hours away in Victoria with the same specialist who diagnosed her Alzheimer's.

"I thought you were taking her and that there would be a respite nurse for the morning and evening routine."

I already take her to her regular doctor, her dentist, her podiatrist. Surely Mr. Lauri wants to be there. To hear how her illness is progressing. To ask questions about her future.

"Can't. I have meetings. I cancelled the respite nurse already. I'd prefer you." He glances at his phone, squinting at the text on the screen. "And," he barely glances up from his phone, "when you get back into town that afternoon, swing by her lawyer's office. There're some papers for her to sign there."

Swing by? And what type of papers? It's none of my business, though.

"Um, sure. She might be kind of tired by the end of the–"

"Here." He shoves a business card toward me with the name and information of the legal office.

"It won't take long."

He goes to find Mummo, and I'm left holding the thick card wondering what on earth I've gotten myself into with this dysfunctional family.

"Do you want me to come in with you?" I ask Mummo.

We're finally at the lawyer, as per Mr. Lauri's request. It's supper time, I'm starving, and I'm more than a little nervous for whatever at home "date" Isaac has planned. I told Mummo that we didn't have to do this extra errand today, but she insisted she was fine and wanted to get it done.

"No. I've known this lawyer for decades; I won't be very long." She squeezes my hand.

With the assistance of her walker, she makes her own way to the glossy reception desk of the law firm. Settling into a surprisingly comfortable chair, I let my eyes drift closed, enjoying the image of a shirtless, shoulder-massaging carpenter that entertains me while I wait.

CHAPTER FIFTEEN

Isaac

Tea lights glow on the formal dining table between us. The chilled bottle of sauvignon blanc is almost empty. Ashlyn finally looks calm after what sounded like a ridiculously long day. Had I planned anything more strenuous than supper at home, I would have cancelled it the second I saw her. I *know* she said tonight isn't a date, but I couldn't help the urge to make this special. When Ashlyn walked in the room an hour ago looking sexy as hell in a pair of high-waisted black jeans and a red top that showed a couple inches of her tan tummy, I knew I made the right choice. She moaned her way through the first bites, making my efforts to keep my mind out of the bedroom near impossible. As we took the edge off our hunger with the food and our nerves with the wine, we talked. I don't remember the last time I talked so much. There was time to finally tell her about the business with Chris, Berg, and Dean, and I detailed everything I'd do with Mummo's property if I ever had the money and time to make it happen. Ashlyn listened, asking thoughtful questions. Her genuine interest made my chest swell with pride.

She shrugs. "I still don't see why he didn't want to go with her to the appointment today. It was important."

"I guess he showed us how important he really thought it was."

I wonder, am I showing Ashlyn how important she's become to me? Putting the way she cares for my grandmother aside, it's hard to imagine moving out of Mummo's house and back into an apartment of my own. Or worse, her leaving first.

"I can't believe it's dark already," she says as we clear the table.

"That's what happens when you eat at a normal time."

"I know, I know. I'm an honorary senior citizen at this point."

She squirts dish soap into the sink, and I slip a stack of dishes in to soak.

"Think you can get me some discounts?"

Ashlyn splats a handful of soap bubbles on my cheek. "Shush."

I swipe off some of the suds and deposit them on her cheek. "Don't start something you can't finish, old lady."

I'm already walking away, trying to get out of the kitchen so I can get my surprise ready for her, when she points the detachable sink nozzle at me with mischief in her eyes, finger over the trigger. "Oh, I'll finish it, Lauri."

I duck out the door before she can hose me down, a grin stretching across my face and warm feeling in my chest.

A few minutes later, the sparks catch on the crumpled-up classified ads, kindling glowing as the flames lick at the neat pile of cedar logs. Slightly damp bark hisses and pops, the hearth heating up for the first time in too many years.

"Isaac? I smell smoke!" Ashlyn bursts out of the kitchen, making a beeline for Mummo's room.

"Hold up, it's okay, come here." I wave her over.

The motion of the dancing flames catches her attention, and she covers her cheeks with her hands, eye shining.

God, I love that expression. This woman can be made perfectly happy with a cup of tea and a fire.

"I thought you might like it."

She kneels on the carpet next to me, transfixed by the growing flames.

"You heard me talking to your dad this morning and did it." She shakes her head. "You actually did it."

"Does that score me points?"

"Major points."

How many? I wonder. I want to earn a million.

What I really want to do is lay her back on this carpet and kiss her senseless. So it's with great effort that I push my hands against my thighs and stand.

"Do you want dessert now? Let's have it in here."

"There's dessert?"

"Is there dessert...what do you take me for?"

161

She shakes her head. "With your sweet tooth, I shouldn't be surprised."

She collapses into the deep cushions of the leather couch and looks so goddamn relaxed that I worry she'll fall asleep before I can plate and pour. I rush around the kitchen to get back to her as soon as possible. Ashlyn is curled up on the couch, awake, still gazing into the fire when I return. I hand her a slice of rich chocolate cake topped with raspberries and take a seat next to her.

"Full disclosure, any semblance of talent I have in the kitchen ended at that casserole and this morning's eggs, so this is from the bakery."

She slides the first bite off her fork, luscious lips running down the tines.

"Who cares who made it? This is delicious," she moans.

I inhale my piece, in part because it tastes so good, but also because I want my hands free so I can get closer to her. I wait patiently for her to scoop every crumb off her plate while she chats between bites about the fire pit she and her cousins used to sit around in the summers in Ontario.

"A fire pit. I never thought about that for the backyard. Sounds perfect for roasting marshmallows."

The warmth of the fire soothes me, leaving me heavy and un-hurried. When I reach my left arm around Ashlyn's shoulders, she melts against my ribs, her hair tickling my neck as I rest my head upon hers. I draw a deep breath of her shampoo and the vanilla perfume she must have reapplied before supper. Having her tucked next to me is perfect.

"Anna will die when I tell her you fixed the fireplace up for me. For all of us."

"You gonna tell Anna all about our date?" I squeeze her. "You kiss and tell, too?"

"I don't see any kissing happening, so..."

The atmosphere of pure contentment shifts. Tension hangs heavy in the room like a layer of thick fog. She meets my eyes, gazing up at me innocently, like she didn't just throw down the gauntlet. Aglow in the fire's light, I watch her pupils expand as she turns her torso enough that I know what she wants next.

"There's about to be a lot of kissing, Ash."

The remaining inch of distance between our mouths vanishes as I crush my lips on hers, harder than I intend. Fused together, neither of us move. Two people pressing against each other, unwilling to yield. When she opens her mouth to gasp for air, chest heaving, I'm back on her in a flash. She tastes like chocolate when I swipe my tongue over her bottom lip. I rake my fingers through the hair at the base of her skull, cupping her head in my palm to keep in her place as I explore her mouth, absorbing the sighs and moans she offers. She's panting now, squirming on the couch like she needs something. I know exactly what she needs, and I'm going to be the one to give it to her. Leaning toward her, hand still buried in her hair, I lay her back on the sofa, manoeuvring myself so we're facing each other on our sides, her tucked against the back of the couch. My dick twitches in my jeans as she rotates her curvy hips against me. Every circle she makes is equal parts pleasure and torture. I snake my bottom arm beneath her waist, slip my thigh between her legs and fit her tight against me for a slow grind.

"That feels so good," she mutters against my mouth.

Her pulse flutters wildly beneath my tongue as I lick and suck my way down her throat to her sternum. I cover her entire chest in one of my hands, her heart hammers against my palm. Her nipples stiffen as she arches her back, forcing her breasts harder against me.

"Jesus, Ashlyn."

The fire burns at my back, and between the increasing temperature of the room and heat radiating off Ashlyn, I'm ready to ditch some clothes. I push myself up one knee, still on the couch, and pull my long-sleeved shirt off over my head, tossing it onto the rug. Her half-closed eyes rove over me from my face to my belt buckle and back again. She makes a damn good effort of hiding that sexy smile, but I know she likes what she sees.

"Get back down here."

"Yes, ma'am." I ease myself over her.

"I'm hot, too." Her cheeks are pink, a hint of sweat forming at her hairline.

"I can help you with that."

I peel her top off, brushing her hair back into place once I add her shirt to the pile. Sheer peach lace covers her full breasts, and as I kiss her collarbones, I inhale more of her subtle perfume. Our hips rock in a rhythm that I won't be able to keep up for long without needing a break to cool down. Her skin is glowing in the firelight, eyes shining as she looks up at me. There's lust painted across her face, but also something more.

"Fuck, you're pretty, Ash. You know how stupid I feel for not calling you?"

She shakes her head.

"Monumentally."

She lifts her neck a few inches so she can kiss me. "Okay, I forgive you," she says quickly.

I bracket her head with my elbows and kiss her back, dipping my head so she can relax back onto the couch.

I break the kiss. "And I'm not just saying that because you're a really good kisser."

She grabs my jaw and pulls me down. "Got it."

I try not to smirk as her annoyance grows. She's going to have to put up with it while I get all this stuff off my chest.

"Or because you're really amazing with Mummo."

I swear I see her roll her eyes and that's a new one for me during a makeout sesh.

Her kisses become more demanding, and she presses her hips toward me so hard that I nearly forget what I'm saying.

"And I think–"

She reaches up and mushes my cheeks between her palms. "Absolutely not. No more. I get it. You're a big, dumb, stupid, idiot who should have called me because I'm a goddamn catch."

"Harsh," I say, my words come out garbled due to my squished face.

"Do you want to fool around or not, Lauri?"

I nod.

"Perfect. Then shut up. I like you a lot, too, dummy."

CHAPTER SIXTEEN

Ashlyn

Making out with Isaac Lauri in front of a roaring fire while he whispered sweet statements against my lips was the biggest green flag of my life. Now I'm dragging him down the hallway, giggling and covering my lips with my finger as we do a terrible job creeping by Mummo's bedroom door. Halfway to my room he scoops me up under the thighs, bridal style, and continues to his bedroom. The sensation of weightlessness as he carries me does more for me than the couple glasses of wine I drank this evening. I'm drunk on my hot roommate. He sets me down and shuts the door. Through the sheer curtains, ambient light from the quiet neighbourhood creeps across the floor, bathing his white comforter in cool shadows. I can only see the outline of his sharp jaw, full open lips, deliciously broad shoulders. The second the brass doorknob clicks closed, Isaac's self-control crumbles. His belt buckle clinks as he undoes it. I want in on the undressing action, so I reach down to help.

"What is this shit?" I ask, fumbling around for a zipper and not finding it.

"Uh, a button fly?"

The buttons are near impossible to work through the thick denim.

"Well, I don't like it."

"When I got dressed today, I didn't consider which clothing items would allow you to access to my dick with maximum speed."

"Regretting that now, aren't you?"

He murmurs his agreement and I have one button conquered, exposing the waistband of his briefs. Isaac's erection strains against the remaining buttons. He moans every time I tug the fly.

"Fuck, Ash. I'll teach you how to do this another time. Please, for the love of God, let me do this."

The shaking desperation in his voice is panty-melting.

"Fine. You do yours, I'll do mine."

The room is filled with the sound of our deep breaths and denim slipping over skin. We're rushing, urgency driving us on. I take everything off, leaving it in a pile at my feet. My clothes are in a heap on Isaac's bedroom floor. No big deal.

He steps toward me. The dim light playing over his chest.

"Are you totally naked, Ash?"

"Uh-huh." I swallow. "Are you?"

Isaac takes one more step, and something tickles my stomach. The tip of Isaac's hard cock just brushed my bellybutton.

"That answer your question?" His voice is low. *Oh, god.*

"Yeah," I rasp.

He walks me backward toward his bed. "Ashlyn, what do you want? Tell me what you want," he pants.

"You. I want you."

The comforter brushes the back of my thighs as he crowds me. When I fall back onto the soft bed he follows, climbing on top of me with his delicious warmth and weight. The erection that grazed my stomach is pressed hard against me now. Isaac is long. Thick. Hot. His hard shoulders flex beneath my fingers, abs twitching as I shamelessly pet them. I'm greedy for more, wiggling my hand between us. He chuckles, putting more of his weight onto his forearms to give me access. I waste no time cupping as much of his package in one palm as I can. My pussy clenches when he groans. The top of my thighs are wet. A shiver rolls through me, goosebumps erupting on my flesh.

"Here," he says, reaching for something then smoothing a soft knitted blanket over my legs.

I'm smiling dumbly into the dark at the sweet gesture. The fabric doesn't stop his wandering hands, and as he shifts to lay next to me, his fingers dance up my thighs.

"How're you supposed to see what you're doing with this blanket?"

"I don't need to see. I can feel."

In the dark, his voice sounds low and sexy, and my chest is heaving when he reaches my pussy. Resting the heel of his hand over my pubic bone, he cups me with his entire palm and holds still.

"I can *feel* that this sweet pussy is warm for me," he whispers, and I melt deeper into the comforter. "I can *feel* that you're already soaked."

The pressure of his hand. The rumble of his words in his chest. The man is going to talk me to a fucking orgasm.

I reach out, wrapping my hand around his shaft and squeezing.

"Fuck me, Ashlyn. Those hands."

I pant against the crook of his neck. "You're so fucking hard."

"That's for you, babe. All for you."

I'm squirming beneath his hot, heavy hand that he's holding frustratingly still.

"Touch me." Arousal and impatience marry together in my voice.

My thighs fall apart, still under the blanket. He's kissing my neck, my breasts, my stomach.

"Isaac," I cry.

"Shhh..."

I'm swollen, writhing, and soaking wet for him. He eases off, two fingers barely gliding along my outer lips.

"Is that better?" he asks, increasing the pressure of his caresses.

My only reply is a needy moan.

A low chuckle vibrates through his chest. "Ashlyn, you're so ready."

I buck my hips. "Mmm-hmm." Anything to urge him on.

"I fucking love *this*," he growls, grabbing my dark curls in his fist and lightly tugging.

A gasp accompanies the pleasure that rushes between my legs. "Really?"

"Let me show you how much."

He swipes his finger down my centre, and my outer lips part effortlessly.

"You're gonna hug me so tight, aren't you?"

I'm nodding my head yes when he works his index finger into my heat.

"Isaac!" I cry out.

He works me with his thick finger. Never have I felt so satisfied by one digit. My breathing grows shallow and fast. The heel of his hand presses against my clit and I writhe at the sensations. When he crooks that finger against my front wall and stimulates my g-spot with a firm, steady rhythm, my pussy clamps down.

"Isaac, I need...something. I can't–" I say, clutching at his wrist, my short nails digging into his skin.

He speaks in soothing tones, bringing me out of my head and back to him. "Ashlyn, I've got you. Don't chase it, just let it happen."

I want to relax. To slow down and unwind and turn my busy brain off.

"Kiss me," I beg.

One gentle lick against my lower lip and then he's sucking it into his mouth, devouring me. I groan, already closer to release.

"That's right," he encourages. "You're so close for me."

My orgasm approaches like a cresting wave. I'm right there.

"Like that. Don't stop. Don't stop," I beg.

"I won't, Ash. I won't."

My pussy pulses over and over around his finger as I cry his name.

"Tell me what I'm doing to your body. Say it," he growls against my lips.

"I'm coming. You're making me come."

I gasp before the wave crashes down. Rolling over me, pushing me down into the depths of pleasure. I'm swirling in it, moving along at the mercy of the current. Isaac is there, he pulls me up to him, expertly bringing me back from the delectation that tried to drown me. I'm still contracting as I clutch at his arm for dear life, at the hand still gently working me.

"That was fucking gorgeous," he says.

Oh my god.

I tuck my face into his neck. I'm not embarrassed, really, but that was raw.

He grasps my chin in his hand, pulling me out of the safe little crook. My eyes have adjusted to the darkness, and I can see the sincerity on his face. "I mean it."

Our tongues rub together, and I moan into his mouth as I massage his impossible hardness.

His forehead meets mine. "Damn it, Ash, you're gonna make me come if you keep that up," he says through gritted teeth.

"That's kind of the point," I whisper.

I no longer need the blanket, so I kick it away. We lay facing each other, his hand on my waist, mine between his muscular legs. Wrapping my hand around his shaft, I stroke him from root to tip. My finger and thumb make a valiant effort to encircle him, but they don't quite meet. I'm jerking him so slowly that the groans escaping him are positively unholy.

"Ash, fuck, I'm already so close from watching you come."

His admission makes my empty pussy clench, and I want his talented fingers again already.

When I smooth over his slit, slickness spreads over the lush skin of his swollen head. I release him, rising to my knees on the soft bed.

He's breathless, "What are you doing? Your hand...that felt so fucking good."

"I have to taste you."

"Jesus," he gasps, rolling to his back and closing his eyes.

"You good?" I ask when I see his strained expression.

"Fuck, yes. Just glad you stopped stroking me before you said that, or I would have come right then."

I giggle at his praise, then kneel by his hips, taking a moment to check him out. Athletic chest, strong core, big dick. Honestly, he's captivating, and I'm about to consume him.

"Ash, do something. Anything."

I breathe against his shaft then lap at his tip with my tongue, groaning as I taste the saltiness. Using the flat of my tongue, I lick the underside, pressing the head against his firm stomach while I reach every spot. Angling his erection toward my open mouth, I slip him past my lips, over my tongue, all the way to the back of my throat.

"Ashlyn," he hisses my name, both his hands coming to the back of my head. "Shit, sorry." He pulls them away, fisting them at his sides.

"Mhm-mhm." I shake my head, trying to communicate with my mouth full of this gorgeous leaking cock.

I want his hands back. To know I'm driving him so crazy he can barely control himself. Reaching out for his fists, I interlace our fingers and intentionally place them on my head.

"Oh my god, okay. Okay, baby," he pants, weaving his fingers into my hair.

I'm bobbing up and down on him now, not too deep. Every few sucks, I get another taste of his precum.

"Fuck, you're doing so good."

My breasts and hard nipples graze the hair on his upper thighs. I move one knee between his and sink down to grind my clit on his muscular leg. My wetness slicks against his skin. As I circle my hips, the warm tugs of another orgasm begins to build.

"Ashlyn. God, yes...I'm gonna come soon. Just...move if you don't want to–"

I stare up at him and slowly shake my head. No. No way in hell am I going to skip Isaac twitching and coming in my mouth.

He groans, his hands tightening and tugging the roots of my hair.

His hips thrust powerfully off the bed, forcing his thigh further between my legs. I whimper around his pulsing dick and at the sensation is sends through my clit. Never have I been this close to coming so soon after another orgasm. The cry that escapes me as I come is muffled by the thickness in my mouth but I don't stop grinding down until I'm satisfied.

"Jesus Christ, did you just come again? Oh, fuck..."

When our eyes lock, he explodes, his climax sending two, three throbbing waves of cum into the back of my throat. I swallow him down eagerly, then tenderly kissing his shaft. Boneless, I flop down on him, that semi-hard dick pressed between us. Covered in a sheen of sweat, my soft stomach sticks to his abs, and our hearts beat against each other's chests.

A contented sigh whooshes out of me, the sound more effective than anything I could have communicated with words. He wraps his arms around me and runs his fingertips along my spine, and I melt like honey on hot toast.

My mind is so pleasantly *empty* for several minutes, and then a switch flips in my brain and the questions creep in.

This isn't my room, should I go?

Will we take turns in the bathroom to clean up?

Why do I get the sense that when we part, that he'll be taking a pocket-sized piece of me with him?

You know how stupid I feel for not calling you?

I roll off him, the sweat cooling on my skin. I grasp the soft blanket and pull it around my body, clutching it close as I stand.

"Where are you going? Stay." He pats the spot next to him, sounding sleepy and sated.

I bite my lip. "I'm going to shower."

He perks up a bit, head popping off the pillow. "Can I come?"

The idea makes me want to drop the blanket and beckon him out the door and into the steamy spray. But bathing together is couple stuff. And staying in the same room? That's not what either of us signed up for.

"No way, Lauri."

I can't miss the slight frown the plays across his mouth.

It takes an immense effort to walk to the door. The comforter rustles behind me, and when I turn, Isaac stands there utterly naked. I try not to let my eyes drop. I really do. Damn my excellent peripheral vision, though, because I can tell he's erect again. A fresh blush spreads across my face and chest.

He reads me like a book, and says, "Babe, you should like that I want you so bad."

I gulp, allowing myself the briefest glance between his legs before tearing my eyes away again. I do like it. Oh, so very much. But it's not the arousal that's currently reviving itself between my thighs that has me turning pink. Isaac offered me the best of both worlds.

Casual sex with someone I can trust.

But what happened between us tonight wasn't casual at all. I step forward and rise on my toes, careful to keep my hips from making contact with his. If his parts touch my parts, I'm a goner. I'll never leave. He looks down at me, a quizzical expression on his face like he's trying to see something right behind my eyes.

"Thanks," I say, pecking him on the lips.

His eyebrows knit together. "Thanks?"

"Yeah, for like...everything."

He puts his hands on his hips, and I can tell he's unimpressed. On second thought, maybe thanks *isn't* the right thing to say in these situations. But, of all people, why would I know that?

"See you," I say, probably making it worse.

He huffs as I turn and open the door.

"Right. See you 'round, pal."

Pal? Oh, god.

I rush down the hall, tripping on the blanket tangling between my legs. How did I manage to take a mind blowing sexual experience and cap it off with the most awkward goodnight of my life? Safe in the confines of the jade green bathroom, I twist the tub tap. Leave it to me to take something sexy and fun and throw a wet blanket on it by *thanking* the guy. I watch the cold water swirl down the drain, and a similar sensation of frigidity settles into my stomach. There's no way Isaac will want to continue after this.

CHAPTER SEVENTEEN

Isaac

*T*hanks.

You know that mind-melting, heart-harrowing, panty-peeling sex we had? Thanks. Something shifted for Ashlyn between the time she draped herself over my body and when she rushed out of my bedroom door. What was it? Fuck if I know. Did I think we'd sleep curled in each other's arms until dawn broke? No. But I sure as *hell* didn't expect a closed-mouth kiss and the cold shoulder. A high five would have been better than that. Ashlyn blew my mind that night, and I haven't been able to forget the good parts for a second. I spend my days in a near constant state of arousal and hardly sleep because the woman I want desperately is mere feet away. She'll barely look at me, and I'm going to find out why as soon as I have a spare moment to do something other than breathe.

Mummo's main ask on her to-do list was something I should have done years ago. Adding a ramp to the front porch is a no-brainer, and with the help of Berg, Dean, and Chris, we got it done in only a few days. The timing couldn't be more perfect, because our business has its first real job. Next week we'll be refocusing our efforts toward a full restoration of a farmhouse porch. The lumber is ordered, the plans are drawn, I'm ready. Nervous as hell. But ready. Between my worries about the project and agonizing about what's going on in Ashlyn's mind, I'm exhausted. The workshop has been my home for days, and aside from going inside for sleep or a quick shower, I've barely crossed paths with Ashlyn or Mummo. I'm not avoiding her, per se, just...giving her a wide berth. Waving bye in the kitchen on my way out the door isn't going to give us the time we need to figure things out. I can only hope that when we do sit down and get to the bottom of her feelings, that it's not too late. Will Ashlyn have rebuilt the wall between us that we worked so hard to break down? I'm finishing up a few things in the workshop when I hear a grunt of frustration outside. I cock my head to hear better and make my way to the closest window.

"What the actual hell..."

Ashlyn is out there dressed in some sort of coveralls, head down and muttering, going to town on a weed-laden garden bed. There's almost no delineation between the once neat beds and the too tall grass of what barely passes for a yard. The tool in her hand is taller than she is, an ancient rake that looks like it belongs in an agricultural exhibit of a museum. I make my way outside and clear my throat as I approach, having learned my lesson about sneaking up on women, especially those holding vintage farming implements.

"What are you doing?" I ask.

She doesn't skip a beat, driving the rake into the dry soil and tangled weeds. "What does it look like I'm doing, Isaac?"

"Struggling?" I bite my lip to keep from grinning as she turns to scowl at me, blowing some loose strands of hair from her face.

"I'm gardening."

She has fire in her eyes, but it doesn't convey complete hatred, so I'll take it.

A voice sing-songs across the yard, "Put your back into it, girl!"

Mummo is perched next to the open window in her bedroom, cheering Ashlyn on. She waves at me, and I raise a hand back.

"What the hell are you using to do said gardening?"

"A rake. I found it in the garage. Mummo said I could use whatever I needed."

I scratch my head. The vast majority of stuff in that garage is destined for the landfill. "Was that during this century or..."

Bits of red-brown rust flake off onto Ashlyn's unprotected palms. I can see that the coveralls are also from the garage. I'm sure Mummo used to wear the exact pair for messy jobs around the yard. Even though the threadbare garment hangs off of her and she has a sheen of sweat plastering her baby hairs to her forehead, she's so pretty. It's been too many days since I've really looked at her. My dick twitches in my Carhartts as memories of last week flicker through my mind.

"Those tools are perfectly good, Isaac!" Mummo hollers from her room.

"She's gonna get Tetanus!" I yell back.

How the hell did she even hear that? My grandmother looks fully entertained, elbows propped up on her bedroom windowsill. With every pull, the tines of the rake snag in the hardy weeds and make a terrible twang as the metal catches. The pile Ashlyn has managed to remove is pitifully small. I clutch the rake with my right hand, stopping her midway through a pull.

"Stop," she says, yanking back with surprising force.

The April sun is beautiful and not nearly as hot as it will be later in the season, but Ashlyn's cheeks are pink with exertion.

I pull back harder. I'm not trying to be an ass. I want her to find a way to work smarter, not harder.

"Isaac," she sighs, "let it go."

I get the sense she's talking about more than the rake. She wiggles the handle around, but my grip is strong. Covering her hand, I gently loosen her fingers off the battered handle. She slackens her grip, and I lower the rake to the ground, feeling like I just disarmed a criminal.

I hold my empty hands out. "Show me."

"This isn't necessary, Isaac," she says, voice cracking.

"It's necessary to me."

She nods and places her hands in mine, palm up. Her hands are red and swollen from the friction.

"Why aren't you wearing gloves?" I keep my voice soft, not wanting to admonish her.

She shakes her head weakly, and I think I hear her sniffle.

"I found some in the garage, but they were way too big. I left mine at my apartment, but they're more for keeping dirt off your hands."

I would have gotten her some if she asked. I'm only at the hardware store every other day.

"Do you want help?"

I'm bone tired but the words fly out of my mouth anyway.

"You don't need to–"

I stop her there. "I *want* to. If you haven't noticed, I enjoy doing things for you, Ashlyn. And if you don't like that...well, tough. If it makes you sleep better at night, imagine I'm doing it for Mummo."

We both glance at my grandmother. She gives us a wave with her fingers.

"I know things didn't really work out with our, um, plan. Don't feel like you have to treat me differently because of that."

I scratch my head, "Wait...just...what?"

If my face doesn't convey my confusion, my utter lack of English skills might.

I try again. "You think that things didn't 'work out' the other night? Were we in the same room?"

She shoves her sore hands in the pockets of the coveralls and nudges the weed pile with her toe.

"We were...but I messed it up at the end."

I step into her space, finding her waist with my hands and pulling her toward me, not caring if my grandmother is watching. She *has* to know how badly I still want her.

"The only thing you messed up was not letting me thoroughly kiss you goodnight so I could taste myself on your lips."

She opens and closes her mouth.

"You can't say stuff like that!" she whispers.

"Nobody heard but you."

She takes a deep breath and closes her eyes, like she's steeling herself for something.

Don't pull away.

"I thought you regretted it after. Because I made it so weird."

Regret? Hardly.

"It's going to take a lot more than that to keep me out of your bedroom...*my bedroom*," I tease. "I'm still down to pick up where we left off. If you are, that is."

"Thank, god." She presses a palm to her heart.

We both laugh, and I can't resist a bit more banter. "That good, hey? We haven't even gone all the way."

"Isaac!" She sounds scandalized again, looking over her shoulder where she knows Mummo is.

Despite how tired I am, it only took ten minutes of staring into Ashlyn's chocolate eyes to forget it.

I release her and clap my hands together once. "Get your things. And get Mummo ready."

"Ready for what?"

"Field trip. We're going to the garden centre."

I'm already heading for the back door to get my wallet and truck keys when she giggles and claps. With that sound every single trace of exhaustion is gone.

"I've never been here before." Ashlyn's eyes go wide as she observes the massive garden centre and busy parking lot. We drove out to a more rural area that isn't far from where we met. The vibe in the April sunshine couldn't be more different than that wind-swept winter storm. This garden centre is open to the public, but it's a favourite of landscapers and more professional-grade operations. Someone with only an apartment-patio-sized garden probably wouldn't have much cause to visit.

"I'm moving in here. You two can fend for yourselves," she says.

I poke her between the ribs. "Try not to drool on the plants."

"No promises."

"You can push, Little One. Let her explore," Mummo says as I tuck a light blanket around her knees.

We brought the wheelchair so she wouldn't have to walk around the giant place and tire herself. We're already interrupting her nap with our afternoon excursion. Ashlyn forges ahead the second we get inside, talking a mile a minute, taking everything in. She left the coveralls at home despite my protests, and I try not to leer at her legging-clad butt as she power walks toward the seeds. I steer Mummo toward some of the more heavy-duty tools, taking note of the things I need to manage the lawn and tough weeds. I'll be damned if I let her spend another summer staring at that absolute disaster. Maintaining a lawn is the least I can do for her.

When I find Ashlyn, she's ogling high-end greenhouses, trailing her fingers along the glass. Hanging back, I lean against a pallet of soil, watching her. I can hear her muttering to herself. She reaches for the price tag and scoffs, dropping the tag like it bit her and taking a small step back.

"A little steep?"

She whips around and finds me. "You can say that again."

I walk over to glance at the tag, eyebrows shooting up. The price is fucking stupid. I could build it better for half the cost. Balanced in her arms are packets of zinnia seeds and, much to my relief, a heavy-duty pair of gardening gloves.

"Hold these." She dumps everything into my arms.

She joins Mummo at an impressive display of a backyard pond. They ooh and aah at the huge koi, laughing together when a golden yellow one jumps to snag a bug from the surface and splashes them. Aren't they two peas in a pod? Ashlyn and I could work together on the yard. I imagine us toiling away, lovingly restoring the space into its former glory. Enjoying the shade of the trees that have grown on the property for a hundred years. I turn away from the women, a tightness in my throat as I swallow the unexpected wave of emotion.

When our supplies are tucked into the truck bed, we take a meandering drive home. Mummo snores softly behind us, the vibration of the truck having lulled her to sleep. We pass organic farms and entrances to vineyards. Tractors and groups of road cyclists. I divide my attention between the road and the happy woman next to me. She's beaming out the windshield, and if she asked me to take her on a road trip that solely consisted of visits to garden centres, I'd gladly do it. In a heartbeat.

"I loved that place, Isaac. Thank you."

I shrug, "No problem, babe."

"I want to tell you something."

I glance over at her as swallow hard, "Okay..."

"The night we met. I told you I was..." a nervous laugh erupts from her mouth, "a horticulturist."

She dissolves into a fit of laughter. It starts out loud but turns into a wheeze, tears leaking from the corners of her eyes.

She draws a breath. "What was I thinking? Why would I say that?"

I'm laughing with her now. Even though it's not funny, it's contagious and damn endearing. All I can do is struggle to breathe and keep my eyes on the road.

"Ash," I say, sides aching, "did you think I forgot that?"

She looks horrified, sobering for a second. "Oh my god! You must have thought I was so weird. I'm so embarrassed!"

I reach over and rustle her hair. "I remembered it the day after I moved in. Why'd did you say it?"

She puffs out her cheeks and exhales. "I don't want to be a nurse anymore," she blurts, covering her mouth with her hands.

Ashlyn is amazing at her job, but her admission doesn't completely surprise me. There's no rule you have to stay in the same career your whole life, especially one as complex as nursing. Hell, I'm going from commercial construction to running my own small business.

"Ashlyn. Gardening, horticulture, plants. That's obviously your passion. You lit up like a Christmas tree in there."

"My family doesn't get it. They think it's a bad move to leave a secure job for something so...changeable."

I empathize with her so hard. When it comes to restoration work, there's no guarantee of the next job. My gut clenches. Does she want to leave? To quit now? I want her to be happy...but I don't want her to go. I can't bring myself to ask.

"When I was a boy, Pappa had an old truck with a full bench seat. I used to sit between him and Mummo on drives."

Ashlyn smiles over at me.

"I'm thinking it's too bad they did away with that style of seating, wish you could slide over here with me so I could put my arm around you."

"You old softie," she says.

"Maybe an old soul. I don't think very many people get as lucky in love as they did."

I didn't mean to turn the conversation so deep, but the thought of Ashlyn leaving has me feeling nostalgic. The whole outing awakened a spot in my soul that was dormant.

"You don't think so?" Ashlyn asks.

"You never hear people say, 'my marriage was average'. It's either amazing, like Mummo and Pappa, or total shit, like my parents." I rub the back of my neck.

"Do you remember anything from the time they split up?"

I shake my head. "No, I was way too little."

"Do you want to know what I think?"

Always.

I nod.

"I think you don't hear about the hard parts. Of course your grandmother and grandfather faced challenges. It's impossible not to."

"It almost feels unattainable."

I catch her grazing her fingertips over her fresh blisters, so I reach over to take her left hand, gently pressing her palm to my lips. She blushes at the gesture, but doesn't pull away, so I settle our clasped hands into my lap.

From the backseat comes the gentle hum of the song "K-I-S-S-I-N-G".

"I think the jig is up," I say.

"You two don't fool me."

A few minutes later, she's softly snoring again, and I'm reevaluating this arrangement. Only having Ashlyn casually? That doesn't seem like enough anymore. Not by half. But how do I tell *her* that? Because it isn't part of our agreement, and I'm so scared she's going to leave.

CHAPTER EIGHTEEN

Ashlyn

"I'm back!" I holler as I lug in the groceries, every handle digging into the flesh of my forearms.

No way in hell am I taking two trips.

"Helloooo. What's the point of having a strapping man around if he doesn't help with the heavy work?" I plod through the living room towards the kitchen, using my hip to push open the kitchen door. I spot Isaac outside at the far end of the backyard.

"Help a girl out!" I call.

He whips around at the sound of my voice, blond hair flying, and starts running toward the house with total golden retriever energy. He's shirtless, so I enjoy a Baywatch moment, thanking my brain for turning the speed to slow motion so I have a few more seconds to ogle the way his obliques taper before disappearing into his jeans.

"Hi," he says, stepping into my space. He smells like fresh cut grass and spring air.

"Hi, yourself." I stretch up to kiss him.

The greeting grows until my cheeks are burning from the friction of his beard. How does this man take me from zero to a hundred so fast?

"Is Mummo still out with my dad for a while?"

His tone is pure trouble.

I glance at the clock. "We're good for a bit. Why...what do you have in mind?"

Some women might want jewellery or fancy nights out, but Isaac Lauri took me to the garden centre of my dreams yesterday and that was *my* idea of a good time. If he wants to get busy right here on the kitchen floor? I'm down. I lean in and resume our kiss, losing myself in the cinnamon and cedar taste of his lips. He holds me back, breaking our kiss, groaning as he does it.

"Hold that thought," he says.

"What?" I nearly snap.

He laughs, "Oh, is someone not getting what they want?"

I scowl at him and cross my arms over my hard nipples.

"Let me show you something."

He motions for me to follow then leads that way out the back door.

"Um, okay? What do you have up your sleeve now? Is there another fireplace somewhere? I *will* jump up and down if that's the case."

"You'll see. Come on."

He tows me along through the yard and I can barely keep up with his long strides. The afternoon smells like fresh cut grass and pollen. Isaac stops and I nearly crash into his sculpted back. Bathed in a pool of sunlight is a gorgeous, three-tiered garden bed made of, if I'm not mistaken, cedar. It's filled to the brim with rich, dark soil, and the grass surrounding it has been mowed.

"What do you think?"

"Is...is it a project for work?" It's so beautiful. I want to believe it might be for me...but it's too much.

He scrunches his face up.

"Ashlyn, I made it for you," he says, like it's the most obvious thing in the world. "The old garden beds are going to take ages to clear, and I want you to be able to plant those zinnias right away. They should be planted soon, right?"

His observation and this gesture touch me in a way I don't expect, and I have to pretend the clouds are beyond interesting for a minute to keep the happy tears at bay.

"I used the cash that appeared in my underwear for the materials."

Victory is written all over his face. I want to smack it right off, but I opt to swat his bare chest instead.

"First off, that was for the tow truck! Second," I soften my voice, "this is the nicest thing I've ever had."

He hugs me, and I really can't think of a better place to be than against his warm chest in this overgrown yard behind this hundred-year-old house. This spot in the abundance of afternoon sun will be perfect for the zinnias this summer. But summer seems far away right now. Will I live here long enough to see them bloom? What if, tomorrow, the perfect place pops up? I'd be crazy not to take that opportunity, right? I push the thought away. It's too painful to bear.

Back inside, I'm placing the last of the cold groceries in the fridge, arranging the pots of yogurt how I like them, when Isaac gasps.

"What!" I startle.

"Lucky Charms *and* Froot Loops?" He holds out the boxes before clutching them to his chest like newborn twins.

It's stupidly adorable, and now I'm thinking about Isaac holding babies. Great.

I tuck my hair behind my ear. "Yeah. So?"

"You got these for me."

"It's not a big deal."

"You know how much I like it. And now you *really* like me so...cereal." He shakes the boxes at me.

"You *might* have been on my mind as I went down that aisle."

"You've been on my mind a lot, too." He sets down the precious boxes. "When I'm working, when I'm laying in bed at night, when I'm showering..."

I roll my eyes.

"Don't roll your eyes at me, Ashlyn Carter."

"Or what?"

It's my new favourite question to egg him on.

"Or I'll pull you inside this pantry and have my way with you."

I inhale and cover my mouth with my hand, eyes wide with false shock. "But what will the root vegetables think?"

I'm joking around to hide the fact I'm kinda freaking about what exactly that means. Are we about to fuck under the watchful gaze of the Quaker Oats guy?

"I'll show you a root vegetable," he says, stalking over to make good on his threat.

I shriek when he hauls my body flush against his, carrying me into the dim pantry. A single bare lightbulb swings from the ceiling, and the competing smells of spices tickle my nose. He smacks my butt hard and shoves me against a relatively empty section of shelving, a palm shielding the crown of my head. My ass stings, the thin leggings didn't protect me from his playful swat. He wastes no time covering my mouth with a searing kiss. The night with the fire and wine was all kinds of romantic, but this is a whole other animal. Our teeth clink together, then I bite him on the lip hard enough to make him swear. Isaac's erection is dead obvious through his jeans, the thick fabric unable to conceal the hardness pressing against my hip.

"Are you always so ready?" I reach down to squeeze him.

Those blue eyes sparkle with mischief. "For you... yes."

He plunges his hand down the front of my leggings, right into my panties, swiping along my slit. As he withdraws it, I whimper at the loss. Even in the weak light, I can see my moisture glistening on his skin when he holds up his hand.

"Are *you* always so ready for *me*?" he counters, popping the finger in his mouth and sucking it clean with delectation.

My eyes flutter closed at the sight.

This man.

"Babe," he drops to his knees and hooks his thumbs into my waistband, "if you told me I could have my pick of anything at all to eat in this whole damn pantry," he inhales my scent, his nose tickling my clit, "I'd choose you."

My thighs tremble. I'm not sure I have the strength to stand for this, especially if he keeps running that dirty mouth. He looks up at me through his unfairly long lashes, peeling my leggings and panties down to the middle of my thighs, lowering his face to my pussy and breathing me in again.

"Sweetest fucking thing in here," he growls.

He presses his lips to my pubic bone, the crease of my upper thigh, my labia. The man isn't eating me out, not yet, he's *kissing* me. What I wouldn't give to lay back on a comfortable bed and let him do this until his heart's content, but I need more.

"Isaac...please."

The moan he makes as his tongue swipes through my lips, parting me, is carnal. If he was kissing my pussy before, he's making out with it now. I hold on to the wood shelving, thanking god for quality craftsmanship. The world needs good carpenters for many reasons, it seems. His hands grip my hips, fingers pressing into the flesh. The pressure of his mouth, the deep groans, the wet sounds. It's stoking something deep inside me.

"Don't stop..."

I've *never* been this close this fast from someone's mouth.

He keeps his tongue against my clit, gently massaging it with steady movements, his breath fanning across me. My fingers knot in his hair, immediately understanding the fascination with hair pulling. I weave my hands into his roots and direct his head where *I* want it. Controlling my own pleasure. This big man is on his knees for *me*.

"Ashlyn..."

I glance down at him when he moans my name. He's dropped his right hand from my hip, and it's splayed over his crotch, squeezing his rock-solid erection through the denim.

Oh, my god.

My pussy clenches as he sucks my swollen clit, his left hand massaging my butt, dangerously close to the spot no man has ever touched.

"I'm gonna come, Isaac. Don't stop."

He shakes his head, the movement only pushing me closer. He fumbles with the buttons on his pants, and I catch a glimpse of his shaft.

"There!"

I cry out, the sensations rushing together into one bright point before scattering like fireworks, radiating through my pussy, down my legs, and up my spine. I'm breathless, knees shaking, but he braces me easily with that one strong arm. He laps up my wetness and pulls himself out of his pants. If he's going to stroke himself to completion right here, I'm going to come again. But he freezes with his dick in his hand before jumping up and hitting his head on the bulb.

"Fuck." He reaches up to steady it, burning his fingertips and hissing in pain. Then I hear what caused his reaction. The front door slams closed and voices drift into our hiding spot.

"Oh my god!" I pull up my pants and smooth down my hair.

He pulls me to him, covering my mouth with a kiss that tastes like me, wasting seconds we don't have.

"Go away with me this weekend?"

"What? Are you crazy?" I squirm in his arms.

We can't go away together. It's too serious. But the temptation of having uninterrupted time with Isaac is strong. Not only to be intimate, but to have the opportunity to simply be in each other's presence without all the stresses of day-to-day life.

"Say yes. I'll arrange everything."

I stifle my nervous, giddy laughter. I'm so screwed. "Fine. Let's get out of here."

"I can't!" He gestures to his raging boner.

"I'll go first. Put all that away."

I exit the pantry with my game face on, mere seconds before Mr. Lauri enters the kitchen, guiding his mother.

"How was your grocery shopping?" he asks.

"Good. Good. A bit of a zoo."

My cheeks are hot, so I busy myself around the kitchen.

"How was your appointment?" I smile at Mummo, wiggling my fingers in our usual greeting.

"Well–" she starts.

Mr. Lauri interrupts her. "Fine, just fine. It was a *family* matter."

I press my lips together. The way he cuts her off sometimes makes my whole body tense.

Isaac steps out of the pantry, and I've never witnessed a father so thoroughly displeased to see his child. Mummo beams, as she always does in the presence of her grandson. He's composed himself, no sign of any obscene bulges. Yes, I looked.

"What's this about an appointment? Where were you dragged off to today, Mummo?" Isaac leans down to kiss her on the cheek.

"I said it's a family matter," Mr. Lauri snaps.

Isaac takes a breath. "It's a good thing I'm family then," he says.

"I take it the ramp out front is your doing?"

My eyes dart between them as they talk. It's the first time I've seen them interact. The tension is thick.

"Did you recognize my top-notch craftsmanship?"

Mr. Lauri scoffs. "Who paid for it?"

Isaac's fists clench at his sides, and I'm starting to think about stepping between them.

"Now that's enough."

All three of us turn toward Mummo. Her interjection does the work for me, Isaac's posture relaxing right away at the sound of his grandmother's voice. Satisfied with the result, she settles into her regular dining chair and begins leafing through her May edition of Home and Garden Magazine.

His father can't leave it alone though. "It's the middle of the day. Don't you have somewhere to be doing your *top-notch* work?" His voice drips with sarcasm.

Isaac offers a winning smile, white teeth on display. "Fixing some wobbly shelving in there for Ashlyn."

"Shirtless?"

I turn to hide my smile. Isaac goes to the sink to pour glasses of water for himself and Mummo.

"That's so helpful. I'm glad my son is handy," Mr. Lauri says.

What? Is it a character flaw to be talented with your hands? I can attest that it isn't. I'm sort of sick of seeing this grown man bully his son.

"He did a really solid job in there."

Isaac chokes his water, spluttering and sending me a 'stop that' death glare.

"You should get on with your day, Isaac. When I was starting Forward, I certainly didn't have time to play Mr. Fix It. Besides, it looks like Ashlyn has some cleaning up to do."

I bite my tongue until it hurts, and Isaac mouths an apology at me.

"Ugh, and Miss Carter? *This* is not the type of food I want to see in this house." He lifts up the box of Lucky Charms, clicking his tongue in disapproval.

Isaac barks out a laugh before he snags his shirt and opens the back door. I plunk the last few apples into the fruit bowl, probably bruising them.

Chapter Nineteen

Isaac

The rock skips once before it sinks beneath the choppy waves. I needed to blow off some steam, so when I left the house and texted Chris, he told me to meet him at a nearby beach where he'd be finishing up his run. Pebble Bay is littered with broken shells that crunch beneath my boots. Faded driftwood decorates the coast, brought ashore by strong winds. I used to come here with my grandparents to have picnic lunches or with other kids in the neighbourhood to beachcomb at low tide. Maybe when our first job is done I could bring Mummo and Ashlyn here on a calm day.

"Your parents still have that cabin?" I ask Chris while he stretches his hamstrings.

"Yeah, it's been empty all winter, though."

"Think I can use it this weekend?"

201

"*This* weekend?"

A group of seagulls screeches nearby, fighting over the remnants of a dead crab.

"Yeah." I give up trying to skip the rocks, trying instead to toss them as far as possible into the Pacific.

"Don't we have work?"

"Everything's ready."

I'd made sure of it. I *could* pour over the plans again and again, stressing myself out, but that won't make a difference. I'm going to go away for two nights and come back fresh.

"It's only two nights."

"You're taking her, aren't you?"

I nod, pulling at the back of my neck.

"Seems serious."

"It's not." I whip another rock into the bay.

Chris tosses one a bit further. "You sure?"

No. "Yep."

"You're so full of shit," he says, fiddling with something to do with his run on his smart watch.

"Wow, thanks for that."

How can I be mad at him for stating the obvious?

"You ran out the door to get her from the bar a couple weeks ago like your first-born child was in mortal danger."

"Excuse me, I had a very important role to play that night."

He snorts, "More like *roleplaying*." In a falsetto voice he says, "Nurse Ashlyn, help me, my dick is swollen."

I shove him toward an incoming wave, soaking his sneakers with icy water. It's gonna be a squishy walk home, asshole.

"Hey, what the hell? I'm playing around."

"Use her name and the word dick together in a sentence again, and I'll drown you."

Chris sinks down on a log, dumping water and sand out of his shoes.

"I'm trying to give her a break," I say, joining him on the log. "Nobody knows better than us what it's like to work for my father."

"Fair enough. I have a set of keys at home, I can drop them off to you tomorrow."

I'm finishing up some errands when my phone buzzes with a text from Ashlyn.

Ashlyn: Coast is clear.

Isaac: Thank God. Sorry I left you with him. That conversation was going nowhere fast.

Ashlyn: 🥕🧅🧄

It takes me a second to interpret her text. Root vegetables. I bark out a laugh that gets lost in the wind.

Isaac: I'm going out with some of the guys tonight. I might be late. But weekend plans are secured.

Ashlyn: Where are you taking me?

Isaac: A cabin in the middle of the woods where I don't have to be subject to blue balls.

Ashlyn: Poor baby.

Isaac: Why do I get the feeling that was highly sarcastic?

Ashlyn: Because you know me by now.

I do know her. How can I not after living with her for this long? She's type-A to the max, but wickedly funny. Flowers and plants are her favourite thing in the world, except for maybe her cousin. By the end of the weekend, I have a feeling we'll know each other even better.

The Tipsy Mermaid is tucked far enough away from the downtown core of West Isle that tourists rarely visit. Most of the customers are long-time patrons looking for a good meal or a cold drink, and the guys and I are amongst the most loyal of those. Dean rubs his knuckles over my scalp as he approaches our table from behind and slides into the chair next to me. I nod at him as I take a deep pull of my cold beer.

"Got one of those for me?"

"You bet, take your pick." I point at the cold bottles in the centre of the table.

He twists the cap off and clinks his bottle against mine. "Cheers."

"What are we toasting?" I ask.

"Health, wealth, happiness...and taking your hot nurse to a cabin." A shit-eating grin spreads across his face.

Fucking Chris.

"First off, she's not *my* nurse. Second, it's not even anything serious so don't worry about it."

I squeeze the tense muscle between my neck and shoulder. I've been riled up all afternoon since getting interrupted in the pantry. The way my dad spoke so rudely to Ash and Mummo made my skin crawl. I can't wait to get her far away from the stress.

"Man, I'm just busting your balls. Life's been kind of shit for you the last few months, so you should take your fun wherever you can get it."

I start my next beer as a waitress delivers calamari and a plate of nachos.

"Berg or Chris gonna make it?"

"Nah, Berg couldn't find a sitter, and Chris has some big hike this weekend so he's taking it easy."

I'd hoped to have all four of us here to treat them to a beer and food before we kick the project off next week. I make a mental note to take them out for an early breakfast or something instead. We dig into the battered squid and cheesy nachos while they're still hot, glancing between the handful of television screens. Four of them play sports games or highlights, but the fifth one, without fail, always plays an ocean-themed movie. It's a stupid tradition, but one that makes the Mermaid what it is. *Jaws* is currently playing with subtitles on. At first, I think Dean's far off gaze is because he's lost in thought, but a smirk tugs up one corner of his mouth.

"Hey, ladies, glad you could make it." His voice is low and inviting as he greets the two women who seem to have appeared out of nowhere next to our table.

One looks at her feet rather than meeting Dean's intense eye contact, the other holds his gaze steadily.

I speak out of the corner of my mouth, "D, what the hell?"

The chairs skid as the women take the seats across from us, the bolder of the two choosing the spot across from Dean.

He leans into me so only I can hear, "You need to have some fun."

The only thing I need is fast asleep at home, tucked into my childhood bed. My pants tighten when I remember the way she tasted this afternoon. I see why Dean didn't mention it would only be the two of us tonight. I've been volunteered as wingman.

"Isaac, this is Katrina," he says, gesturing to a curly blonde across from me.

I offer a tight-lipped smile. "How you doing?"

She places her purse on the edge of the table, and I can't help but wonder if she has a condom for her night out like Ashlyn did. From the way her friend leans across the table and toys with the wet neck of Dean's beer bottle, I'd say *she* does. Dean flags down our server and orders some more drinks, talking easily with his date. This is awkward. I feel like a grade-A asshole every time she smiles coyly and I scowl in return. Time plods along, and the only thing getting me through listening to Kristen, no, Katrina talk about how peanuts aren't actually nuts, but members of the legume family, is the rum and cokes I'm slurping down. I'm taking Ashlyn away this weekend, and, technically, I'm on a date with another girl. I imagine Ashlyn's face if she walked through the door right now and saw us and my stomach churns. Nothing about that sits right with me. When they excuse themselves to the washroom, I turn to Dean.

"I did not sign up for this, D."

"You don't date anymore? You off the market?"

Fuck it.

"You know what? I think I am."

Pretty sure I have been for a while.

He whips out his phone and starts typing.

"What are you doing?" I lean over to see his screen.

207

He swerves out of my view. "Notifying Chris and Berg that they owe me fifty bucks each."

"What the *hell* was the bet?"

"That if I brought you a hot girl, you'd turn her down because you're basically wifed up."

I balk at his words. "Wifed up? Jesus Christ, D. She's..."

Titles are hard. I think she and I have both learned that we suck at keeping things casual. Even though we haven't fooled around very much, things between us are intense. Yet...I don't hate that. I rake my hands through my hair.

"Tell me she's nothing. Tell me she's just a hookup. Do it."

"I..."

I fucking *can't*. Ashlyn has quickly become so much more than I bargained for. Objectively, Katrina is hot. She's one hundred percent the type of girl I might have hooked up with in the past. But tonight? There isn't a thing she could say or do to interest me. All I can think about is the woman who's dreaming away with that fuzzy pink robe at the foot of her bed. The woman who treats my grandmother like family. The woman who bought me the breakfast food I love without me even asking. I bump the table as I stand, nearly tipping the empty bottles.

"I've gotta go, man."

Now that I've decided to go to her, I can't get there fast enough.

"You've had a lot of drinks, you need a ride?"

"No. I'll walk."

Hell, I'll run to get there faster.

Ashlyn will be in bed by now, but the idea of sleeping in the room next to her is all I need.

CHAPTER TWENTY

Ashlyn

Mummo went to bed ages ago, and I'm standing in my room, completely overwhelmed, so I've called in back-up.

"You don't need that." Anna tosses a pair of jeans out of my small weekender bag.

I place a pair of flannel pyjama pants inside.

"Or those," she says, throwing them out too.

I toss my hands in the air. "What *am* I allowed to bring?"

"It's a sexy cabin getaway. You literally only need yourself. And him, but you can't pack that. Speaking of packing...is he?" She bounces her eyebrows at me a few too many times.

I ignore her, surveying my room. Clothes are strewn about, and it's giving me a mild anxiety attack.

"What about those?" I ask.

Our eyes settle on the condoms on my dresser. The box that's opened...but still completely full, the condom from my clutch the other week having been returned to its home.

"Nowwww you're getting the hang of it," she says, waving me off to retrieve it.

"What? You can't get it?"

"No. I only take things out." She uses her hands to gesture removing things from the bag.

"Super helpful."

"Isn't it early to pack for a trip for next weekend? I wouldn't exactly put it by you to pack a week in advance though."

"It's *this* weekend, Anna. Tomorrow. In twelve hours. He called to set up a nurse and told my boss I needed some time off for personal reasons. Who knows the web of lies he's spun regarding that. Basically, I'm the least professional nurse in the history of ever. Do you know how long I usually plan trips in advance?" I try to take a deep, cleansing breath, but it comes out staccato.

"I do. Because when you decided you were moving to British Columbia, you talked about it for a year. The only reason I decided to come with you was so you'd shut up about it."

I roll my eyes because that couldn't be further from the truth. Anna came with me because we're not simply cousins, we're best friends, and her mom and stepdad are...overbearing. I wanted to move. She needed it.

When my half empty bag is packed and Anna's gone, I try to read before turning out my light. I can't stop thinking about

Isaac's hands and lips on me earlier. Visions of Isaac Lauri on his knees, one hand on his erection. Sleep isn't coming nearly as easily as I did on his tongue. I bite my lip in the dark, swallowing at the memory. My fingertips are sliding down my stomach when I hear the backdoor thud. Butterflies beat in my stomach. Isaac's footsteps sound heavy as he walks around the house. I'm used to his routine of ensuring everything is locked. I get a stupid smile on my face when he guards over me like that. He's coming down the hall now, almost at my door. I clutch the comforter to my chin, heart pounding, weirdly turned on by the idea of him stalking through the dark house. I snatch my phone off my end table.

Ashlyn: We have unfinished business.

In the hall, I hear his phone chime with my message. His heavy footfalls pause in front of my bedroom door. Anticipation weighs on me as I clench my thighs together. The creak of the turning knob steals my breath. A sliver of light stretches across the floor, stopping short of my bed. Isaac's shadow is imposing, his head nearly grazing the doorframe. Reaching up, he grips the trim.

"You're up late, babe."

Fuck, his voice sounds sexy in the dark.

"Coming in?"

He takes a slow breath as though struggling to control himself. I hope he doesn't. When he slips inside, shutting the door behind him, I silently rejoice.

"What's this about unfinished business?"

Now that he's so close, my boldness fades.

I try to convey my thoughts, "In the pantry...when you were kneeling..."

He curses under his breath, "Christ. You want me to eat that sweet pussy again?"

Oh, god. I'm getting wetter by the second.

"No. Not...necessarily." How do I voice what I have in mind? This type of talk is so out of my wheelhouse.

"No? Did you not come all over my tongue, Ashlyn?"

As if I need the reminder. It's a wonder I got anything done the rest of the day with the way my brain was so set on replaying that orgasm.

I blurt it out. "You touched yourself."

Blood rushes up to my cheeks and down to my pussy.

"You like seeing me handle myself?"

I nod before remembering he can't see me well. My hand shakes as I reach for the bedside lamp. Much of the room still sits in shadows, but now we can see each other's bodies, our facial expressions.

He repeats himself, "Ashlyn, I asked if you liked seeing me stroke my cock?"

That word in his mouth absolutely destroys me.

He grits his teeth, and I have the feeling he's losing that control. "Answer."

"Yes," I whisper.

"I'll jerk it for you. But I'm not kneeling this time."

I'll take him any way I can get him. And he knows it.

He walks to my bed where I'm still resting with my head on my pillow. His fingers work the leather belt and deftly open the buttons on his fly. His hardness is apparent even through his jeans.

"Have you been laying here thinking about my hard dick, Ashlyn?"

He smells like his smoky body wash and hard liquor. Removing his black ball cap, he rakes his hand through his thick hair then slips it on backwards.

And if that's not sexy enough, he pulls himself out of his jeans and briefs in one swift move.

"Here you go," he says with a smirk.

At the sight of the hard flesh stretching out toward me, I whimper. Only inches from my face, my fingers itch with the desire to reach out and touch. Wrapping a huge fist around the base of his shaft, he squeezes and gives himself a long stroke all the way to the swelling tip. Isaac tosses his head back and groans, the column of his muscular throat exposed. A bead of pre-cum shines in the faint light, but is swept away by his thumb, smeared across the dark pink skin. My mouth remembers his salty taste and I consider extending my tongue for more. His grip loosens, allowing himself a slightly faster stroke.

As if he reads my thoughts, he says, "No touching. If you touch me, I'll fuck you right here. And I'd really rather wait until the cabin."

I moan at the thought of *that* sliding inside of me. Tomorrow may as well be next year for how far away it feels.

"Keep your hands where I can see them. Seeing you touch yourself will have a similar result. I have very little willpower left when it comes to you."

Never have I felt more desired...and he's not even touching me. I'll follow his rules, but he didn't say anything about showing.

I push the comforter down my body, revealing to him that I opted out of pyjamas tonight. My hands grip the edge of my pillow, and I hope I have the wherewithal to live up to his challenge.

His eyes narrow as he tries to see me better in the shadows. "Goddammit, Ashlyn."

He strokes himself faster, a grunt falling from his lips. "How the fuck am I supposed to sleep right there," he jerks his chin to the wall behind me, "when you're over here like this?"

He eats up the sight before him, dragging his eyes over my bare breasts and down to the apex of my thighs where I know I'm so damn wet.

"Spread your legs so I can look at you."

Cool air whispers over my pussy as I comply. Laying here naked under his gaze, knowing he won't lay a finger on me, is empowering in a way I've never experienced.

"That's my girl."

His girl? I briefly consider jumping him, cabin getaway be damned.

He stares at my exposed flesh, concentrating his loose strokes on the head of his cock. Breathing fast, his eyes are laser focused. With every sound he makes it becomes harder to keep my hands to myself.

"Isaac..." I whine, as though I'm the one rushing toward an orgasm.

"Gonna come for you, Ashlyn."

My thighs clamp together, I need the pressure. No matter how tight I squeeze them, it does nothing to extinguish the rising flames of arousal.

"Fuck...gonna come."

His pelvis juts forward, strong jaw open, big palm ready in front of him. My eyes go wide as I watch him spill into his hand, spurt after spurt of cum leaving that gorgeous cock. His head hangs heavy, chin to chest.

"Too fucking good."

Thank god, I think. What's going to happen next? Will he eat me out again?

Instead, he leans over me and kisses my forehead with tenderness.

"Don't you dare touch yourself tonight."

My mouth falls open. "What?"

He's going to leave me hanging?

"Now we're even. One for you in the pantry. One for me here," he says, matter of fact. "The next time you come will be tomorrow in that cabin, and it will be *my* doing. Understand?"

I want to say something smart and indignant. To tell him to fuck right off and that I'll do with my body what I please. I know full well, though, that anything I do to myself tonight in the dark will be a poor substitute for the orgasms he can give me.

Instead, I nod like the needy girl I am and listen to his footsteps as he retreats from the room. Tomorrow can't come soon enough.

Chapter Twenty-One

Isaac

After a straight stretch of highway, we wind our way through a mountain pass high above the Pacific before heading deeper inland toward the backcountry. As the steep road flattens, we're spit out into a clearing surrounded by dense conifers that seem to swallow us on our approach. The cabin rests far down a narrow drive, a stovepipe protruding from the navy metal A-frame roof, giving the otherwise simple structure a modern vibe. We ascend the shallow steps to the covered patio, stomping off the snow from our boots.

"This is more snow than I expected," Ashlyn says, sliding her hand into mine.

"Right? We gained a lot of elevation."

That must be why I'm so light-headed every time I look at her.

"Shall we?" Ashlyn looks ready for adventure, her bag over her arm.

"I'll go first. It's been empty for a while."

I expect her to roll her eyes or fight me on it, but she steps aside, "Be my guest."

The solid oak door swings open, and I wait for my eyes to adapt to the dark. A black wood stove dominates the living area, squatting on four metal legs. The air is dusty and stale, the long-cold flooring groaning under me. This will do, this will do just fine. I'm about to call Ashlyn in when motion catches my eye, and a shadow zooms across the floor towards my feet.

"Holy shit!" I jump a foot and turn tail for the safety of the front porch.

"What! What is it!" Ashlyn backs herself up against the railing to make space for my rapid exit.

"You know, I think a hotel might be nice this time of year. What's another couple hours in the truck? Grab your bags!" I hop off the porch, striding away from the cabin.

"Hang on a minute," Ashlyn calls after me, hot on my tail, trudging through my tracks.

"Rat, Ashlyn. *Gigantic rat*."

"And that's a problem because...?" The question hangs in the mountain air.

"I don't do rodents."

"You don't *do* rodents? My big, strapping, carpenter man can't handle a teensy tiny critter?"

I don't miss that she called me 'hers' or 'big' or 'strapping'. That's interesting.

"It wasn't 'teensy tiny'. And I *can* handle it, I just don't want to." I examine the tips of the trees towering over us.

She folds her arms across her chest, pushing her breasts up in her sweater in a way that has me reconsidering the use of the cabin...at least for a while.

"I'll take care of your rodent."

"You're gonna take care of it?" I rub my hands up my arms to chase away the chill of the air and the thought of long, hairless tails.

"You wait here."

She rummages around in the bed of the truck, for what, I have no idea. I keep the interior clean but have odds and ends kicking around back there. It's a work truck, after all. She comes out holding a five-gallon bucket and heads for the cabin where the front door is still ajar. Before entering, she grabs an old straw broom with splayed bristles from the porch. When she disappears, I wonder if I'm still getting laid after this display of cowardice.

"C'mere, little guy." I hear her say inside.

You've got to be kidding me. She's talking to it?

A brief shriek is followed by a series of muffled bangs, and Ashlyn marches out triumphantly, holding the bucket aloft.

"You ready to start our vacation, big guy?" A gorgeous grin is plastered on her face.

I tentatively join her, shaking my head in disbelief.

She tips the bucket, and onto the fresh snow falls a tiny grey mouse, miniscule pink paws curled against its chest. After a few seconds, it flips back onto it's feet and takes off for the brush.

"There goes your big, scary *rat*, Lauri."

In an effort to redeem myself, I restock the wood pile with remarkable speed while Ashlyn tidies up inside. Beads of sweat cool on my brow, and my flannel clings to my lower back. Each strike of my axe echoes around the forest, a pileated woodpecker joining the rhythm, and grey wood smoke puffs lazily from the stovepipe. As twilight approaches, I call it a day, stacking one last log on the pile and leaning on the polished hickory handle of the axe to admire my handiwork.

"Okay, Paul Bunyan, dinner's ready!" Ashlyn calls from the porch.

"Yes, dear," I joke.

Is there anything more domestic and charming than this? A man chopping wood while the woman cooks over an actual fire? And I thought we'd been playing house before. Ashlyn in her leggings and red, fuzzy sweater has me thinking about another type of wood. I get my ass in the cabin and latch the door for the night.

The fire crackles, and the smell of onions and chicken permeate the air. A simple kitchen with knotty wood cabinets and butcher block counters make up one corner of the cabin.

Mismatched furniture, mostly plaid, fills the rest of the space. Throw pillows of all shapes and sizes cover overstuffed couches and chairs. A large propane tank and generator provides electricity and hot water for the cabin which makes the rustic retreat damn cushy, if you ask me. Chris undersold the place.

"How'd you make this so fast?" I accept a steaming bowl from Ashlyn's hands.

"I made homemade chicken soup yesterday and reheated it."

"Clever. I'd have brought hotdogs." I blow on my spoon before slurping down the salty broth. I groan in appreciation, the hot liquid warming me.

She chuckles. "That's what we're having for lunch tomorrow."

Side by side on the plaid sofa, we devour our meal. Ashlyn's supper hit the spot so well I had two servings of soup and two glasses of chardonnay with it. I hope my dessert is going to be the snow bunny that kicked off her slippers and has her feet tucked beneath my thighs.

"Isaac!" Ashlyn straightens her spine.

"What's wrong?" I grasp her leg while visions of rodents fill my head.

Where the hell was the broom?

"It's snowing." She points out the largest window. Sure enough, large flakes drift past and accumulate on the narrow pane.

"So it is."

"Comfy couches and fires are kind of our thing, don't you think?" She relaxes, sighing as she snuggles against my ribs.

"I do." I lay my right arm over her shoulders, drawing her tighter to my side. Any closer and she'll be in my lap.

Not a bad idea.

I scoop her up and settle her sideways onto my thighs.

"Hello, there..." She loops her arms behind my neck, her eyes settling somewhere near my mouth.

"Hi. I seem to remember kissing the last time we sat by a fire." I brush my lips against hers.

"I think there was also some nudity..."

"Don't rush it." I quiet her, putting some pressure against her mouth, pulling her against me.

She straddles my hips, moaning as she settles her weight right over my zipper. The last couple days since getting cockblocked in the pantry have filled me with a level of sexual frustration unlike anything I've ever experienced. Here, there will be no interruptions or distractions. Alone.

I gaze at the woman in my lap, ready to sink my teeth into her. Hell, I'll sink balls-deep into her the second she asks. I thrust up instinctively, but it's not enough. She whimpers against my lips, tugging eagerly at the hem of my shirt, frustrated at the layers separating us. I smirk against her lips as I strip down, only parting from her when I pull my sweater and shirt over my head. Curious fingers trace the curled hairs there, short nails scratching lightly over every inch of my torso. I pull off her sweater next, leaving her in a simple white satin bra. The thin fabric shows the texture of her nipples, hardened despite the fire behind us. Her hips roll in my lap, and I fight the urge to lay her back on the couch and take her right there.

"We gotta move, babe," I say.

We take quick turns in the washroom, and I head up the ladder first, waiting for her.

The loft houses a queen-size mattress and several layers of plush bedding. I lay back against the lush down duvet and feather pillows, barely resisting the urge to stroke my cock. The ladder creaks a second before Ashlyn's head comes into view. She freezes on the top rung.

"Coming up?"

Slowly, her gaze lifts to my face. "Enjoying the view."

"Oh?" I give in and stroke myself over my pants.

"I'm talking about the snow." She smirks, pointing to the tiny loft window.

I don't buy it.

Instead of flopping onto the bed like I did, she gets on all fours, fucking *crawling* towards me like a goddamn predator. I recline on my elbows to watch her approach. Her hips, higher than her shoulders, sway seductively with each move, the white satin panties that match her bra cling to her ass. She has sex in those big brown eyes as she stares me down. When she reaches me, she climbs onto my lap. I'm all for her riding me, but not tonight. She gasps when I roll us and her bare back meets the cool duvet. I pin her with as much body weight as I dare, savouring the pressure of her breasts against my pecs. I blaze a trail of kisses from her lips down to her throat to the swell of her chest. I'm a goddamn adventurer, and her body is territory I fully intend to explore. The satin straps of her bra fall easily from her shoulders and she shamelessly arches her spine, shoving her tits right into my waiting face. I honour her wordless request, licking and teasing her nipples. Dragging my mouth across her heaving chest. The white bedding wrinkles in her fists, so I brush my lips across her knuckles until they relax.

"Relax, Ashlyn." I speak into her left palm before licking it with the tip of my tongue. The taste of wood smoke and salt on her skin makes my mouth water.

I push back onto my heels.

"Where do you think you're going?" she asks.

Based on the heat in her eyes, I doubt I can fend her off for long. I'm gonna take a wild guess that she listened to my instructions last night and kept her hands off herself. Her hand is around me in a second, clutching me through my thin cotton pyjamas.

"Jesus, Ash."

The pressure at the tip of my dick and the throb in my balls intensifies. I groan long and loud as she gropes me through my clothes. The only way I manage to pull myself from her eager hands is because I'm desperate to taste her again. She's perfect, painfully close to naked. When she parts her thighs ever so slightly, I reach out. Almost imperceptibly, I brush my index finger across her panties. Even this gentle touch makes her squirm and sigh my name. I repeat the feathery touches up and down the gusset, heat radiating from her centre. I know she's pink and puffy for me beneath the scrap of fabric.

"Can I look at your pussy, Ashlyn?"

I tear my eyes from the curve of her touching thighs to see her nod for me, mouth open, panting. As good an answer as any. My fingertips sink beneath the seams of her panties where they push against the flesh of her rounded hips. Arousal clings to the fabric as I peel them away from her pretty pussy.

I close my eyes to get a hold of myself.

Knowing I do that to her? No better feeling in the world.

"Isaac, please." Her begging would bring me to my knees if I wasn't already on them.

"Turn over, babe." I coax her onto her stomach.

She's putty in my hands and goes willingly, open to whatever I offer. When she settles onto her tummy, I groan at the sight of her round ass curving up from her waist. I take a plump cheek in each palm and squeeze, spreading her cheeks. The sight of that darker shade of pink between makes my dick twitch hard in my pants. I need to get these things off. Now. At the momentary loss of my hands, she whines in protest.

"Just a second, baby. One of us is still wearing way too many clothes."

"Be fast."

I return to her side, my erection grazing her thigh as I straddle one of her legs.

"Is that..."

"My cock on your leg?"

"Oh, god."

She's squirming now, pressing herself into the mattress to get some relief.

"I've got you," I tell her, spreading her legs to get access to what I want.

I slide my fingers from her tailbone, down her cheeks, lower and lower until I reach her centre. "You're warm like fucking honey, Ash."

"Isaac, please touch me!"

"I *am* touching you."

Arching her ass off the bed, she offers herself up to me in the most primal of ways, allowing me an angle that shows off every fold and seam.

I slip two fingers inside her and lean forward to whisper in her ear, "Is this what you wanted?"

The sound she makes is stifled by the pillows.

"How do these fingers feel in your pussy?" I start moving inside her, curling my fingers to find the spot that needs my attention.

Her ass clenches, dimpling the soft skin as she alternates between driving her hips into the bed and pushing herself back onto my fingers. My name is the only intelligible thing I hear as she tries to fuck herself on my hand.

"Isaac..." she moans, right before she squeezes me and comes all over my hand.

She turns herself over, and her dishevelled hair frames her swollen mouth and shining eyes.

"You're so beautiful," I say.

"Thank you."

There's not an ounce of self-consciousness as she lays before me, nude and wet with her pussy still throbbing. She spreads her legs invitingly, staring at my dick like she didn't get off a minute ago.

"You side-tracked me, beautiful. I was trying to taste you."

I dive between her legs, surprising her with my mouth.

"That tickles!" she screams, trying to close her legs against the sensation.

I grab her knees and hold them open as I lick and suck at her.

She stills beneath me. "Oh." Her ticklishness apparently subsided.

She tastes glorious, the remnants of white wine on my tongue mixing with her heady sweetness. I reach down to stroke myself, and she raises her head off the pillow, catching me in the act.

I growl into her pussy, "Watching me jerk myself again, babe?"

Ashlyn moans, twisting the sheets.

"You want me to come right now with my tongue buried in your cunt?"

She cries out, "I want you inside me, Isaac. Please, can we?"

She's desperate. Like my cock is the only thing that will satisfy her. I come up and brace myself over her, elbows on either side of her flushed face. I kiss her forehead, her cheeks, her lips. Then we dive in opposite directions, each returning with boxes of condoms from our bags. We laugh, and she tosses hers aside. I rip one off the strip and sheathe myself. As soon as I'm done, she clutches my arms and pulls me down into a searing kiss. We paw at each other, the grabby neediness driving me wild.

"I'm ready now," she breaths against my lips.

"I've been ready for months."

Her eyes are round and glassy as she processes that. Is now the time to explain that I'm crazy about her? That casual was never the right word for what I wanted?

"Ash–"

She kisses me sweetly. "Now, Isaac."

I adjust the pillows behind her and use my knees to spread her legs. She doesn't need to guide me. I know exactly where to go, the tip of my cock easily finding her slick heat. Pressing into her the first inch, she moans. I give her another inch, pausing when her brows knit slightly.

"Ashlyn, I'm trying to go slow for you. But you feel so damn good."

"Stay still for a second," she breathes, "it's been a while."

I kiss and lick at her throat until her muscles relax and her hips move. That's my cue to give her the rest of me. The torturous pace as I enter her all the way both pleasures and pains. Never have I taken so long to enter a woman before.

"Move," she commands.

So I do. I keep my thrusts shallow. A slow pace will allow her to climb higher towards her next release but keep me from falling over the ledge too soon. Coming too quickly is an undeniable possibility with how good Ashlyn feels, with how far into my head she is. I slip my tongue into her mouth and move it in the same rhythm as my hips. Trailing a hand down my chest, through the centre of my abs, she reaches between us. I watch as she grazes her clit and swollen outer lips.

"Fuck yes, touch yourself, Ashlyn."

I fucking love that she's comfortable enough with me to play with her pussy while I thrust in and out of her. She must find something she likes because she flutters around my cock.

"Faster, Isaac," she gasps, lips parted.

I oblige, picking up the pace. The glazed expression on her face tells me I've got the right rhythm, and when a smile stretches across her face, I decide I'll do anything in the whole goddamn world to recreate it.

"I'm getting close, Ashlyn," I warn. I'll have to slow way down if she needs more time.

"Me too," she whispers right as she tightens around my shaft and lets out the most contented moan I've ever heard.

"Ashlyn!" I call as I find my release, continuing to thrust erratically inside of her while I draw out the last bits of our pleasure. I drop my head to her chest, listening to the thudding of her heart, kissing her there.

"So, that just happened," she giggles.

I smirk up at her. "What's so funny?

"I have no idea. I'm happy."

We're both giddy from the wine, fantastic orgasms, and the long drive. Man, I love it when she laughs like that. I rest with Ashlyn in my arms. Content.

Chapter Twenty-Two

Ashlyn

I stretch so deep I quiver, a goofy grin plastered on my face. The smile has been there since I opened my eyes and the memories of last night swept in. That was the best sex I've ever had. Isaac's side is empty, the duvet pulled up and tucked in neatly. Through the window, I see the dark snow clouds have cleared and the forest floor is covered in pillowy layers of powder. The pine branches hang heavy, and tiny birds flit from perch to perch, gentle puffs of snow falling where they land. Throwing a hoodie over my sleep set, I descend the ladder and use the washroom, splashing my face with water and brushing my teeth. The wood stove crackles, and I'm planning to spend as much time next to that glorious warmth as possible today. I have vague memories of Isaac leaving bed last night, kissing me on the cheek and whispering that he's going to add fuel to the fire.

The rhythmic thwacks of steel versus cedar guide me to him. I kind of think he'll chop the whole forest down if I tell him I'm cold. I slide on my snow boots then step onto the front porch, squinting against the light reflecting off the crystalline snow. Isaac wears jeans and a hoodie, a red toque on his head, axe in hand. He's sporting the same unrelenting focus he applies to projects in his workshop back home.

Home.

Since when did I consider Mummo's house home? More importantly, when did I start calling her Mummo? That's not my house or my grandmother, not by a long shot. Technically, it's not Isaac's home either. We're both imposters playing house.

"Mornin', beautiful." His devilish grin sends a flurry through my stomach.

My brain beelines to last night, his solid form above me, the fullness of him inside my body.

"I asked if you had anything planned for breakfast?"

I snap out of my sultry daydream. "Breakfast, right. I have oatmeal and lots of toppings."

His face falls the tiniest bit.

"It's like adult cereal, you'll see. I have chocolate chips for you, Little One." I tease, using his grandmother's term of endearment.

"Nuh-uh." He shakes his head. "I'll eat the oatmeal, but you can't call me that."

"Mummo does."

"She's my grandmother. It feels wrong when you say it."

"Ha!" My bark of a laugh echoes through the trees, scaring off a group of finches. "What shall I call you that speaks more to your manliness? Big guy? Master?" I list the options on my fingers.

"You can call me Isaac."

He buries the axe in a log with one powerful swing, and instead of taking the stairs like a normal person, he climbs smoothly over the porch railing. He crowds me against the cabin, hemming me in with a hand on either side of my body. Taller than tall, I have to tilt my head to gaze up at him. He looks down at me with enough heat in his eyes to melt every bit of snow in a hundred-mile radius.

"But say it like you did last night when you were coming on my cock."

My knees almost give out.

"What are you thinking?" He smirks knowingly.

I swallow. "I'm thinking the oatmeal can wait."

"Perfect answer, babe."

He wrenches open the cabin door and stands aside. "Get your ass in there."

"Yes, master," I sass.

"God help me," he says before the heavy door slams, blocking out the innocent chirps of woodland creatures.

We're on each other in a flash, winter boots thudding against wood planks, Isaac's belt buckle jangling. Smells of fresh chopped cedar and sweat cling to his skin. I do my best to reach his luscious lips, but he grunts in frustration and cups my ass, lifting me effortlessly, walking us toward the loft ladder. Somewhere along the way, I lose my hoodie. We lean against the rungs, making out so deeply that my cheeks will be pink with beard burn later. I break away, glancing up at the loft.

"Do you want to..."

He presses himself against me, jeans splayed open already. His thick cock is on display through the material of his white briefs.

Yeah, he wants to.

I turn to face the ladder, reaching for the rungs.

"No."

He places his hands on my hips, effortlessly preventing me from climbing. I push my ass against him, because I can, peeking over my shoulder to see the effect. He sheds his hoodie and shirt and I drink in the sight of his slightly sweaty torso. Another roll of my hips, and he barks out a simple command: "Go face the couch."

Wordlessly, I go, eyes on the plaid cushions.

I can't see him approach from behind, but I hear the grind of the heavy coffee table skidding several inches across the floor, as he shoves the furniture out of his way to get to me. One hot hand presses between my shoulder blades, forcing me forward. A whimper passes my lips. I fold in half, hands sinking into the couch cushions, ass in the air. Fabric rustles, and when he takes hold of my hips and runs his hardness over my cheeks, I know he's ditched his boxer briefs. A damp trail forms as he paints my skin with his precum, wet and leaking for me. I moan, dropping my head so it hangs between my shoulders. My breasts have popped out of my white tank, and Isaac's strong, bare thighs are visible behind me. I crane my neck to try and see more of the beautiful man. All that height plus who knows how many inches hanging between his legs.

"Should we take these off, Miss Carter?" He tugs lightly at the waist of my tiny sleep shorts.

"Yes, please."

I'm ready and willing, and he wants to talk and tease? *Damn him.*

"Hmm, they aren't exactly in the way."

My shorts are twisted and riding up. He rubs a palm over my exposed pussy, patting me gently to prove his point.

"You're so fucking ready for me, Ashlyn," he praises.

A thick finger presses inside me with no warning. I don't want his fucking fingers, so I tell him as much. "No, I want you."

"Tell me what you want, Ashlyn. Say it." He pushes himself against my ass.

"I want to sleep with you."

He tuts his tongue in disapproval.

"I want you to...fuck me."

"There we are. Good girl."

Fumbling in the pocket of his jeans for protection, I watch him get ready. We're both panting unabashedly by the time he grinds his hard dick against my ass and pussy until, at last, he slams into me in one smooth push.

"Isaac!" I cry.

"Jesus, you're tight."

His left hand steadies me in my precarious position, and his right reaches to toy with my clit. My miniscule shorts hide very little. He has a perfect view of his dick slamming in and out of my pussy, glistening with my wetness, and the tight hole above that. My cheeks burn with the thought, but his praise emboldens me.

I twist my neck to meet his gaze, "Are you gonna make me come on that cock?"

His cock twitches. "Ashlyn..." he warns.

I bend deeper, a delicious stretch in my hamstrings that matches the stretch of my full pussy.

He groans at my gratuitous display of flexibility, moving the hand working my clit to keep me on balance.

"Ashlyn, I can't last much longer."

Fine by me. This brand of fucking isn't designed to last or be contained. Our climaxes are at the precipice of a towering waterfall. There's no coming back from the edge now that the current swirls around us.

"Prove it," I push.

"God damn it, Ashlyn." He shoves his knee into my straightened legs, and they buckle, forcing me to collapse onto the couch. Hauling me up with a thick arm around my waist, he positions me on my hands and knees, facing one end of the couch. His right knee drops to the low couch for leverage, then he's thrusting with a renewed intensity that has me seconds from release.

Being manhandled by Isaac is a fucking delight. He ruts at me, balls slapping deliciously onto the backs of my upper thighs. A light sheen of sweat coats my skin, and I couldn't stop the impending orgasm if my life depended on it. His wild thrusts and grunts turn animalistic.

"Ashlyn! Fuck!"

We come together, riding it out as if to leave nothing behind, declarations of pleasure on our tongues. Isaac eases me down off my hands and knees, scooping me into his arms before falling onto the couch with me cradled against his naked body. Spent and sated, I rest my head against his sweaty bare chest and wait for our ragged breaths to slow.

"Why, in the ever-loving hell, have we been sleeping in our own beds?" he asks, head tipping back against the couch, eyes closed in bliss.

Because you promised this was casual.

"I have no idea."

"You're sleeping with me when we get home," he states.

There's that word again. Home.

That's not your home. It's your workplace.

I can't move off of him. I'm boneless and weak-willed. I search through my mind and soul to find one good reason why I shouldn't move my clothes into the master bedroom tomorrow. Logic eludes me. Everything pulls me toward Isaac Lauri.

CHAPTER TWENTY-THREE

Isaac

Another snowball explodes between my shoulder blades, and I yelp as the cold flakes fall into my collar.

"You brat!"

Damn, she has a good arm on her.

I grab a tightly packed ball from my stash and peer through the trees for signs of movement, but all is white and still. The trees aren't massive, but neither is Ashlyn, so she has the advantage of hiding during this stealthy, cutthroat snowball fight. A branch snaps on my left. I hold my breath, lungs burning, like that'll help me. My ass sticks out so far beyond this tree that a four-year-old would have a clear shot. I hear the sound again and grip the snowball lightly in my ski glove.

Movement catches my eye, a doe emerging from some dense foliage and into our small clearing. She glides silently, sniffing the air, knowing exactly where we are. Ah, there's my girl. Ashlyn's crouching behind a trunk, watching the same live episode of Planet Earth that I am. Our eyes meet across the clearing. She points at the deer with a mitten covered hand, then places a finger to her lips. The deer's eyes are round, ready to bolt at the slightest whiff of fear. Two braids peek out beneath Ashlyn's pink toque, a matching pom-pom swaying in the light wind. Puffs of vapour escape her mouth, reminding me of her hot breath. My phone buzzes against my thigh a second before it rings. There's no way I can get it out of my pocket in time to silence the noise, and the interruption startles the deer. Her head snaps up to assess the situation then she darts away, pushing powerfully off her hind legs. Ashlyn scowls as I remove my glove, mouthing an apology.

"Hi."

"Isaac. I was at your grandmother's today." My dad starts.

"How is she?" My heart speeds up, sensing confrontation.

"Why is she talking about Ashlyn going to some cabin? You told me she needed time off for a family matter."

The thought that Ashlyn does seem like family comes naturally.

When I don't answer, he continues, "I think you've overstayed your welcome when it comes to squatting at the house."

"Squatting? Really?" I work hard to keep my voice level, but he riled me up in one minute flat. Every word with him is a weapon, every sentence an articulated attack.

"What else do you call it if you're not paying rent and it's not your house?"

"It's not your house either, last time I checked."

"That's only a matter of time."

My voice lowers an octave, "What the fuck is that supposed to mean?"

"Watch your tone when speaking to me, young man."

Ashlyn leans against a birch tree, resting her cheek on the grey bark, chewing her bottom lip.

"Yes, why not do some parenting now? I'm only in my thirties? It's never too late!"

I have no idea what it's like to parent a child after your spouse walks out. Something tells me my first instinct wouldn't be shipping my kid off to the grandparents. My future kids won't even have grandparents on my side. Not if this is how my dad continues to conduct himself. To always keep me at arm's length. That works me up even more.

"I allowed it at first, but I don't think it's appropriate for you to be living there," he says.

"Once again, it's not your house. And appropriate for who? I love spending time with Mummo, and she's keeping me busy around the house."

He pauses before letting out a fake laugh. "You're busy I bet. And I imagine it's with the little nurse."

My free hand forms a fist, and I press it against the tree nearest me, trying to stay cool. Ashlyn falls back into the snow to make a snow angel, oblivious to the conversation.

"Don't be disgusting. Ashlyn does her job perfectly."

He lets out a low whistle. "That good, eh?"

From her spot in the snow, she calls out, "Everything okay? Get over here!"

I squeeze my eyes shut. Because I have crap luck, he hears her over the line.

"You've taken her away this weekend, haven't you? That's why she took some vacation time. You can tell her I'm not paying her to fuck my son."

If he were here, I'd have him by the collar.

"Your issues with me have *nothing* to do with her." My jaw clenches so tight I fear I'll crack my teeth.

"I should fire her for this. It's completely unprofessional."

Fuck. His words are a sharp sting. It's the one thing she was concerned about. If he lets her go because of our relationship, or whatever the hell this is, she'll never forgive me.

"We have something to discuss when you get back. You might want to start thinking about packing your bags and getting your shit off my property. Workshop is looking pretty full."

My molars grind as I hang up on him and shove the phone deep into my pocket. I'd rather hurl it into a snowbank. Ashlyn stands, brushing off the snow from her pants and jacket, watching me warily.

I can't reach the cabin fast enough. Ashlyn calls after me to wait up, but anger clings to me like something I can't shake. One second of eye-contact with her, and she'll read the pain on my face in an instant. The woodpile is the perfect outlet for the rage creeping up my throat, threatening to strangle me. I'll work the feelings out of my system and then lose myself in Ashlyn for the next day and night. He won't ruin this. It might be all the time I have because when we get back, I'm not sure how much longer I can keep this going.

The whole last day and night Ashlyn and I christened the cabin. Each time our bodies came together, it was unlike anything I've experienced sexually or emotionally. Based on Ashlyn's screams and the time she leaked hot tears onto my chest after an intense, eye-contact-laden orgasm, I'd say she feels the same. Her body is a haven, but she can only briefly quell my worries. I wrack my brain over that phone call and open my mouth a thousand times to bring Ashlyn into the loop. The words stay locked inside me behind a cage of dread. What does he want to talk about? Will he kick me out of the house? Can he even do that? Every penny I have is sunk into the business. Moving in with Mummo was a choice initially, but staying with her now is an absolute necessity.

The snow was fun for a weekend, but the green lawns and blossoms that appear as we drive out of the mountains back down to sea level are a welcome sight. Like any trip, the mood on the way back is subdued. As we approach the house, I sit up taller in my seat. Something's not right. Blocking the driveway are multiple white pick-ups I recognize by their logos immediately. Forward Construction.

"What's going on?" Ashlyn asks.

"Fuck if I know." I hop out of the truck. "You," I bark at the first person I see.

It's a middle-aged guy I don't recognize. He's balancing surveying equipment in his hands and turns to watch me approach. "And you are?" he says.

"I'm Isaac Lauri." I watch the wheels turn when he hears my last name.

He clears his throat. "I'm Ralph. I'm in charge of surveying the property."

"Cool, nobody asked."

Surveying. You only need that for a few reasons. One of which is in the planning and designing phase of construction projects. Dad is getting too fucking bold. I brush by the man, heading toward the backyard. I'm by the garage when I hear someone yell.

"Bring me the bolt cutters! Boss wants to get in here."

Bolt cutters?

I push past someone walking on the gravel path. He says something to me, but my ears are ringing, and nausea grips my stomach. He's doing it again. He's pulling everything out from under me, right as I'm getting my footing. When I pass the garage, I see a man with bolt cutters securing the jaws around the padlock on my workshop door. My grandfather's workshop. The crunching sound of metal on metal sets me in motion, eating up the distance to the asshole that just broke into my space. When I draw my elbow back, I'm not thinking straight. And when my knuckles connect to the guy's jaw, I'm not thinking at all. I barely register Ashlyn's scream from somewhere behind me.

"Isaac, stop!"

Someone bands their arms around me, and I try to shrug them off, but I'm tired. The fight's all out of me already.

Berg speaks in my ear, "Easy. Easy lad." His slight Scottish brogue acts like a balm on my frayed nerves, and for the first time in several minutes, I draw a proper breath.

"I'm calling the police," someone says.

"Fuck, no. I'm fine. I'm fine!" The injured guy says, pushing someone away from him.

He's sitting up now, holding the right side of his face. There's no blood. Too bad.

A quiet falls over the yard as my father exits the house. His mouth is a hard line, but his beady eyes are gleaming like he loves the chaos.

"Isaac. You're back." His voice is flat. "Let's go inside."

The house is dark and cold after the warmth of the yard. I lean against the formal dining table that Ashlyn and I ate at together while Dad paces along the perimeter of the living room, looking at the art and photos hung on the walls.

"I thought long and hard about our conversation."

"It was *yesterday*," I grit out.

He scratches his head. "Seems like longer."

"Can you get to the point?"

He shrugs. "Or what? You'll sucker punch some more of my employees?"

I didn't even recognize half of those guys. Berg, Chris, and Dean all reported weird levels of turnover not long after I was fired. Things at Forward Construction seem rough. Sighing, I rub my eyes, suddenly tired from the drive, the drama, the half-truths. I cross the room and sink down on the leather couch, letting the cushions do the job of holding me up.

"I don't *want* to do this with you anymore, Dad."

I haven't called him that in years. What can I say? I'm trying to appeal to the softer side of Matt Lauri. If that side even exists. He won't meet my eye, so I think it might be a lost cause.

"This type of property lends itself best to demolition. It's over an acre, Isaac. You do the math."

My mouth hangs open for several seconds before I find my voice. "This is Mummo's *home*. You grew up here. We both did."

This is a transaction for him. A cash grab.

"Your grandmother's health has deteriorated. I'm actively searching for a spot in an assisted living facility for her."

My heartrate ticks up. *No.*

"She's not going to want that! We can, *I* can care for her."

"You don't know that. It might be a good environment for someone her age." He holds his hands out to me like I should level with him here.

Maybe. Or it could be cold and understaffed and lonely.

Before I can open my mouth to speak, Ashlyn comes through the swinging kitchen door.

She puts her fists on her hips and turns to my father. "This was a ridiculous display of...of I don't know what. Posturing? Power? You greatly upset your mother today." Her nostrils are flaring, her voice tight.

I move toward her to comfort her, but she takes a step away. The motion hurts.

"I'm going to pretend you didn't just speak to me like that," he says to her. "I have a meeting. Isaac, I'll keep you posted."

"Fucking hell," I mutter as he walks out the front door, and I hear his BMW zoom away.

I pace the length of the room, tugging at the roots of my hair. Ashlyn stands by the fireplace with her arms crossed.

"Do you have anything to say for yourself?" she says.

I shrink under her line of questioning, staring at my feet like I'm ten again.

"Me?"

"Yes, you. I can't...be with someone who's punching people out when they get mad."

For the first time in a day, my shoulders loosen. I'm sure I'm focusing on the wrong part of her sentence, but I can't let it go.

"With me? You're...with me?" My voice sounds high.

LOVINGLY RESTORED

She looks everywhere but my eyes. "I *want* to be Isaac. All weekend I thought about it. Tried to find a way to talk to you about wanting more. But you told me yourself that you're only going to be getting busier. I didn't want to be *that* girl who immediately wanted more than you had to offer. Hearing no...that would hurt."

I'm trying not to let a smile spread across my face because she looks so fucking pretty. But warmth is spreading through my chest at her admission.

"I didn't know how to tell you. I want to be with you too."

"I want to be happy about that, Isaac. I really do, but this is too much drama for me."

I step toward her, and, thank god, she doesn't move away. She stays rooted to the ground so that when I brush her hair off her face, I can get a good look at those chocolate eyes.

"I wasn't thinking. It was stupid and could have cost me a lot. It's just...my workshop? Really? There was no need for him to cut the lock and go in there to survey the property."

Shit.

"The workshop. I've got to secure it before it's dark."

She steps in front of me, smoothing her hands over my shoulder. "Relax, Berg already put a new lock on it. I saw him working while I was with Mummo."

"Okay." I nod and blow out a breath. I'm still too wound up. "That's good."

"He was coming by to stick some forms under our door when he saw all the trucks and commotion. You're lucky he did."

I owe him one, for sure.

Ashlyn sighs, and I can tell she's calming down, too.

"Guess you're not so good at casual yourself, are you, big guy?

"I guess not," I say, shrugging and pulling her in for a kiss.

"One kiss...then I need to look at that hand."

"It hurts real bad," I say, smiling against her lips.

"I'll fix you up, Lauri."

I make that one kiss count, pressing her against the brick hearth. Only Ashlyn could take the worst day ever and turn it into the best.

Chapter Twenty-Four

Ashlyn

"**D**o you want to talk about it?"

I'm sitting cross legged in an old armchair in the corner of the workshop, an open book in my lap. Isaac's been pissy all week. Dodging my questions and doing a damn good job of distracting me when we fall into bed each evening. In *his* bed. Just like he said.

"No."

He switches out the dying battery on his drill. Despite the fact Berg already replaced the broken lock, he insisted a secondary lock was necessary. Personally, I don't think Mr. Lauri will try to pull that crap again. He proved his point...whatever it was. He finishes and hooks his thumbs in the tool belt fastened around his waist.

"Don't think you can get out of this conversation by doing *that*."

He widens his eyes and pushes his pelvis forward, smug at the effect he has on me.

I snap my book shut and cross my legs. "Spill it."

His broad chest rises and falls, and I can tell he's ready to talk.

"Fine. It was a hard first week. I knew it would be...but it's still a challenge. I'm learning from my mistakes."

"Nothing too serious?"

What can I say? I'm invested in this project, too. I want success for Isaac. He's talked me through it twenty times.

"No, no. Backorders and general issues. I'm handling it."

"I'm proud of you."

He smiles and stands straighter. We've barely seen each other the past week. He's either at the job site, in the workshop, or on the phone. I only came out here with my book to spend some time in his presence. When the pouting and stomping around persisted, I resolved to drag it out of him.

"You know we could..." He winks and gestures to the table behind him.

"In your dreams, Lauri."

"These are healthy," Mummo says, rubbing the vivid green stalk between her fingers.

She's in her wheelchair next to my cedar planter with an umbrella attached to the handle to keep her out of the sun. She wanted to get out into the garden, and I was happy to oblige, even if it took some creativity.

"Thank you. I think some of the credit goes to you. This place has some major gardening magic."

She laughs. "I won't disagree. I wish that magic worked on the weeds."

"Wouldn't that be nice." I take a sip from my water bottle.

I fall off my knees onto my butt, the blades of grass poking my bare thighs.

"What do you want to do for the rest of the day, Mummo?"

"It's Sunday?" she asks.

I nod. "Sure is."

She makes a show of looking contemplative, steepling her fingers.

We make eye contact and, at the same time, shout, "Backyard Shakeup!"

The television in the living room is easily the newest electronic item in the whole house. Purchased by Isaac a few years ago for his grandparents, it hasn't had a lot of use. Mummo is the picture of comfort on the couch with a padded ottoman under her feet and a pillow behind her back for support. After introducing her to Backyard Shakeup, a Home and Garden Television show of over-the-top yard makeovers, it became her favourite. We've watched all the old episodes and new ones air on Sunday evenings. We're sharing a bowl of popcorn when Isaac comes home.

I shush him as soon as he enters the room, "Shh, it's almost the big reveal."

"What are they revealing?" he whispers, sitting so close to me on the couch that I sink towards him.

"This guy did a huge backyard makeover for his parents. Outdoor kitchen, pond, the works."

"Fancy-schmancy," he says, using his inanely long arm to reach over and steal our popcorn.

"How was your day?" I just told him to be quiet, but I can't help myself.

"It's good now." He lifts his arm and settles it around my shoulders.

"That was smooth as hell, Lauri."

"Shhh," he says, "it's the big reveal."

CHAPTER TWENTY-FIVE

Isaac

I'm dead on my feet, but the farmhouse porch restoration is done. Every spindle sanded; each strip of wood stained. I have happy customers giving glowing reviews. My chest swells each time I think about my work. I race home to Ashlyn. No matter how long my days last, I'm coming home to my girls. Finding Ashlyn toiling away in the last semblances of light, making good use of the tools we purchased at the garden centre in the beautiful May weather makes my heart squeeze. I haven't been able to get working on the yard like I hoped. Unless I'm going to take up nocturnal landscaping, it's still going to have to wait. The urge to give the girls the perfect space is powerful.

Ashlyn kneels in the grass by her beloved garden box. Hair piled atop her head in a messy bun, she's wearing my old Ford t-shirt that's so long it covers the shorts I can only assume she's wearing beneath it. Blades of grass cling to her bare feet, the soles nearly black. She hums as she bends to reach a stubborn weed.

"You know we have neighbours, right?"

Her head whips around, shining spade in her hand.

"Don't throw it!" I raise both hands in surrender. I crouch, kissing her deep, tension melting off my shoulders. "How's my favourite plant mom?"

She rolls her eyes. I've overheard her whispering to her fledgling garden, but if that's the weirdest thing I discover about Ashlyn, so be it.

"Speaking of neighbours. Jackson next door invited us for a drink."

"Who the fuck is Jackson?"

There was a time when people on this street weren't strangers. Most of the occupants of the neighbourhood from when I was young sold long ago. So many families are priced out of living in areas like this one with large, single-family homes.

She points at the two-story next door. "Jackson. We were talking earlier. He offered to help mow the grass back here."

And the tension is back.

"And who does Jackson live with?"

"Himself."

Shocking.

"Why does a single guy need a whole house for himself?"

She laughs, taking a small bit of pleasure in the jealousy leaching into my words. "Isn't it your literal dream to own this house?"

"That's different. It's smaller. And I wouldn't live here alone."

Her eyebrows rise. Lately, whenever I picture owning Mummo's house, someone else is sharing it with me. But those fantasies are premature. She doesn't question me further.

"Anyway," I steer the conversation back to the nosy neighbour, "I bet you ten boxes of Lucky Charms that Jackson was only inviting you. And you can tell him I'll mow my own fucking lawn."

Her floral gloves fist on her hips. "What are you so riled up about?"

"I don't much like the idea of *certain people*," I raise my voice loud enough for any neighbours to hear, "watching you out here. It's not even summer yet, will you be doing it in a bikini by then?"

"If I'm still working here. You can bet I will."

Will my dad find an assisted living space for Mummo by then? The thought of Ashlyn being gone by summer is a bigger gut punch than picturing Jackson leering at Ashlyn from his big empty house.

"Good thing I know a guy that can put up a twelve-foot privacy fence."

She gasps, moving to guard her plants. "You wouldn't dare. That will be way too much shade for them."

"We're at an impasse." I fold my arms, eyebrows furrowed.

"Think of the children." She strokes a tender green leaf.

"Plant mom. Told you."

She rubs her eyes, smudging dark dirt across her rosy cheeks and forehead. "Oh, Isaac?"

I melt at her sultry tone. "Yeah, baby?"

"Don't *ever* tell me what to wear again." She reaches out and swipes the rest of the damp dirt across my cheek before taking off as fast as her bare feet will take her.

"I'm showering first!"

"What's for dinner?" I call after her.

"Do I look like a chef?" She sticks her tongue out at me over her shoulder. "I'm just the nurse!"

Wet hair hangs over her shoulder, saturating the fabric of her clean shirt like the night we met. Cross-legged, fresh from the shower without a stitch of makeup on, it's hard to ignore how natural this is. To come home to someone and discuss our days. We're sprawled on the living room rug eating Hawaiian pizza straight out of the box. Ashlyn convinced me to start a tiny fire even though it's warm.

"So, Mr. Modesty, do you know what you look like every day?"

I wipe grease from my mouth with a paper towel. "Um, like an upstanding member of the community and a small business owner?"

"Right. So you buying medium shirts when you very obviously need a large. That's what? An oversight? And you remov-

256

ing said snug shirts at the faintest hint of sunlight? What do you think that does for the *community*?"

"I like to think of it as an act of philanthropy. Why, you been checking me out?"

"You wish," she mumbles, mouth full of ham and pineapple and a generous dip of ranch. "I'm done. No more. Take it away!" She closes the pizza box and pushes it along the carpet towards me, patting her full tummy.

I tuck the box behind me. "I'll take that for work tomorrow."

Tomorrow. How many of those are we going to have?

After tossing the pizza boxes in the recycling and turning out the kitchen lights, I return to put out the fire.

"You ready to turn in?" I stop in my tracks, the kitchen door hitting me in the ass. Ashlyn is on her stomach by the fire, nude on the wool rug, hands beneath her chin, legs swinging playfully behind her. I harden against the zipper of my work pants in three seconds flat. A million tomorrows won't be enough. I've got to start thinking in months, years.

"It's so hot in here," she fans herself, batting her lashes.

Her breasts press into the fibres of the carpet beneath her.

"That's because you demanded a fire and it's May," I tell her.

"If it's this hot outside this summer, I think I'll be gardening in a very skimpy string bikini."

"You think so, do you?" My voice is hoarse at the thought.

The little vixen.

I walk to her, stopping in front of her elbows, forcing her to gaze way up as I loom over her.

"Sounds like you need a cold shower, Miss Carter."

She rolls over, stretching out like a cat. I grow harder at the sight of her bare breasts.

"I've already had one."

"But I haven't." I scoop her up in her nakedness and settle her over my shoulder in a fireman's carry.

"Isaac!" she shrieks, forgetting someone sleeps down the hall.

"Comfy up there, babe?" I bounce on my heels to shake her around a bit, wishing like hell I could see what this looks like from behind.

"Not really, but the view is glorious," she pinches my ass.

She squirms, but her attempts are futile and only result in me slapping her bare cheeks. I enter the bathroom and close the door behind us.

"You're *not* serious," she says.

"You better believe it."

I set her in the green porcelain tub, watching her nipples pebble from the cool surface beneath her feet. Icy water rushes towards her as she shuffles away from impending doom.

"I said I've already showered! My hair is still wet!" She grabs a handful to prove it.

I finish stripping and step in beside her, pulling the diverter and cranking the temperature just shy of scorching. The protesting stops when she sees how turned on I am. Relenting, she kisses me. I groan and pull her towards my aching cock. The room fills with steam, wrinkling our skin, and we do everything but get clean.

Chapter Twenty-Six

Ashlyn

"**C**'mon, Mummo, you're killing me."

Another meal that she's barely touched.

She waves me away. "I'm not hungry."

I sigh, "You've got to have something. How about a nutrition drink? I found the strawberry flavour you love at the store."

When she shakes her head, I can tell I won't win this one. The last couple days she's not had her normal appetite, and her afternoon naps are stretching longer. Her doctor ruled out any serious problems. I set out the things I need to give her a simple manicure. It was my bargaining chip for her having three bites of lunch.

"You choose your colour. I'll be right back."

I scrape the uneaten food into the compost. Through the window, I notice Isaac, Chris, Berg, and Dean—the whole group—drinking coffee in folding lawn chairs outside the workshop doors. Isaac's telling a story with grand gestures and animated facial expressions, and before long they're all howling. He throws his head back, the deep boom of his laugh reaching me through the glass of the windows.

"That man," I say, under my breath.

Something about him puts me at ease, a certain relaxed quality that rubs off on me. I try to remember the last time I gave him a hard time about the chore chart. Is he actually doing all the things under the Isaac column? Or do I just not care what time of day the laundry gets done any longer? My things are scattered all over the house, my flowers are growing in the yard, and my affections are expanding unchecked. Not only for Isaac, but for Mummo too.

I scream, jumping several inches off the floor when the land-line phone on the wall rings.

"Oh my god." I cover my hand with my chest as I rush to answer the old phone that I've never heard ring.

"Hello?"

A woman clears her throat. "Good afternoon, I'm looking for Mr. Lauri."

"Can I ask who's calling?" I lean against the wall by the phone.

"This is Breezy Shores Retirement Home. Is he available?"

"I..."

Retirement home? I glance at Isaac still goofing around and having a good time outside. She must mean Isaac's dad.

"No. No, he's not available. Can I take a message?"

With shaking hands, I draw a pen out of my apron pocket and stretch the curling cord of the telephone across the kitchen to grab my notebook.

"Sure. This is Rita from Breezy Shores, like I said, and we're pleased to inform him we have a spot available for his grandmother. We need the decision right away. These spots get snapped right up. You know how it is."

She said grandmother. A heavy weight sits in my stomach like I swallowed a rock. I squeak out a goodbye, taking note of the call in a haze. Mummo doesn't need to move to a retirement home. She has me. I'm...I'm the one who takes care of her. Isaac and I, together. Does he not feel the same way?

"Ashlyn, I've made up my mind!" Mummo calls, pulling my attention back.

"C-Coming!"

An hour later I blow on the frosty pink polish, attempting to accelerate the drying time.

"There. Picture perfect."

"Thank you, sweetie." Her voice wobbles, and I switch my focus from her fresh manicure to her shining eyes.

"You are so welcome." I squeeze both her hands.

Ask her. Just ask her if she knows anything about this Breezy Shores place. Surely, Isaac wouldn't make decisions without her input. He loves her more than anything.

"Don't leave him."

"Who Mummo?"

"The boy."

I place the polish in its basket and tilt my head. She's confused, thinking of Isaac as a child. Memories of his mother leaving haunt her, and she's been bringing it up with increasing frequency. Isaac says he has no recollection of that time, but his grandmother does.

"Isaac will be fine. He's all grown up now, right, Mummo?"

She grasps my hands with surprising strength. "You'll stay with him."

I'm unclear as to whether her mind is still in the past. The realization that I *would* stay with Isaac if he asked washes over me like a rogue wave.

"You're very special to me, Ashlyn."

I swallow, trying to smile. I'm getting pretty wobbly too.

"Like a granddaughter. I never had one of those."

No.

I fight against the muscles in my face that want to scrunch up and push the tide of tears from my eyes. My own grandparents passed away when I was tiny. Isaac is beyond lucky to have her in his life. The thought of him planning to move her into a care facility without consulting her, or me, stings. I can't bring myself to ask her about it. She's already barely eating.

"Mummo. I appreciate that. I'm your nurse. And your good friend." I add, adding a layer of protection between us.

Ever so shrewd, she asks, "Is Isaac your good friend?"

"Yes?"

A moment passes where she seems to peer through me. That blue-eyed stare is so much like Isaac's. She looks fragile. Her already slim build can't afford the missed meals.

"I don't know," I admit.

A friend, or a boyfriend, wouldn't keep something like this from me. A tightness covers my chest, like I've been laying on my stomach too long and can't take a good deep breath. It's clear as the morning dew that, yet again, I've treated a patient like a family member. Soon, I'll have to bear the weight of losing her.

I help her move from her chair to her bed, tucking blankets snug around her.

Her words are slow, eyelids heavy. "He can't stay here all by himself."

I want nothing more than to place my head on the quilt next to her and cry. Instead, I choke down a bitter ball of sorrow and rise from my chair.

"Have a good rest, Mrs. Lauri."

I can't bring myself to call her Mummo. Not anymore.

She's not my grandmother. That's not my garden. And Isaac isn't my boyfriend. Not like I thought. *You've done it again, Ashlyn,* I think. *You got way too close.*

I'm lying in my own room. The shadows of my palm play across the ceiling, the tall tree swaying in the draught from the open window. I looked up Breezy Shores. It's an assisted living facility over an hour away. I shake my head, scoffing in disgust. Isaac is out and I don't have the slightest idea how to bring this up. Instead of waiting up for him, I'm hiding out in here, which is stupid. This is the first place he'll check when he doesn't find me in his bed. I can't help but wonder if Isaac's been convinced by his father that demolishing this house and developing the land is the best bet. Surely those two would never agree on anything, but what do I know? I'm the newcomer here. The odd one out. Isaac must have snuck in quietly. I'm too lost in my own thoughts to hear anything other than the nasty voices in my head.

"You here, babe?"

I wince at the pet name. Isaac's sweet, light energy is at odds with my own emotions.

"Are you asleep?"

Pretending to be out cold would be the easy way out.

"Ugh, no." I kick my feet to untwist them from the sheets. I've been tossing and turning for hours.

"Do you want to tell me why you're in here?"

Before I can answer he's lifting up the comforter and sliding in next to me. He maneuvers us so I have the great privilege of using his firm bicep as a pillow. My body relaxes automatically, but my mind still vibrates with unanswered questions.

"Turn on the light, please."

He stretches to twist the lamp switch, his familiar spicy scent drifting over me.

I reach for my notebook on my end table. It's already opened to the page with the name and phone number of the lady who called earlier. The pages rustle when I toss it on his chest harder than intended.

"What the–Ash, what's this?" He scans the page. He scowls. "What the hell is Breezy Shores? Rita?"

Please let it be this easy. Just a misunderstanding. He can carry me to his room, and we'll fall asleep and deal with whatever this Breezy Shores thing is in the morning together.

"You've honestly never heard of it?"

His gaze is direct. "I've never heard of it."

My shoulders relax as I let out a deep sigh of relief. I snuggle closer to Isaac's side.

"It's an assisted living facility. I looked it up."

Isaac's arm goes rigid under my head.

"Shit. Did you call my dad? Give him the message?"

"No. Of course not. Why do you sound like this isn't surprising?"

He groans. "Because it isn't. Listen, babe, the day we got back from the cabin, my dad said he was trying to find a spot for her. I didn't...I didn't know how long that might take. Or if he was even serious about it. *Fuck.*" He scrubs his hands over his face.

I'm sweating under the comforter. Isaac is radiating too much heat. I should be relieved to hear that Isaac wasn't the one to contact this Rita woman, but I'm not. Something isn't adding up, and it's turning my stomach. Every cell in my body is alert. Struggling out from under the covers, I sit up.

"Are you okay?"

I shake my head. I don't think I am.

"You knew that your father was looking to move her? That my job was in danger? For weeks?"

He tugs at the roots of his hair, sitting on the bed across from me. "I thought I could figure it out. Find some way to stop him?"

I'm shaking my head at him. In disbelief or disappointment? I don't know which.

"Maybe the right place could be good for Mummo."

I blink at him. "What?"

"And it would let you do what you've been planning. Switch to floriculture?"

My lungs deflate. "Not like *this*!"

He's minimizing the effect this is having on me.

My voice is weak when I say, "You promised."

"What? What did I promise?"

He's giving me puppy dog eyes, and, for the first time, they don't have an effect on me.

"You promised me the night this all started that no matter what happened between us my job wouldn't be in jeopardy."

"That's not in my control, Ashlyn."

I throw my arms out wide. "Then you shouldn't have promised it," I whisper-scream. I *know* that Isaac isn't responsible for his father's actions. That's not why I'm mad. "You should have informed me. I don't need your protection. I want your honesty. I'm well aware I'm not a member of this family–"

"Ash, don't say that." He tries to take both my hands in his, but I slip out of his grasp.

I sniffle, "Well, I'm not. I know I'm not a member of this family, but you should have kept me in the loop. It doesn't need to be you versus your father all the time. Coming to me when you found out about this might have allowed us to take it on together. I'm friends with people at so many assisted living facilities. Maybe I could have..." I shake my head, "Maybe I could have found her a closer spot? I would have liked the chance to try."

I keep my eyes cast down as I grab my weekend bag from the closet.

"No, Ash, what are you doing?"

The quiver in his deep voice physically hurts me. A few changes of clothes is all I need. I can send Anna to collect everything else. Tears blur my vision as I walk out of the room and reach the living room.

"Jesus, where are you going?"

"*Home*. My real home." I barely recognize my raw voice.

He weaves his hands through his hair and holds them there on his head.

"I screwed up, Isaac. Some of this is my fault. I'm not too stubborn to admit that."

"No, Ash. You didn't do anything. You're perfect. I–"

I hold up my hand, afraid what words he might say in an attempt to get me to stay. I close my eyes, still avoiding his gaze. "It wasn't my intention to get this close."

"I don't know what that means."

"Yes, you do," I whisper.

The muscles in his jaw twitch. "So, we're closer than ever, and your reaction is to push me away?"

"Don't put this on me. You chose to keep secrets. I can't stay, Isaac."

"Not even for Mummo?"

"Mrs. Lauri is important to me."

His jaw goes tight. "*Mrs. Lauri?* Give it a rest. You haven't called her that in weeks."

It takes every ounce of energy I have left to keep my voice calm and reasonable. "It sounds like I'm out of a job, Isaac. What would you have me do?"

The longer we stand here and hash things out, the more painful this break up, or whatever it is, will be.

"You could fucking look at me for a start!"

"No!" I sob, no longer able to keep the burning hot tears back.

"If you can't even afford me that respect, then it's best you go."

I'm not avoiding looking at him out of a lack of respect. It's pure self-preservation. If I see the wounded expression on his face, I'll crumble and stay. As I hang the house keys on the hook by the front door, I hear his heavy footfalls behind me.

I hold a hand out to stave him off. "The whole thing was my mistake. When you moved in, I should have known this wouldn't work. I let a...a crush get in the way of my work. I'm sorry."

I accidentally look up, and I'm hooked by the intensity of his eyes. I was wrong. I don't see hurt or sadness there. He holds his chin high, nostrils flaring. He's *pissed*.

"Don't be sorry, Ashlyn. I'm not." When he continues, his voice is as cold as the winter rain the night we met, "We were both here anyway. Easy access, you know?"

I splutter but can't form any words. My heart pounds and the edges of the room blur. For the first time that day, a fresh wave of tears does not accompany my emotions. Hot fury takes over as my dry eyes narrow at the equally angry man in front of me. I couldn't be more shocked if he shoved me out the door with two hands. And that reminds me why I'm standing at the threshold of the house that accidentally became my home. I don't have to stay and listen to this shit. I wrench open the solid door and cross the threshold, leaving it open behind me. Providing him the smallest opportunity to come after me and make it right. To at least make sure the last thing he says to me isn't a bald-faced lie.

Not like this. Please don't let that be the last thing he says.

And then the door slams. The bang sends me running down the stairs and onto the rough path. Blood rushes in my ears, my fingers tingle, the front yard is too dark for me to notice the uneven paving stone. I fall hard, my kneecaps and heels of my hands breaking my fall. I cry out, barely allowing myself a moment before scrambling to my feet and running the last metres to my car.

You better fucking start.

When it does, I take off down the road.

Away from my garden.

Away from Mummo.

Away from the man I've fallen in love with.

Knees stinging, heart aching.

CHAPTER TWENTY-SEVEN

Isaac

I slam the door with such force that the walls rattle and something in the dining room plummets to the floor. Avoiding the glass surrounding the frame, I pick up the fallen photo. The image is a crushing blow. I've been so busy, I didn't notice this. Ashlyn had the picture of Mummo and I on the porch swing developed. She chose the frame with care, it blends beautifully with the other family photos.

"Shit." I run my hands through my hair.

I place the damaged memory on an end table. Did I ever screw that up. The reality of what happened settles over me.

"Isaac."

I jump at the sound of Mummo's voice.

"I'm sorry I woke you." I turn to escort her back to bed, but she doesn't seem sleepy in the slightest.

"Are you sorry about the way you spoke to her?"

Fuck. Did she hear everything?

"Hmm?" she prompts, "Are you sorry?"

"I don't know."

It's the truth. Even though my words were harsh, awful lies, they slipped out easily. Hearing her say that this was a mistake? No fucking way.

"Isaac," I note she's not using my nickname, "I don't know how I raised your father to be such a vulture. Circling around this house, trying to get his claws in it, closer and closer. Do I look dead to you?"

I hate to hear her talk like this.

"Mummo. Don't say that, please."

"Death is a part of life."

I shrug.

She continues, stronger and clearer than I've heard her in a while, "When your father acts like a fool, I'm used to it. But you...when you disappoint me like this, it hurts."

The adage that a parent's disappointment stings more than their anger is painfully true. I shrink under her gaze. Ageing backwards at a rapid pace.

"She's gone, I take it?"

I nod. Not able to voice that fact quite yet.

"You should pack your things, too."

"Me?"

She looks around the room, "Yes, you. The boy who just said unspeakably foul things in *my* living room."

"Mummo, you can't be serious."

"Can't I? Don't infantilize me."

My cheeks burn from the weight of her glare. She means it. The blue eyes that usually remind me of my own are icy. Is that the same cold glare I gave Ashlyn?

"Okay."

What else can I say? I walk down the hall, dragging my feet. If I go slowly enough, Mummo will surely reconsider. As I pack my things, though, my grandmother remains silent. Minutes later, with the same heavy duffels on my shoulder that I brought into this house only months ago, I stand shamefaced in front of the woman who raised me.

"The shop, Mummo…can I still work out of it?"

I chew on my lip. She doesn't have to say yes to me.

"That was Pappa's. He'd want that."

"Thank you." I stare at my feet.

Stooping under the weight of my bags and Mummo's disappointment, I walk to my truck. The only place I ever considered home, at my back. This morning the three of us were happy. Now, I'd stubbornly tried to handle everything myself and screwed it all up. So much of what we just said to each was bullshit. Her calling me a crush. Me calling her an easy access hook-up. I cringe, shaking my head to clear it as I drive through the quiet neighbourhood. With a deep sigh I dial my dad's number and get ready to hear 'I told you so'.

I glare at the lumpiest sofa in the history of sofas, the one I've been getting shitty sleeps on for the last two weeks. Crashing on Chris's couch is a new low. One I deserve. If I'm not at work, or on the torturous couch, I'm at the gym, depleting myself in some semblance of self-induced torture. Unfortunately, it's doing fuck all to heal my soul or my heart or whatever the source of pain and discomfort that resides in the region behind my ribs. Chris comes in his front door from a run, raincoat hood pulled tight around his head, drip drying all over my open duffel bag.

"Quit leaking all over my stuff, man."

He shakes the rainwater off like a dog.

"Should have come with me." He pours himself a glass of water.

"Nah, I did legs last night."

He raises his eyebrows. "Again? I'd ask who hurt you but that's obvious."

"Pretty sure I did most of the hurting. All she did was walk out the door." I rub my knuckles against my chest, trying to assuage the ache.

"Yeah, but that stings, too."

It's not lost on me that I might have compared Ashlyn's running out the door with my mom leaving me as a kid. I don't have to remember the details of that day for it to affect me.

"It did. But I went out of my way to be shitty. And I really disappointed my grandma."

Fuck.

He gestures to my phone on his coffee table. "Did you call her yet?"

"I texted an apology." I cross my arms.

"Think she's been on a date yet?"

"Christopher..." I warn.

At least he said date. Had he chosen another four-letter verb, I'd drown him in one of the many muddy puddles right outside the door. I can't sleep on the damn couch much longer. I'm wearing out my welcome. Affording another condo is an option, but that means accepting the truth and the defeat that goes with it. If I live out of a bag long enough, things will magically right themselves. I'll wake up one morning, stretch the stiffness out of my back, and return to the life I thought I deserved.

That's not delusional at all.

"I dunno what strings you pulled or who you sucked off, but you got it done, man." Berg claps me on the back, a delivery truck beeping its way down the driveway.

"That's, uh, vivid, man. Thanks for the image." I shake my head at him.

I might have begged and borrowed, but I didn't steal, and I hadn't sucked anyone off to get the delivery in time. It doesn't matter how I did it, just that it arrived, and that if we bust our butts, our current project stays on track. I nearly screwed this one up by fumbling an order, but I called in some favours and saved my ass. Even if everything else in my life is crumbling, at least this is solid.

Pure embarrassment has kept me away from Mummo's house the last couple weeks, but I spoke with her on the phone a few days ago, and she told me to visit her today after work. I've offered several apologies, but I need to make one in person, tail tucked between my legs, before she'll regain any respect for me. If I had more guts, I'd find a way to give Ashlyn a face-to-face apology too. The only good thing that came out of Ashlyn answering the phone that day from Breezy Shores is that my dad didn't get the message and Mummo lost the spot. She's still at home with a nurse, but it might not be like that for long, and I don't want to think about it. I rush up the porch stairs and knock, deciding to not test my luck by using my key. I snap my fingers as I strain to hear footsteps, or anything, inside.

"C'mon."

Impatience wins, and I let myself in, but the house is quiet.

"Hello?"

I think back to the day I found Ashlyn in the kitchen, scaring the crap out of her. I chuckle, but the sweet memory is overshadowed at the reminder I'll never see her in the kitchen again. It only takes a moment to confirm nobody is home. Mummo specifically told me to visit after work today. After locking up, I ease into the porch swing.

"Hey, everything okay with your grandma?"

I find the source of the voice, a dark-haired guy about my age on the sidewalk walking a big black dog.

"Uh, hi. Why do you ask?"

He twists with the dog leash in his hand. "Ambulance ripped out of here not too long ago. I heard the sirens."

An ambulance? Fuck. I get off the swing so fast I lose my balance. Recovering, I jump off the porch stairs, jogging to my truck.

"I take it you're Jackson?" I call as I climb in.

"Yeah, I live next door."

Guess nosy fucking neighbours are good for something.

I rub my thumb across the back of one of Mummo's hands, the one without the pulse oximeter and the IV that delivers her fluids and antibiotics. My lower back throbs from sitting in a chair at her bedside all night. I drove like an asshole to reach her yesterday. When I arrived she was asleep in an emergency room bay, oblivious to my presence. A few hours later she was admitted with acute pneumonia which, the doctor explained, is very serious in a woman her age. A sharp rap signals the arrival of the day nurse.

"Morning. Here to do a few checks on your grandmother," she says.

I watch her work, efficiently taking Mummo's temperature and blood pressure readings.

"Should I open these?" She gestures to the curtains.

I shrug and grunt.

"Let's let a little sunshine in."

Yeah, cause that'll help.

I shade my face to prepare for the unwanted light, but the sky is angry grey and rain streams down the windows. My phone's almost dead, no sign of a message yet from my father. His assistant told me he was on a trip. I clench my fists. He left town and didn't even have the decency to give her new nurse my number. What if she needed someone? What if she needed me? I stand to stretch, walking to the window with the view of a sprawling parking lot. My work clothes smell and I'm starving, but I can't leave. A deep rattling cough has my ass back in my chair so fast, taking Mummo's hand back in mine.

"It's okay, it's okay." I try reassure her.

She opens her mouth, and I strain to hear if she's speaking or simply trying to breathe. Beneath the thin blue sheets and blankets, her legs move restlessly. If I get a chance to leave, I'll bring her slippers and quilt from home. Mummo's eyelids twitch before her eyes open.

I squeeze her hand. "Mummo. I'm here."

"Little One."

I smile at the sound of her voice, but a wave of emotion steals it off my lips.

"Hi, Mummo, I'm here. I'm so sorry about everything that happened with Ashlyn. I wish…I wish I could take it back."

"Nurse."

"She was just here. Are you in pain?" I scan the room for the call button.

"My nurse."

"Okay, Mummo, hang on."

The call button is roped around the bed rails, but I hesitate, thumb hovering. She means Ashlyn. Of course. If I call her, will she come? I want to believe she will, but I won't blame her if she doesn't. I owe it to Mummo to make an attempt.

I grab my phone. "I'll try to get her, Mummo. I'll try."

Chapter Twenty-Eight

Ashlyn

Isaac's sharp words run on repeat through my mind as I unpack my things. Anna was a life saver by going back to get my plants and leftover belongings.

Easy access, you know?

Was it easy for us to live on top of each other as strangers?

Was it easy to keep our relationship from his dad as long as we did?

It didn't seem easy at all to build me a planter box and take a trip three hours away so we could be alone.

I carry another plant to my windowsill; the ceramic pot barely fits on the ledge. The lack of outdoor space, the small windows, the noises from neighbours. Everything about my apartment seems too tight. Like it isn't the correct fit for me anymore and I'm outgrowing my surroundings. I miss the comforting creak of the porch swing in the evenings and the way Mummo hummed between sips of her tea each morning. And at night, each time I roll to a new space in my bed, the sheets are cold. My body can toss and turn all it wants, it won't find Isaac's warmth. I groan, pressing my palms hard against my face.

Had Isaac been open and honest with me we could have worked *together* to find a solution. I think knowing that he didn't see me as a teammate that could work with him on a problem is what hurts the most. I sigh, giving up on finding a decent spot for the philodendron. Some of the leaves are yellowing anyways. My phone chimes, telling me it's time to nap before work tonight. Sitting around living on my savings won't do me any good so I took some work at an assisted living facility. Night shifts are as brutal as I remember. An unruly philodendron vine falls off the windowsill. Impatient, I tuck it back up, but I nudge the pot and it slips from the ledge. I surprise myself when I catch it easily. A bubble of anger inflates in my gut.

Easy access, you know?

"It's not fucking easy!" I scream, wrenching my arm back and throwing the plant at the ground. Cracks appear in turquoise ceramic, but the result is underwhelming, dulled by the carpet. I sink to my knees, hovering over damp soil spilling across my living room.

"Damn," I whisper, bowing my head at the extra work I created for myself.

Nothing about breaking up with Isaac Lauri is easy.

I glare at the sealed cereal box on my two-seater kitchen table. The colourful parrot mocks me from his sugary, two-dimensional perch. After working a night shift, I should really eat some breakfast before trying to get some sleep. Yesterday I ate my last two eggs, but when I stopped at the grocery store on my way home from work, I didn't head for the cooler. Instead, I found myself staring at rows and rows of cereal, tears streaking my faded makeup like a total basket case. When a grocery boy asked me if I was alright, I grabbed the closest item to me and hightailed it to the self-checkout. So, now it's just me and my feathered friend having a sunrise showdown.

"Dammit." My forehead thuds against the table.

I'm still not used to the night shift or taking care of a floor full of patients. Most of all, I'm not used to my empty apartment. How did I manage to get so comfortable sharing a bathroom with three people? To brushing against Isaac in the kitchen while he brewed coffee and I steeped tea. Screw it. Hunger wins, and I tear open the top of the cereal box, not even caring that I didn't neatly slide my finger beneath the seal. Milk sloshes onto the table when I pour. The first bite is the perfect combination of sweet and cold, the frosted o's crunchy.

"Oh, why does it have to be *good*?"

A salty tear drips into my meal. I devour the whole bowl, drinking the pastel-coloured milk, too. Did he have the same thing for breakfast? The bowl joins the other unwashed dishes in the sink, and I move on autopilot to my room. I barely remember showering, but the vanilla smell of my wet hair on my pillow reassures me that I at least cleaned myself. One more night shift then days off. That's when I'll climb out of this. It's time to pull it together. As I weave together more lies, a fitful sleep creeps over me.

My lungs burn as I shoot upright and suck in a breath. I'm too hot, pulling at the collar of my tee, fanning my face and neck. I can't have been asleep for long because I'm still exhausted.

My phone buzzes on the nightstand. Skittering across the surface.

"Oh my god! I'm trying to get some sleep," I say, reaching for the sound that infiltrated my less than peaceful slumber.

"What!" I snap.

"Ash?"

Isaac. I squeeze my eyes shut and suck in a breath so shaky he can probably hear it on his end. He's called before, and I've let it ring.

"Ashlyn, are you there?"

I take another ragged breath. "Yes. I'm here."

I'm here, and you're there.

"I'm at the hospital."

All traces of warmth leave me.

Is she already gone?

I don't have it in me to ask.

"Listen, Ashlyn. A quick visit is all I'm–"

"I can't, Isaac. I'm sorry, but I can't."

Does he want me there to sit with him while she goes? I'm not sure I can be that person for him.

Those last sweet memories of Mrs. Lauri are the ones I want to cling to. That's how I'll remember her. And it's easier to keep the angry version of Isaac in my mind. If I go to the hospital, how can I hate him when I'm in his powerful arms while he mourns?

"She's only been here for a day and she's asking for you, Ashlyn. She wants you."

Shit. I'm screwed. I'll never punish Mrs. Lauri for the sins of her grandson.

I sigh, defeated. "I'm coming."

He lets out a long breath. "Thank you."

When I arrive, Mrs. Lauri is sleeping, and Isaac is nowhere to be seen. I watch her rest, longing for my own bed. Barely any time passed between when I drifted off and when I woke abruptly to Isaac's call. My eyes burn with exhaustion. At least he had the foresight to know I wouldn't want to sit in this cramped room with him. He takes up too much space, physically and otherwise. It's pneumonia, and her prognosis isn't good. She's close. Anyone can see that. Kernels of guilt for having left her nudge at me. I should have been the nurse to bring her in. Why couldn't I have sucked it up?

You were protecting yourself.

I laugh coldly. "Protecting myself from what? Love?"

I draw her chilled hand to my mouth and blow warm air across her knuckles. Her nails are bare, and I remember the last time I did her manicure. There's a subtle pressure around my fingers. Did she squeeze my hand?

"Hello, sweetheart." Her voice is weak, her eyes open only a sliver.

I didn't know how badly I needed to hear her voice again until this moment. How could I have even considered not coming to her?

"Hi. Hi, Mummo. I'm sorry I left you," I say, sniffling while I cling to her hand.

Her breaths are shallow. When I offer her a sip of water, she blocks the straw.

"I'm the one who owes you an apology for the things my grandson said to you."

My stomach clenches. She heard us? I'm mortified.

"Don't you worry. I gave him–" She coughs, "Gave him a good tongue lashing."

My laugh is watery, nose running. The thought of that big man being dressed down by his diminutive grandma is comic relief I sorely need. I hope she really let him have it.

"He wasn't going to live with me after that." She shakes her head. "No, ma'am."

My mouth falls open. "You kicked him out?"

I can't believe it even when she nods.

"Wow."

The way she stood up for me is touching. It's what a real grandmother would do. My eyes flit up to see Isaac hovering in the doorway, a styrofoam cup in each hand. Talking to him on the phone was one thing, but seeing him stand here has me torn. Duelling emotions war within me. The urge to storm out is as powerful as the one that tells me to let him envelop me in his muscular arms. I stand, the defensive part of me taking over, making the decision easy. Bending over the hospital bed, I press a long kiss to the forehead of a woman who isn't my blood, but who cares for me an awful lot. A grandmother. A Mummo.

"Goodbye, Mummo. I love you."

CHAPTER TWENTY-NINE

Isaac

Ashlyn is a sight for sore eyes after staring at the same four walls and my weakening grandmother all night. If I thought she'd smile when she saw me, I was sorely mistaken. Her arms lock across her chest, shadows of exhaustion under her eyes. She looks like she rolled out of bed with her oversized sweats and messy ponytail. I hold out a cup of cafeteria coffee, the lamest peace offering in the history of ever.

Her voice is only a whisper, "I think it's time for me to go."

"No, not yet."

I don't want to stay here alone anymore. Not for this. I'm not strong enough.

"I've said my goodbyes."

She means to Mummo, but is this her last goodbye to me too? That cuts deep.

I wince at the reminder of my insults, the weight of it landing across my shoulders. I lashed out at her that evening and then watched her go. The best time for that apology was right after I said it. The second best time is now.

"Ashlyn, I'm so sorry. Please, stay."

Her arms stay tight over her chest, and she nods slightly. I doubt it's an acceptance, but at least she acknowledged me. Before I can continue my half-assed semblance of sorry, she rushes from the room. This time when she leaves, she doesn't leave the door open. If there's any hope in the whole goddamn world that I can right things after all the shit I said, I'll have to do more than wrench open some doors. I dump the crappy coffees in the garbage and settle into the chair next to my grandmother, laying my head down on the bed next to her, memorizing the familiar scent of her perfume while tears sting my eyes.

I glare at the cold brick hearth, grief sullying the nostalgia I usually experience in my favourite place. After hanging on for weeks, Mummo passed last night. My thoughts and movements are painted with a thick coat of sadness. I came straight here from the hospital, desperately seeking a comfort that seems to have left this world when Mummo did. As I wander from room to room, numbness envelops me. If this is the way living in this house will be, my father can fucking have it.

Light streams through the window over the kitchen sink, illuminating an etching in the table's leg. I sink down to examine it. Scratched right into the wood are the initials I.L.

What a brat.

A spark of a memory appears. Crouching beneath the table with a tool from my pappa's shop. A boy, five or six, who thought it would be a good idea to mark his grandparents' furniture with his name. Pappa and Mummo *had* to have known, but they never said anything. I run my fingers over the messy carvings of a child who was probably proud as hell of his work before he realized he screwed up. We'd shared so much at this table. Meals, stories, laughter, and tears. Keeping my dad from demolishing my home isn't possible, but I'll be damned if he takes the memories inside it. I rush out to the workshop, trying real fucking hard not to think about losing the building, and grab what I need. Detaching the legs off the table is easy and I carry them out to the truck in one trip. The top is a real bitch to squeeze out the back door. But it's *my* fucking table, thank you very much. It has my name on it, so try to tell me otherwise. I back down the driveway and turn onto the street. My foot hovers over the gas pedal as I spot the porch swing swaying in the breeze. I throw it into park. That fucking swing is mine, too.

"Hey, next time can we not carpool?" Dean asks from the back-seat of my truck. "I'm curled up like a pretzel."

"Quit whining," I say.

We need to find a new workshop and office space because it's only a matter of time before my father takes a wrecking ball to it all. I insisted we all go together, cause comradery. Berg rides shotgun; Dean and Chris have the back. He needs to quit complaining. There's plenty of space. Berg screws around with my phone until a sappy country song comes on.

"Turn that shit off, Berg."

I'm suddenly regretting this field trip.

"Our boy is lovesick, that's all, Papa Berg," Chris says.

The steering wheel creaks under my grip. "I'm literally going to leave you all on the side of the road."

Dean leans forward and wraps his big arm around my throat. "Keep driving, bitch."

"Get off." I wrestle out of his grip, managing to keep the truck in my lane.

"We're all awfully sorry about Mummo," says Berg, turning down the volume, "but Chris is right. You're pining, but you're not doing a damn thing to fix it."

"What do you guys know?" I pull at the back of my neck.

"Here, give me the phone. I'll choose something."

Berg relinquishes it to Chris, the AUX cord stretching to the back seat.

"Okay, we could do 'She Fucking Hates Me' or 'We Are Never Ever Getting Back Together' or, this is a good one, 'Since U Been Gone'."

"Why are we friends?" I ask.

We looked at three potential spaces, none of which worked. I drive toward town full of defeat. The guys finally shut up, and Chris chooses something mellow, but my mind is busy replaying what Berg said. It's an echo of Mummo's last words. Our last scattered conversations were hard to follow. She mentioned Ashlyn, Pappa, the garden, all the things she loved. But there was also mention of apologies. At first, I wondered what my grandmother could possibly have to atone for, but then I figured she was talking about me. By the time she started talking about lawyers, which greatly agitated my father, I didn't have a clue what she meant. My phone chimes a few times.

"Um, Isaac? You've got a few messages here."

"That's fine. Just put it on silent. I'll get to them later," I tell him.

I watch Dean lean toward Chris in the rearview mirror.

"You probably want to take a look at this now."

"Oh, for the love of God." I pull over on the shoulder of the highway and reach back for my phone.

There are texts and emails and missed calls. I'm not sure what to open first. The texts are from my father and feature a lot of caps locks and expletives, and those can be dealt with later. I don't recognize the phone numbers, so I pull open an email while Dean and Chris whisper together in the back seat. The message is from a lawyer I'm not familiar with. Everything about the email looks legitimate. If I'm understanding what I'm reading...then my wildest dreams have just come true. I turn in my seat, and everyone in the truck is looking at me carefully, waiting for a reaction. I punch Berg in the shoulder, and a high-pitched yelp erupts from my throat. A grin splits my face, then I'm pulling a U-turn in rush hour traffic. My heart is in my throat as I process what I've just learned.

Mummo's house.

Mine.

Dean claps me on the shoulder. "Home is the other way."

"I know, I know. But we have another stop to make first."

I pull into Ashlyn's favourite huge garden centre a few minutes later. This time, instead of a grandmother and a nurse, I have my best friends with me.

"You guys ever heard of Backyard Shakeup?"

CHAPTER THIRTY

Ashlyn

"Wow... I like what you've done with the place," Anna says, picking her way through the piles of laundry and take-out containers on my bedroom floor. I've been dodging her for a few days, but she bullied her way into my neglected apartment.

I cover my face in shame. "I can't look at it. Who even am I?"

"You're still in there... somewhere."

I'm working my way through cleaning my depression den. It's not as bad as it was a couple days ago. My first day off was completely designated for crying and eating what I promised was my last box of cereal. Each day I'm finding more strength.

"Do you still want to go out with me? We could just...clean." Anna nudges a potted plant that's been rotting with me in the dark.

After leaving Isaac, I allowed myself a decent period of heart-break. I thought I did a decent job of keeping it together. I exercised, I worked, I cried...a lot. Each hour I swung between wanting to run back into his arms and wanting to slash his truck tires. The normal stuff. After I got the word Mummo died? That broke me. Isaac had left a voicemail in the middle of the night, and the utter pain in his voice did me in. Was Isaac alone in his grief? Who would comfort him? Certainly not his father. I rub my chest, another rock stacking on top of the shame pile. Are ribs even strong enough to hold up to this type of pressure? We didn't talk about heartbreak in nursing school. Anna rips open my bedroom curtains, and the light hurts my retinas more than is reasonable.

"I don't want to cancel. It's time to get out there."

"Good. Get in the shower. I'm going to pick your outfit then I'll blow out your hair for you. We're getting mani-pedis and having a meal together..." she nudges an empty pizza box, "a meal that includes at least two vegetables."

"Pizza has vegetables."

She narrows her eyes. "We both know that was an extra cheese pizza."

After a full day out with my cousin, it's apparent I have more in common with flora than I thought. Some sunlight, some water, and I'm almost myself. Anna drives us along the oceanfront. Rollerbladers whizz by on a walking path, kites tug on their strings, and the seaweed scent of retreating tide floats in the open windows.

"It's so beautiful," I say, the briny June air blowing my waves against my lip gloss.

"One more stop," Anna says, fiddling with the clasp of her necklace as she turns down a road that leads away from the oceanfront.

The streets start looking very familiar.

I turn down the radio. "Anna?"

"Are you freaking out? Don't freak out."

I twist my hair in my hands, messing up Anna's blow out.

"Isaac messaged me because you're ignoring him."

My mouth falls open. "It's not like that."

I should have replied. I'm *going* to. I've read his heartfelt apologies a hundred times.

"That's kind of what it seems like..."

She's not wrong. There must be some sort of time limit on these things. What if he stops looking for my replies? What if I accept his apology but it's too late?

"He wants you to pick up your planter."

I rub my temples. "I don't want it."

"He won't even be there. He said to go around back and get it. It's yours."

I should be relieved to hear that this errand isn't going to turn into an awkward encounter, but instead a pang of disappointment rolls in. The planter *would* be pretty tucked up against one end of my balcony, flowers springing from the soil.

"It's a nice memory of Mummo."

As soon as I think of her, my mind is made up. I have nothing to remember her by, except for a few photos.

I bite my lip. "It's heavy. I suppose the flowers will be dead, though, so we can dump out the soil."

The poor things will be shrivelled and brown from weeks of neglect, frying my poor zinnias to a crisp. Some gardener I am. Plant mom, my ass. Bitterness spreads over me every time I see a poster for a summer market or a roadside stand selling bright orange or pink gerberas. That's supposed to be *me*.

My heart rate ticks higher the closer we get. I don't want to see the house in whatever state of demolition it happens to be in. I avoid the passenger side window at all costs. Seeing a hole in the ground will ruin me.

"You're going to have an awfully hard time making it to the backyard if you won't even look at the house." She elbows me.

"I'm going."

Why can't he have left the freaking box out front? He paid someone to have a whole car delivered to my house once. Why not a few pieces of wood?

"You want me to come with you?"

"No, I just need a few minutes."

"Okay. I'll be here."

I push the car door open, forcing myself to be brave. Songbirds sing of approaching dusk, a lawn mower drones nearby, the fresh cut grass smell strong in the heat.

Get it over with.

LOVINGLY RESTORED

The house I ran from looks...the same. I shade my eyes from the late summer sun. Perhaps all the renovations are inside. When I try to picture the living room without its wood burning fireplace or the bathroom without the jadeite fixtures, I can't. It's all wrong. The gravel path between the house and garage is shadowy and cool, and I pause when I see the English Yew thriving there. Isaac told me that we all have our own areas of expertise and the memory paints a soft smile on my lips. When I round the corner, I take a step back, blinking rapidly. This can't be real. The moss-covered cement pavers and creeping weeds are gone. Neat interlocking bricks have taken their place. I raise my head, squinting against the low-lying sun. Is sudden onset colour blindness a thing? Because there isn't a single brown, dry, dead object in sight. In fact, there's barely anything I recognize except for the fence and the workshop and the mature trees along the property line. Maybe I've developed severe double vision, too, because there's my planter, but it's multiplied.

The once barren backyard is in the throes of a landscaping transformation. A dozen garden beds cover the neat grass, each box filled with dark, moist soil. One area of the yard has been churned up into a large, in-ground bed surrounded by deer fencing. Dominating the unfamiliar landscape, opposite the workshop, is a completely new structure. A greenhouse. It's not even close to the one I admired at the garden centre. It's *better*.

My fists tremble in the fabric of my dress. The gigantic, glass-covered greenhouse glitters in the golden hour rays. I barely dare to breathe, lest the mirage before me disappear. Lured by the sparkling light, I press my shaking hands to the hot glass. Inside are empty rows of sturdy shelves. A familiar creaking sound surprises me, and I rip my hands away like I've been burnt. Isaac emerges from the workshop, a wood plank balanced on one shoulder. He's dressed in cargo work shorts and an honest-to-goodness leather tool belt around his hips. Shirtless and sweaty, rows of abs flex as he exits the workshop door with the board in tow. He halts when he sees me, free hand steadying the plank as his momentum changes.

"You came." His voice is gravelly, like he hasn't spoken for a while.

"I think I was hand delivered. I'm guessing Anna is in on this." I wave my hand behind me. "Whatever *this* is."

He comes closer, affording me a better view. My heart thumps heavily as I look at him. Slightly sunburnt nose, hair longer than usual, maybe a bit slimmer than normal. He blows a falling strand of hair out of his face.

After not seeing him for weeks, the effect he has over me is stronger than ever.

I smooth my hands over my dress.

"Is this the part where I have to listen politely because you've been toiling away for me?"

"Something like that." He shrugs with the shoulder that isn't weighed down.

"Do you want to put that board down first?"

He shakes his head. "Nope."

"It looks very heavy."

"Not for me."

"You're shaking." A muscle in his left bicep twitches, a bead of sweat rolling through the shadow between his pecs.

Show off.

He grunts. "Fine." He places the board at our feet, dividing us. An angry red line marks his shoulder. "Only because I'm gonna need my hands in a minute."

I'm already warm, but a fresh flush blooms across my cheeks at the thought of him touching me. Is a well-worded apology and a shirtless man all it takes to win me back?

He clears his throat. "The things I said to you before you left were abhorrent. They were untrue, all of them, and I'm ashamed. Most importantly, I'm sorry I kept you in the dark about things that affected you. It wasn't fair or right."

My chin is already wobbling. He said as much in his messages, but to hear him say it in person is a relief. It's what I needed to hear.

"I'm truly sorry for your loss, Isaac."

"I'm doing better, but how are you?"

"I'm..." I try to nod enthusiastically, but my chin starts to wobble, and the movement transforms into a shake.

I'm a bad liar, and I'm still grieving.

"Oh, Ash. I contributed to you getting so close to another patient. If I'd have left you alone maybe you wouldn't have been hurt."

"I would have fallen in love with her whether you'd ever moved in or not. She was perfect." My throat swells, "I miss her so much."

His eyes shine. "Me, too."

This is more than an apology, it's penance. The amount of work is mind-blowing.

"I don't understand all this. Did your dad rent you the house? I mean, this is a crazy amount of work for a temporary living situation. What if he changes his mind?"

At any moment, Mr. Lauri could rip this away from us.

Him, not us.

"This is all mine. The yard, the house. She left it to me." He spreads his arms wide, and I nearly run into them.

"And your dad?"

Surely he received something as her son.

He presses his lips together. "Yeah, according to her lawyer Mummo handled all this a long time ago, but my dad kept trying to convince her to alter things. She left him some money, but my guess is that it won't go far. Turns out the Government of Canada and him have a very different idea of how taxes and business expenses work."

I cover my mouth but a burst of laughter escapes anyway. "Oh my god. I shouldn't laugh–"

"Laugh away. I sure did."

So, I do. I probably look unhinged standing here in this nearly unrecognizable space laughing. When the tears of sadness and the tears of joy are mixed and I don't know which are which, I glance at the house. "This is everything you ever wanted."

Isaac is the type of man who will fully appreciate this gift.

"No, it's not."

I frown. "But now you don't have to worry about the workshop and you can do all the renovations...what more could you want?"

He reaches out, and we weave our fingers together. His warm skin against mine is a salve. Oxygen dives deeper into my lungs than it has in weeks.

"I'm obsessed with old houses; I wouldn't work in the industry if I wasn't. Mummo and Pappa's house is so special, and, God, I was so bitter when I thought my father was going to ruin it. To demolish it."

He rubs his rough thumb back and forth over my hand.

"The house is plenty nice, Ashlyn, I love it. But my attachment to this place doesn't have a damn thing to do with the fireplace or the workshop or the hardwood. My grandparents' relationship and the memories I built with them here is what always brought me back. Without that love, without someone to build new memories with... it's simply another house on another street in another city."

Tears are rolling down my cheeks, but I don't care.

"Living here alone sucks so bad. It has all these memories of my grandparents, and they're gone. And then I have memories of you and...well, you're gone too–"

I can't keep quiet any longer. "No, I'm not gone. I'm right here!"

He laughs. "I know, baby. I see you. Stay. Be my girlfriend and move back in with me. If that's too fast or serious, then don't move in, but use the space. I only need the workshop. The rest is useless without you."

I don't know what to say because he offered me everything.

"Don't say anything if you aren't sure. Even if you can't forgive me, I still want you to use the space, we'll figure something out. But you should know," he pauses to step over the plank, so our hands are pressed between our bodies, "that I'll be working right there," he points to the workshop, "every single day, and I won't stop trying to win you back."

Mummo once told me Lauri men were nothing if not relentless.

"Can I garden in my bikini?"

His hips shift toward me, stopping short of the folds of my skirt.

"That depends." His voice is husky.

"I mean...that won't be a distraction for you while you work?"

I've tortured the poor man enough. I laugh, relief and joy and a million other emotions evaporating in the heat. His bare chest is hot beneath my hand, and the moment he registers my touch, he yanks me against him.

"Isaac! You're all dirty!" I wiggle beneath his grasp, his sweat transferring to my dress.

"Sorry, not sorry. I've been toiling out here for weeks trying to redeem myself, remember?"

"I'm always going to be out here. I am never going to be indoors, not until winter."

"Does that mean you'll move back in?" He holds me at arm's length, searching my face for an obvious answer.

"Yes. Under one condition. No, two conditions."

"Anything."

"One, I need a stand for the front yard. To sell my flowers. The season isn't over yet!" I clap my hands excitedly.

"Has anyone ever told you that you're a bit greedy?" Our hips meet, and I press myself against him, as much as I can with a tool belt in the way.

"You have *no* idea." I catch him off guard with a kiss.

"Mmm, what's the second thing?"

"Tell me you love me."

I'm searching his eyes for a hint of what he'll say next, and it's so obvious I could cry.

"I love you so much, Ashlyn. All of this is for you."

"I love you too," I whisper.

I step forward between his legs, and he mirrors my movement, stepping back. The workshop door is wide open, and I pepper his mouth with kisses as I try to march us into the privacy of his man cave. I want him inside those four walls.

He tries to speak against my lips. "Ash–"

We trip inside, the space so dark after being in the bright light. I shut my eyes and lose myself in the smell of his skin, the way he tastes, absorbing his energy and trying to make up for lost time. When I rise onto my toes my heels pop out my sandals. I try desperately to press us closer together. The tool belt might look hot as hell, but it's not conducive to proximity.

I tug at the soft leather, looking for some type of buckle or clasp. "This is like a goddamn chastity belt, Lauri."

"Ashlyn, would you stop for a second." He seizes my wandering hands.

"What!" I snap.

A trio of chuckles comes from the corner where Chris, Berg, and Dean stand with open beers. Berg is sufficiently mortified whereas Chris and Dean look like they need popcorn. My cheeks burn as I bury my face in Isaac's warm chest.

"Get out!" Isaac roars, gesturing to the door.

"You heard the boss." Berg claps his hands together and leads the way out of the workshop.

They file out quickly.

Isaac's hands skim over my hips, squeezing. I moan appreciatively at the strength of his big hands.

"Um, Ashlyn?" Chris says from the doorway. "Should I tell Anna to leave?"

"OUT!" Isaac snarls.

"Yep, sorry." The door bangs behind him, shutting out the summer heat, and then we're alone.

CHAPTER THIRTY-ONE

Isaac

H aving Ashlyn attempting to claw her way inside my clothes is something I envisioned for way too long and much too often. With the audience gone, I can finally act out the fantasy.

"You have a lot of complaints about my clothing. First the button fly jeans, now the tool belt," I tease.

"Only items that prevent me from accessing your...um..." She licks her lips and looks down between us.

"Cock?" I offer.

Damn, I missed the way that word causes redness to spread across her cheeks.

"I thought there was no horseplay in the workshop," she says sweetly.

"Rules change, Ash. I made that one up to keep from throwing you down in a pile of sawdust and making you mine when I knew you weren't ready."

Her lips pop open in surprise at my admission. She traces a route down my abs with my index finger, following the trail of body hair. Bright pink-red nail polish matches her toes, something I've never seen on her.

"Listen, babe," I reach to unbuckle the tool belt from around my hips. "If you want me to talk real sweet, we can go inside, and I'll shower and light some candles and lay you on the soft bed, and I'll make love to you so, so slow you'll beg me to go faster."

The belt clunks against the floor.

"Or," I take hold of her roving hand and push it south, pressing her hand firmly against my rock-hard erection, "I can take you right here, where I know you've always wanted to be taken…but it's gonna be dirty."

Her eyelids flutter.

I laugh. "Yeah, that's what I thought."

I turn her, press against her round ass from behind, stooping to reach the hem of her dress. gathering it up until all the material bunches around her hips.

"Ashlyn," I grit out. "Where the fuck are your panties?"

She doesn't have a damn thing under the sweet white dress. Nothing but a tan-lined ass staring back at me. When she fails to provide a reason, my mind runs wild with the possibilities.

"It's a straightforward question, babe."

"The linen shows almost every colour right through it. I only have one pair that works with this dress, but they're missing."

I'm having a field day with this.

"So, instead of changing your outfit, you've had a bare cunt all day?"

She gasps, but I don't miss the way those hips tilt at my words.

"I told you if you want to stay in here I'm talking dirty."

She nods, arching her low back so far that I can see the seam of her ass that I'll be spreading apart any moment. I unbutton my shorts, unzipping them and forcing the elastic of my boxers down beneath my balls. She peeks over her shoulder at the sound of the zipper.

"Hold your dress up."

She obeys, for once, taking the fabric from me, neck still wrenched around to hungrily stare at my cock. She leans over the workbench, and I shove her legs apart with my thigh. Debris and dust press into my knees when I sink down to the floor, filthy from weeks of non-stop, after-hours work. It's a small price to pay for the spectacular view of her lips shining with readiness. My cock twitches, begging for me to jerk it.

"Isaac, do something, please," she begs, her sweet smell calling to me.

"I've got you." I place my whole palm over her sex and squeeze.

This isn't the place or time for a lengthy preamble. I told her if she wants it slow and sweet that we'll go to the house, but that isn't the option she chose. Thank God.

"Take it off. I want to see all of you."

She has to let go of the hem of her dress to reach for the straps, temporarily robbing me of my view. When she pushes the material down over her breasts, she's braless too.

"Jesus Christ." I scrub both hands over my face.

The idea of her wearing dresses around town without a bra and panties fills me with a possessive jealousy. All it would take was a cool breeze to make her nipples harden or to lift her skirt in a way that someone might see. The idea of another man seeing those parts of her... I can't bear it.

She stands naked before me, looking confident in her skin but sheepish about a location so clearly unsuitable for making love. Good thing that's not what we're doing. This table is the perfect height. If it isn't, I'll saw the fucking legs off.

"How do you want me?" She fucking hops on the table and licks her bottom lip.

I occupy the space between her bare thighs, the tip of my cock brushing her clit, the only part of her accessible to me as she sits upright on the workbench.

Warm rays of light illuminate her tan skin. A sunbeam plays on her ribs, and I trace the edges of the light with my fingers, the darkness that's shadowed me for weeks starting to dissipate. Ashlyn coming back into my life symbolizes a restoration, an opportunity to begin anew. The chance to lovingly restore not only a home, but a relationship with a person I want forever.

Her heart thumps against my hands as I roll her nipples between my fingers until she cries out. She wiggles on the hard surface of the workbench like that might provide her with relief. My fingers are too dirty to put inside of her, so I position my hands around her curvy thighs instead, her flesh moulding beneath the pressure of my fingers. I grin at her and watch her melt while I lean down to kiss her between her legs. She moans, and I answer, groaning into her hot pussy. Trying to reach all the places I desperately missed touching and tasting.

"How are you so fucking wet already?" I growl, looking up at her.

I suck her clit until she's close then pull away, standing, and wiping my lips with the back of my hand. When my cock is lined up with her, I glance down...shit. Condom. I wasn't expecting *this*. I'll have to get my shorts back on, walk all the way to the house, leaving her ready and willing.

As if she can sense my turmoil, she says, "Isaac, just do it."

I shake my head. "I don't have a condom."

"I know."

She grasps me and guides me closer. The heat of her is exquisite against my bare tip.

"Are you sure?"

"Positive. I'm on the pill and I haven't been with anyone else. H-have you?"

I groan. Barely holding it together.

"Absolutely not."

I push forward and fill her in one smooth motion. She cries out, head tilting back.

"Oh my god, Ash. You wrapped around me is heaven."

I languidly pull all the way out then join our bodies again. The texture of her pussy against my most sensitive skin is bliss, gripping me on each withdrawal. Holding her securely with one arm, careful not to force her off the edge, I speed up, setting a rapid pace. With my other arm, I caress her cheeks, her lips, the hair falling in her face. The dual sensations of my hard cock and my gentle fingers cause flutters within her that have me hanging on for dear life. Despite the decidedly unsexy environment, the woman on my workbench has made it so that I don't have a chance of lasting many more thrusts.

"Isaac. I needed you."

Her body, her sweet words. I can't last.

"You gonna come with me, babe?"

She mewls under the persuasive pitch of my voice.

"Yes, that's right. Tighten around this bare cock. Gimme that sweetness."

She tilts her head back, her neck straining. "Oh, god, Isaac."

I chuckle, but it turns into a series of uncontrollable grunts. She clamps down tight as my balls contract so that they no longer slap against her sticky inner thighs.

"I'm coming, Isaac."

"Fuck, Ashlyn..." I grit out, my thrusts wild as I empty myself into a woman for the first time.

I'm so caught up in her. She's here. She's back. She's mine. Those warm brown eyes bore into mine.

"Come on." I pull on my boxers and scoop her into my arms.

She snatches up her dress, using it like a blanket while I walk us out of the workshop, into the dusky yard.

Ashlyn whispers in my ear. "Take me to your new home, Isaac."

"This is *our* home now, babe," I correct.

"Ours." She presses a kiss against my cheek.

I think about the two people who brought me through my life to this point. Tomorrow, I'll show Ashlyn the plaque on the other side of the greenhouse. The bronze one with the raised lettering that reads:

In Loving Memory of Pappa and Mummo

"Hey, Ash?" I say as I carry her into the kitchen. "You know how I said you could choose between dirty workshop sex and me making love to you deliciously slow?"

She looks up at me and nods.

"We're gonna do the other option now."

"Well, hey, if you're going to do something..." she trails off.

We finish the adage together, "Do it right."

This time? I know I've done it perfectly.

THE END

About the Author

Kelsey Woods is the author of debut novel, Lovingly Restored. She wrote her first book on a typewriter at five years old. While 'Sugar The Adventurous Hummingbird' was lovely, she now prefers using her Microsoft Surface to bring you spicy contemporary romance.

Kelsey can be found attached at the hip to her emotional support Kindle or in recreation centre workout classes with women in their seventies.

Mother of two daughters and a police wife, she lives on beautiful Vancouver Island and will brag about her proximity to the Pacific Ocean at every opportunity.

Social Media

Connect with me on these platforms!

tiktok.com/@kelseywoodswrites?t=8e8Zcu8A4qk&_r=1

instagram.com/kelseywoodswrites

amazon.ca/Kelsey-Woods/e/B0CB54HJ9W/

goodreads.com/author/show/40851616.Kelsey_Woods

Acknowledgements

Thank you to myself. For not standing in my own way or listening to the voices that said I couldn't do this.

Thank you to my husband who endured every idea that popped into my head and stepped in to be my own personal IT guy and book formatter when things got tough.

Most of all, thank you to the women I met through the Indie book community on Instagram. You have truly been the definition of sisterhood as we go on this journey of sharing our spicy stories with the world together.

Manufactured by Amazon.ca
Acheson, AB